The Hangman's
Beautiful Daughter

SHARYN McCRUMB

The Hangman's Beautiful Daughter

CHARLES SCRIBNER'S SONS
NEW YORK

MAXWELL MACMILLAN CANADA
TORONTO

MAXWELL MACMILLAN INTERNATIONAL
NEW YORK OXFORD SINGAPORE SYDNEY

Charles Scribner's Sons
Macmillan Publishing Company
866 Third Avenue
New York, NY 10022

Maxwell Macmillan Canada, Inc.
1200 Eglinton Avenue East, Suite
200
Don Mills, Ontario M3C 3N1

Macmillan Publishing Company is part of the Maxwell Communication
Groups of Companies.

Library of Congress Cataloging-in-Publication Data

McCrumb, Sharyn.
The hangman's beautiful daughter: a novel of suspense /
Sharyn McCrumb.
p.   cm.
ISBN 0-684-19407-4
I. Title.
PS3563.C3527H3   1992
813'.54—dc20   91-46057

10 9 8 7 6 5 4 3 2 1

Printed in the United States of America

To Charlotte T. Ross,
a keeper of the Legends

ACKNOWLEDGMENTS

The epigraph in Chapter Five is taken from "Hanlon Mountain in Mist," by Jim Wayne Miller, from *Dialogue with a Dead Man* (Athens: University of Georgia Press, 1974); rpt. Green River Press, 1978. Reprinted by permission of the author.

The epigraph in Chapter Eleven is taken from "The Hillbilly Vampire," by Amy Tipton Gray, from *The Hillbilly Vampire*, Rowan Mountain Press, 1990. Reprinted by permission of the author.

The author would like to thank the following people for their generous help with the technical matters touched upon in this novel: Dr. Jean Haskell-Speer, chairman of the Appalachian Studies Department at Virginia Tech; Dr. Charlotte Tyler Ross, Appalachian State University; Terry L. Brown; David Kellcher; J. A. Niehaus, Kettering Ohio Police Department; Charles and Mary Thomas Watts; and especially David K. McCrumb, for his help with the environmental issues, and my editor, Susanne Kirk, who has been with me every step of the way on this novel, beginning in a cabin in the hills of Georgia in 1990, when we all sat around and talked about ghosts, the Sight, and the lore of the Southern mountains.

The Hangman's
Beautiful Daughter

PROLOGUE

Summer for the living,
Winter for the dead
——THE RULE FOR SOLSTICE ALIGNMENT OF STANDING
STONES IN PRE-CHRISTIAN BRITAIN

Nora Bonesteel was the first one to know about the Underhill family. Death was no stranger to Dark Hollow, Tennessee, but Nora Bonesteel was the only one who could see it coming.

She was well past seventy, and she lived alone in a white frame house up on the part of Ashe Mountain that had been Bonesteel land since 1793. Across the patchwork of field and forest, eye to eye with the Bonesteel house, was the outcrop of rock called Hangman, looking down on the holler with a less benevolent eye than Nora Bonesteel's. They perched on their respective summits, the granite man and the parchment woman, in a standoff older than the pines that edged the meadows.

She seldom left her mountain fastness except to walk down the gravel road to church on Sunday morning, but she had a goodly number of visitors—mostly people wanting advice—but they'd come bringing homemade blackberry jelly or the latest picture of the grandbaby so as not to seem pushy about it. Folks said that no matter how early you reached her house of a morning with a piece of bad news, she'd meet you on the porch with a mug of fresh-brewed chicory coffee, already knowing what it was you'd come about.

Nora Bonesteel did not gossip. The telephone company

1

had never got around to stringing the lines up Ashe Mountain. She just knew.

Dark Hollow folk, most of them kin to her, anyhow, took it for granted, but it made some of the townspeople down in Hamelin afraid, the way she sat up there on the mountain and kept track of all the doings in the valley; sat up there with her weaving, and her pet groundhog, and her visions.

The night that Garrett Webster died in that wreck on the road to Asheville, Nora had the carrot cake baked to take to the funeral by the time somebody stopped in the next morning to tell her about the accident. She had a dream, she said, while she was sleeping in that old iron bedstead with the hollow pipes at the head and foot of it. Suddenly, she had heard a clang and felt the bed vibrate, as if somebody had hit those footboard pipes with the point of a sword. She'd sat up in bed, looking to see what woke her, and there was Garrett Webster standing at the foot of her bed, smiling at her from inside a glow of white light. When he saw that she'd seen him and knew who he was, he faded away, and the room was dark again. It was eight minutes past five, Nora said, and she got up right then to start fixing that cake for Esther Webster and her boys. The state trooper's report said that the wreck between Garrett Webster's car and a semi on Route 58 had occurred at 5:08 that morning. It also stated that Webster never knew what hit him, but Nora Bonesteel reckoned he had.

She knew other things, too. Who was pregnant, when to cover your tomato plants for frost, and where your missing wedding ring would turn up. She could cure nosebleeds by quoting the sixteenth chapter of Ezekiel, sixth verse; and she knew how to gauge the coming winter by the bands on a woolly worm. But that was nothing to marvel at. Every family had somebody with the simple gifts; even ones who knew when there had been a death within their family, but what made Nora Bonesteel different from others with the Sight was that for her it wasn't only a matter of knowing about close kin. The fate of the whole community seemed as open to her as the weekly newspaper. Even newcomers, like the Underhills, outsiders who had bought an old farm and had come as strangers to settle between the mountains, were within the range of her visions.

Nobody in Dark Hollow ever mistook her for a witch. She taught Sunday school to the early teens, and she kept her place in an old leather King James Bible with the feather of a redbird's wing. Nora Bonesteel never wished harm, never tried to profit by her knowledge. Most times, she wouldn't even tell people things if it was bad news that couldn't be avoided. And if she did impart a warning, she'd look away while she told it, and say what she had to in a sorrowful way that was nobody's idea of a curse. She just knew things, that's all. In the east Tennessee hills, there had always been people who knew things. Most people felt a little sorry for her, and were glad they could go through life with the hope that comes from not seeing the future through well-polished glass.

CHAPTER

1

There is no death! The leaves may fall,
And flowers may fade and pass away—
They only wait, through wintry hours,
The warm sweet breath of May

—J. L. McCREERY

The road was dark. What moonlight there was from a dime-sized crescent moon was shrouded by the cluster of pines choking the one-lane blacktop. Laura Bruce drove the winding mountain road as quickly as she dared, her eyes straining into the darkness in search of deer that might dart out in front of the car. There was enough death abroad tonight in Dark Hollow without hitting a straggling doe.

There is a lot of blood at the scene, Sheriff Spencer Arrowood had said when he phoned her. *I had to tell you that so that you would be prepared for it. We have enough to contend with as it is. But if you think you can stand it, I need you to come.*

Her fingers tightened around the steering wheel. Thirty-five miles an hour. She might have gone faster if she were more familiar with the road, but she had only lived in the area for a year, and this road leading nowhere but deep into the hollers was a route she seldom traveled. She was still a little frightened of the wilder sections of Wake County, where no electric lights diminished the brilliance of the stars, and miles of forest separated each human habitation. It wasn't the people she feared but the isolation. Suppose the car broke down? Will, her new husband, had no such qualms about the mountain road. He loved to drive it in late spring when the mountain laurel turned the shady hillsides pink and white, and in the autumn, when an occasional break in the trees would reveal an endless vista of forests of rust and gold spreading out across the hills below. Will knew each mile of the route, and every householder along the way, from the visits he had made to families back in the hollow, in time of sickness or bereavement. Laura had never gone with him. The role of minister's wife was new to her, and there was still a strangeness to it. She could not see herself a mother to the community, and she was deliberately vague about her own religious views in the face of the parishioners' literal belief.

Her hometown, Roanoke, Virginia, lay four hours to the east. Life in a city with a symphony, a zoo, and several colleges had left her ill equipped for the role of parson's wife in the hills and hollers of east Tennessee.

She was a pharmacist's daughter who grew up in the Kmart/Long John Silver/Brady Bunch culture of suburban Americana. If there was some other world, older and more substantial than hers, in the hills that surrounded Roanoke, she never discovered it. That had come to her late in life, when she met Will Bruce of Wake County, Tennessee.

Will looked every inch an Irishman, and he probably was, given the Appalachian gene pool. They were a study in contrasts: He was blond and stocky and cheerful, and she was dark and serious and filled with doubt. The most comment, though, was caused by the fact that he was only twenty-nine, to her thirty-eight. They resolutely ignored the remarks that this occasioned among their more forthright acquaintances.

Will wasn't very "ministerial," as far as she could tell. Their first date was a Statler Brothers concert, and after years of sneering at country music, Laura was surprised to find out how much she liked it, and how much of it she could relate to. Will was unselfconscious in his enjoyment. After a year of commuter dating down Interstate 81, they decided to marry. It was only later that she realized that marriage to Will entailed greater than ordinary obligations: He came with the spiritual baggage of two hundred souls of Shiloh Baptist Church. She told herself that she would begin by going through the motions as pastor's wife, hoping that the emotions would eventually follow.

So far, they had not. She had visions of an eternally smiling Donna Reed gliding among the congregation like a ministering angel, but she still found herself standing awkwardly at Will's side, wondering if she was overdressed and trying without notable success to think of something she could possibly discuss with these people who seemed neither to read nor travel.

She wished that Will were home now, so that the sheriff's call for assistance could have been answered by more capable hands than hers. There was a quiet strength in Will that made people want to confide in him, knowing he wouldn't be shocked no matter what was said. These mountain folk were his people, and he understood them. She wondered if he would have been shocked at this.

"I can deal with the bodies and the crime scene," the sheriff had assured her. *"But I haven't the time or the temperament to tend to the living. I'd be grateful if you'd come."*

The sheriff was a stranger to her, but she could hear the concern in his voice, and she agreed to go at once. What excuse could she have made? It was as if Will Bruce had left the valley in her care, and she must do her best to comfort these strangers in trouble. Surely, she reasoned, if the sheriff could have found anybody else to go out there, he would have asked them. Or did he assume that the minister's wife was the logical substitute when the minister himself was unavailable?

As she drove through the silent woods, she took her mind off her destination by mentally composing a letter to her husband, on temporary duty as an army chaplain in the Middle East, ministering to the troops left behind after the Gulf War.

Dear Will, she thought. *Nora Bonesteel was right. A couple of weeks ago I thought she was crazy when she showed me that awful graveyard quilt and told me about her fears. But she was right. The deaths have come. And since you're a continent away, I am stuck with the task of ministering to the living, as the sheriff put it. I will do my best, but Lord knows, they deserve better.*

She slowed at a crossroads to read the small white road sign—a four-digit number almost impossible to make out in the glow of headlights. Turn left here. As she eased the car up the steep washboard of a mountain road, she thought of the last time she had driven that route. It had been several weeks ago, when she had gone to see Nora Bonesteel. Will had been stationed in the Gulf two months by then, and Laura had decided that it was time to stop feeling sorry for herself. She needed to get on with her normal routine.

In her mind an image of Donna Reed informed her that the minister's wife had a sacred duty to see to the parishioners, including the paying of an occasional home visit. She laughed at her own sanctimonious fantasies. Surely no one would care if she called on them or not, as awkward as she was conversing with them. But it would give her something to do. Jobs in Wake County were almost nonexistent for a thirty-eight-year-old woman with a college degree.

Every morning since Labor Day, she had gotten up, put on her blue wool suit, and waited by the telephone from six-thirty until eight, but calls for a substitute teacher were rare. She averaged three times a month, filling in for one of the county teachers who had the flu or a funeral to go to. The rest of the time, she eventually took off the suit, put on her old clothes, and cleaned the already clean house. One person alone didn't make too much of a mess. Today the phone had rung at 8:35, but it hadn't been the school system. It was the doctor's office. After spending twenty minutes staring at a congealing plate of eggs, she had decided that she needed to get out of the house. She would go visiting.

On less than a year's acquaintance, Laura Bruce still wasn't able to confide in her husband's parishioners. Their lives and their concerns were different from her own. Most of the women in Will's congregation had married in their late teens, settled down within hailing distance of parents or in-laws, and raised a brood of children. They had lives of accustomed hardship, but it would never have occurred to them to call themselves poor. They owned their own land and supplemented their income with garden-grown food and game from the mountain forests. They made their own clothes and seemed immune to the credit snares of their city cousins. They were all right as long as the world kept its taint out of their lives, Laura thought. But let their husbands take to drink, or find a younger woman and divorce them, and the smoothly working social system broke down. Even if there were jobs for unskilled women—fast-food places in Johnson City or a factory job in Erwin—they couldn't afford the commuting and child-care costs to take them. It seemed to Laura that every woman in Dark Hollow was exactly one man away from welfare.

She and Janet Underhill were the exceptions. Poor Janet Underhill. That's where Laura was going now. To the Underhills'. "There is a lot of blood," the sheriff had said. Laura and Janet were both outsiders, both college graduates, but beyond that they had little in common. When the Underhills first bought the old Tilden farm on the river, Will had gone over to welcome them to the community and invite them to church, but only their teenage daughter, Maggie, came with any regularity. She was now a member of the choir. Besides Maggie, the Underhills had three sons, but they weren't much on churchgoing. The family turned up at morning service every six weeks or so, for no particular reason that Laura Bruce could see. They didn't seem to mix well with their neighbors, although there was never any trouble. They just kept to themselves.

Maj. Paul Underhill was a short, wiry man with a graying crew cut and sharp little eyes like a ferret's. He was retired from the army now, but he would call himself major forever after. Janet never had much to say for herself. She seemed to be composed entirely of shades of beige, and her colorless smile had all the warmth of a winter moon. She didn't seem to want friends, and her husband had an impatient way about him that kept most people at a distance. Laura knew that the major had decided to farm when he retired from his army career. She wondered if they were happy in their choice of Dark Hollow as the place to call home.

So far, the rest of the community had been reserved but friendly toward the Underhills, and toward Laura, a woman with the right accent but city ways, and she found them reminiscent of the folks back in her southwest Virginia home, and therefore easy to get on with in a superficial way. As for Will getting called up by the Guard—people had been very sympathetic about it. They used a lay preacher, as they had in the old days, before seminaries began using rural churches as "starter parishes" for their graduates. Some of the oldest church members still remembered the time when a circuit rider on horseback had been pastor of six or seven far-flung churches, visiting one each Sunday in succession. Will's great-grandaddy had been a circuit preacher, traversing the green mountains on a shining bay saddle horse. In his black suit and string tie, with a Bible and a hymnbook in his saddlebag, he had ridden a six-church circuit until he was eighty, baptizing and burying generations of mountain Christians.

Perhaps it was not strange that Will's congregation had been understanding about his absence. Patriotism ran deep in the hills; Tennessee seceded, but Appalachia had been staunchly Union throughout the Civil War. Country was a duty never questioned; government policy was not debated. But when Uncle Sam got to meddling (prohibition, for example), the law was conveniently ignored. Half the time Laura wished that she could accept life as trustingly as the local people did, and the rest of the time she thought them naive, natural victims of a corrupt and greedy system. Still, their certainty that Will was right and honorable in serving his country gave Laura strength, but she had a feeling that before long she was going to need more than that. She might even need some advice from the parish prophetess Nora Bonesteel.

That day, when her curiosity about the old lady had won out over her fear and skepticism, she had asked directions at the general store and set off on a parish visit. As her car rounded the first steep bend and began the sharply angled climb to the summit, Laura could see most of the Dark Hollow valley out the passenger side window. Although it was early November, the weather had not yet been cold enough to kill the grass, so the meadows that stretched out below her were still green, with rolled stacks of hay lined up against the fence, awaiting the inevitable winter. Far below she could see the Weavers' Angus herd grazing on the bank of Dark Creek. The valley was a succession of low, rounded hills, stretched out vertically between the spines of two mountain ranges. The far one, she thought, would be North Carolina mountains, but from here there was no discernible boundary, only an endless roll of blue hills in a haze stretching toward the horizon.

The remoteness of the mountain vista reminded her that Nora Bonesteel was elderly and lived alone, which made it even more thoughtful to check on her between Sundays every now and then. In this part of the county, neighbors were well out of hollering distance, and hospitals were an hour away in any direction.

By the time Laura's car had crested the mountain, opening up all the spreading vastness of the Little Dove River two thousand feet below, she was worrying more about herself than about Nora. Would Nora expect her to lead a prayer or anything? Would the old woman sense what was troubling her? Should she even talk about it with a parishioner? She wished Will were here to advise her.

She stopped the car on the summit to think and to look out at the comforting wilderness. The Little Dove Valley was a tapestry of autumn browns and gold, with only the Underhills' pastureland and the pine trees on the hills to give it a touch of green.

Brownest of all was the river. Laura's gaze hardened as she stared out at the swath of dead, dun-colored water, oozing through the cut in the hills. She wondered if animals tried to drink there anymore. This is what comes of never questioning the government, she thought angrily. They won't give a damn about what happens to you. Will had read some of the newspaper articles about the environmental hazards of the river, and he thought that the community should hold a meeting about the Little Dove River. He had talked about petitions, and letters to the district's congressman, but another cause had captured his attention before he could appeal to his flock for action. Now Will was facing action of a different sort, and the Little Dove rolled on as before, bringing its poison into the valley. Laura sighed, unhappy to be reminded that no wilderness is really very far from the taint of civilization.

She might have mentioned her pregnancy to the sheriff tonight when he asked for her help, but even as her mind framed the excuse, she sneered at her own cowardice. She wasn't even showing yet. She remembered an old *Life* magazine photo she'd seen as a child: Ethel Kennedy playing a vigorous set of tennis in her eighth month. Besides, agreeing to go was easier than explaining to this harried-sounding stranger at a death scene about something so personal as her unborn child. Even Will didn't know yet. Laura heard herself telling the sheriff to give her directions to the farm. She would be there as soon as she could.

She slowed the car as she came to the Ashe Mountain Road turnoff. A left turn and two miles of gradually steepening incline led to Nora Bonesteel's home in a mountain meadow. Laura peered up through the trees to see if she could discern any lights ablaze on the summit above, but all was dark. Should she come back in the morning and tell Nora Bonesteel of the night's events? Local legend claimed that she would know already.

As she drove on in the darkness, Laura thought back on her visit to Nora Bonesteel on that clear autumn day. Even then, she thought, the old woman had seen death coming.

Nora Bonesteel lived in a two-story white house that dated back further than anybody could remember. It sat in a meadow on the top of Ashe Mountain, shaded by century-old oaks, with an apple orchard, a pond, and a view of all creation. The dirt road was cut into the mountain above Nora's land. To reach her house, you parked on the side of the road, near the ditch full of tiger lilies, and you walked down a lavender-lined path to her front door. The meadow itself seemed to hang on the side of the mountain, like a precariously balanced Christmas ornament. From that meadow, the world fell away to a woven pattern of dark green and beige, seamed by the ocher river, all stretching away to the slate-blue mountains on the horizon.

In the summer it was a tapestry of greens, embroidered with laurel and redbud; now it was a sepia print of a landscape washed in autumn. On the oak-tangled mountain across the valley, the craggy face of the Hangman stared back.

When Laura Bruce's car pulled up beside the lone mailbox on Ashe Mountain Road, Nora Bonesteel was already standing on her front porch, waving for her visitor to come down. In the clear mountain silence you could hear the rumble of a car engine a quarter of a mile away. Even at her age, her lean body looked wiry rather than frail. She wore a plain gray dress with a homespun crimson shawl wrapped about her shoulders to keep out the wind. She was a spare, hollow-cheeked woman, and although she was well past seventy, her hair was still dark, lightly peppered with gray. She kept it pulled back from her face and fastened with tortoiseshell combs in a bun at the nape of her neck. She waved to Laura and motioned for her to come into the house.

Laura Bruce was careful to wipe her feet twice on the rush mat outside before she ventured onto the age-darkened oak floor of Nora Bonesteel's front room. Because that front parlor faced up the mountain and was shaded by the porch, the room was always in shadow, despite a large front window. An old horsehair sofa and a dark braided rug were left in the room for form's sake, but no one ever sat there. It was only a space to pass through on your way to the back of the house—the part that faced the downward slope of the mountain, rooms of light and air that seemed to be built on clouds.

A few years back Nora had gotten a jackleg carpenter to take out most of the east wall of the back parlor and replace it with huge glass windows, so that the first thing you saw when you came into the room was the gentle slope of the back meadow, ending in woods, and beyond that, a thousand feet below, the sprawl of field and forest and the distant blue mountains of North Carolina on the horizon.

The room ran the length of the house. In one corner, surrounded by weeping figs and potted ferns, stood the frame of a handmade loom threaded with white strands for the day's weaving. At the other end of the room, a flowered sofa and two shabby green wing chairs faced the stone fireplace. A cracked china pitcher, filled with mums and asters, the last of the fall flowers, stood on the carved oak mantel. From the kitchen came the smell of brewing coffee and faint strains of classical music from Nora Bonesteel's portable radio.

Laura Bruce walked to the window beside the loom and looked out at the valley and the haze of hills beyond it. "You can see a long way from up here," she said.

Nora Bonesteel set two pottery mugs of coffee on the white pine table in front of the sofa. "Yes," she said. "I can see a long way."

"The valley looks beautiful spread out below. I can't even see any houses. It hasn't changed since pioneer days."

Nora Bonesteel shook her head. "Lord, that isn't so. The old folks wouldn't know this land at all if they were to come back. It would about nigh break their hearts. Fifty years ago, every valley and mountaintop you see would have been covered with chestnut trees. In the spring they flowered white like snowcaps on the top of every mountain, and every autumn their leaves would turn those hills into a shower of gold. Place names like Yellow Knob and White Top hark back to the old days when these mountains were covered with chestnut trees. Those trees were our wealth. We lumbered the old ones for hardwood, and we fed the livestock on the wild chestnuts that fell in the pastures. And then one day they began to die."

"The chestnut blight," murmured Laura. She remembered

17

a table she'd seen as a child at a great-aunt's farmhouse. It was a homemade kitchen table of black-swirled chestnut wood, and the old woman polished it every day. Laura remembered her saying that she prized the table because her husband had made it of chestnut wood and now both were dead and gone forever. "All the American chestnuts caught a disease. It was in the thirties, wasn't it?"

"That's when it reached here, I reckon," said Nora, staring out at the mountaintops taken over by pine and scrub oak. "Do you know where it came from?"

Laura shook her head. "I thought it just happened."

"The New York Botanical Garden imported a tree with the disease, and they allowed the fungus to escape. It traveled from tree to tree, and when it was done, it had killed every chestnut tree in America. Fifty years, and they still haven't found a cure. They keep trying, though." She pointed to two bare trees that were little more than twigs, encircled in stones a few feet down the slope.

"Are they chestnuts?" asked Laura.

"Three years old," said Nora proudly. "The blight doesn't kill them right off, you know. Some trees got to be seven, ten years old before it took them. This is a new strain I got mail order. We're hoping to raise up a blight-resistant chestnut. It's too soon to tell, though."

"Don't you know?" asked Laura. She reddened as soon as the words were out of her mouth, because she felt that the Sight was something you didn't talk about to Nora Bonesteel. It was like noticing someone's handicap.

"I never get things that have much to do with me," Nora replied. "Sometimes I can't make out what they do mean until what they foretell goes and happens. Once when I was seven years old, I started crying in a neighbor's house, saying I smelled smoke. Well, they searched that house from rafter to root cellar, and never did find anything afire. But two days later, some cinders stuck in the chimney during the night, and burned that house to the ground. It didn't do anybody any good, my early warning. My best friend Nellie died in that fire."

Laura shivered. "What an awful thing for a seven-year-old! You must have felt terribly guilty."

Nora looked away. "Nellie told me I wasn't to blame. I'd see her now and again. Till I grew up. Course she never did."

Laura sat openmouthed, wondering what she could possibly reply to that. What would Will have said in such an odd conversation? Would he have denounced Nora's ghosts as a pagan superstition, or would he have humored a frail old woman? He might even have believed her. It was something they had never discussed. There was too much to say about everyday matters: housekeeping and social obligations; politics and financial affairs; church business and parish problems. There was no time to worry about those who were dead and gone.

"I hardly ever get anything I'd set a store on knowing," Nora continued. "Take soap operas, now, for an instance. Do you watch them? That Brittany Devlin on the two o'clock one, I just can't figure out what in the world—"

Laura blinked at this unexpected turn in the conversation. Alas, she could not discuss soap operas, either. Gently she turned the conversation back to Nora herself.

"So you won't know if you're ever . . ." Laura hesitated. Talking of death to an old person seemed impolite, indelicate. "Going to become ill?" she finished lamely.

"Likely not. It doesn't interest me much, anyhow."

"Just as well that I came to see how you were," said Laura briskly, mistaking Nora Bonesteel's simple statement for self-pity. "Besides, to tell you the truth, I was a little lonely myself. I miss Will." She hoped that the old woman

19

would say something—however insincere—like "He'll be back soon." She would have treasured such politeness as a prophecy, but Nora said nothing.

"How are you feeling?" asked Laura after another moment of silence.

"I'm tolerable in body but low in spirit," said Nora Bonesteel. "I dread the shortening of days in the autumn. It's more night than we need in this world."

Laura smiled. "Yes, but for about ten days the trees are the most beautiful shades of red and gold. There's nothing more beautiful than autumn."

"It isn't worth it," said Nora Bonesteel. "When you're my age, you feel the cold all the way through you, and every year makes you less certain that you'll be around in the spring, when the world comes back to life. Pretty soon old Persey will leave me, too. I've seen her scratching around in the backyard there when the wind blew cold."

She pointed to a fat, white-muzzled groundhog curled up in a cat basket among the houseplants. Persey, who was clutching a half-eaten Stayman apple in her paws, watched the visitor with smoldering eyes, ready to run with her prize.

"Does she still hibernate?" asked Laura, staring back into the plump little face.

"Oh, yes. She has to. It's nature's way. She's with me all summer, eating me out of house and home, and then come late fall, she digs her hole out back, and tries on death until the spring comes. But Persey's old now, too, and I'm always afraid she won't be able to make it back from the grave."

Laura ignored the shiver that rippled down her spine. "Well, I'm sure you'll both be here in April," she said briskly. "Look, I've brought you some of our garden seeds so that we can swap stock." She held up the small paper bag.

Nora sat down in one of the wing chairs, and pulled a length of quilted cloth out of her sewing basket. "I'm glad for some company, Laura Bruce. I don't get about much these days. You don't mind my sewing while we talk, do you? I see better in daylight."

Laura took a sip of her coffee. "Please do. What are you making now?"

Nora Bonesteel looked down at the dark fabric in her lap, and her expression became somber. "It's an old-fashioned quilt. I reckon. I've been working on it for a few weeks now. Something has been troubling me lately. It devils me when I try to sleep, and when I'm awake, it hovers just on the edge of my thoughts, where I can't get a good look at it, but it's a dark shape. I can't quite put my finger on what it is. So I thought I'd start a quilt, and see if occupying my hands would ease my mind. I didn't think about any set pattern; just set to working to see could I find out anything by what I was called on to make. This is what I got."

She held the quilt up by the corners so that Laura could see its design. A three-inch border of black velvet framed the quilt, and against its green background she had embroidered a scene: a wavy swatch of blue fabric suggested a river, placed below rounded rows of dark blue and green satin mountains. The foreground of the picture contained a full-leafed oak tree towering over gray satin crosses and rounded gravestones, surrounded by an unfinished web of black stitchery resembling a wrought-iron fence.

"It's a cemetery," said Laura, staring at the textile landscape. "It's very well done, but . . . what are those things on the bottom hem?"

Along the bottom of the quilt, Nora Bonesteel had tacked six coffin-shaped pieces of black satin. "Caskets. I think they're meant to go in the center of the quilt by and by," said Nora, speaking dispassionately, as if it were someone else's work.

"I've never see a quilt with that design," said Laura. The

design was executed in rich velvet and satin, and the stitchery was flawless, but she found herself reluctant to touch
the fabric. "Did the making of it ease your mind?"

"No, but it centers the feeling. When I put that heavy
material across my lap to sew on it, it gives me chills."

"What do you think it means?" asked Laura, staring at
the white needlepoint crosses in the quilted scene.

"Death, of course," said Nora Bonesteel in the voice she
might have used to tell you the name of a wildflower. "But
it isn't coming sudden and accidentallike, the way a truck
might smash into a car next week. This death got rolling a
good while back. Just lately it's been picking up speed."

"Who?" asked Laura. Her thoughts, a litany of *crazy old
woman, crazy old woman*, did not drown out her fears.

"I'll know when it hits them."

CHAPTER

2

I am a brother to dragons, and a companion to owls.

—JOB 30:29

The red shine of two eyes above the road surface ahead warned Laura of the danger in time to brake and allow the doe to cross safely. Sitting motionless behind the steering wheel, she watched the deer, illuminated by the high beams, sidle across the blacktop in no apparent hurry. It was a small doe, probably a yearling, and unlikely to be traveling alone. The car must mask the human scent, Laura thought, still waiting for the deer to leave the pavement. At last, she blew the horn, causing the animal to disappear into the underbrush in one arching bound. The noise would warn the others to keep their distance until the car was safely past their crossing.

Laura seemed to be afraid of everything tonight. When she came to the narrow stretch of road that curved under the concrete railroad trestle, she sat there for several agonizing minutes, unwilling to proceed in the dark when she could not see around the bend. At last, she blew her horn and edged forward into the deserted country road. She did not speed up again until half a mile later, when she passed the shabby frame church that was the snake handlers' domain. This sect of solemn fundamentalists took their beliefs from one verse in the sixteenth chapter of Mark, in which Jesus describes the attributes of his followers: *"They shall take up serpents; and if they drink any deadly thing, it shall not hurt them; they shall lay hands on the sick, and they shall recover.''* The believers kept to themselves in the re-motest hollers of the county. Laura had never met a snake handler; she had never heard anything said against them, but on this harrowing night the mere sight of their church chilled her. She fiddled with the radio, trying to find a lively all-night station to distract her, but on the one clear channel she found, the stentorian tones of the speaker told her within seconds that she was hearing a sermon. Impatiently, she switched it off, only then remembering Will, and the fact that she had thus far neglected to pray.

She was nearly there. The ruins of an old country store and gas station on the left side of the road were her signal to turn onto a gravel side road that wound down the hillsides between pastures and pine groves into the narrow valley cut by the Little Dove River. The old Tilden place, now owned by the Underhills, lay in rich bottomland a few hundred yards from the silent river. One more downward twist in the road and she would be in sight of the farmstead.

The house was ablaze with lights shining far into the darkness of the surrounding valley. On the road, a shelf of gravel a quarter of a mile above the home place, Laura could see the white shapes of sheriff's department cars and the rescue-squad ambulance parked on the lawn in front of the Underhills' front porch. Even in the silence she could sense the hurry and confusion behind the glow of the house lights.

She edged her car off the gravel driveway, and parked it beside a spreading lilac bush, out of the way of the official vehicles. She reached for Will's big leather Bible on the pas-senger seat, but in the end she went in without it.

The Underhills' place was a two-story white frame house with narrow columns divided by a small upstairs porch. The front door stood open, and now she could hear voices from within. She wondered whether to call out to let them know she was there, or to go in as unobtrusively as possible so as not to disturb them. *There's a lot of blood*, the sheriff had said. She stopped on the threshold of the Underhills' front hall, a spacious entryway paneled in shining chestnut boards. Each wall contained a closed door. The muffled voices seemed to be coming from above. Laura walked to the base of the stairs and called up toward the upstairs hall, "Mr. Arrowood! It's Laura Bruce, from the church."

A moment later a scowling, dark-haired deputy appeared on the stairway landing. "Are you here to see about the kids?" he demanded, clattering down the stairs. His blue eyes never left her face, and she felt a momentary twinge of free-floating guilt. On his khaki uniform the silver name bar said *J. LeDonne*.

"Yes, Officer . . . LeDonne," she stammered. "The sheriff asked me to come."

He nodded. "They're in here." He nodded toward a closed door to the left of the stairs. "I'll take you."

Laura stood still. "First I need to know what happened. The sheriff didn't seem to want to go into detail on the phone. Are they all right? I'm not even sure which . . . who . . . who's left."

LeDonne glanced for a moment in the direction of the voices in the front parlor. "They'll be bringing the bodies out soon," he said. "But I'll tell you the gist of it. We got a call about eleven from Maggie Underhill, the teenage daughter."

"Yes," said Laura. "I know her from the church. She sings in our choir."

"She acts, too. She and her brother Mark were down at the high school practicing for the class play. *Hamlet*. While they were gone, some kind of altercation took place here on the farm. We haven't pieced it all together yet. When Mark and Maggie Underhill returned from play practice, they discovered the bodies of their parents in the living room." He jerked his thumb toward the room to the right.

27

"Both had been killed with blasts from a shotgun. They called us, and while they were waiting for us to get here, they checked the rest of the house, and found their other brothers, also dead." LeDonne paused, as if debating whether to say more. Her shock, which he took for calmness, encouraged him to tell her the rest. "The older boy's wound was self-inflicted. Right now we think that he killed the rest of the family and then committed suicide."

"They're all dead?" Laura repeated, trying to take it all in. What, all my pretty chickens and their dam? No, that wasn't the right play.

LeDonne nodded. "Except for the two who were at play practice. I don't know why he didn't wait for them. The sheriff has talked to them a little, but they're in shock, and we have the rest of the crime scene to attend to. If you'd just keep them company, we'd appreciate it. They don't need to be alone."

"You don't want me to find out anything, do you?"

"No, ma'am." LeDonne was patient. "If they volunteer anything, fine. But we asked you here as a family friend."

"But I didn't—"

"I know. Nobody around here knew that family worth a damn. Maybe if they had, this wouldn't have happened."

He opened the door for her, and when she hung back, he edged through ahead of her and led the way into the front room, an extra bedroom that doubled as sewing room and study. "It's all right," he murmured so that the youngsters couldn't overhear. "There's not much blood in here."

Laura saw flecks of blood on the white wall near the window. Had someone been trying to open the window to escape from the gunman? She tried to imagine the Underhills' terror, facing their own son turned executioner. Would there be room left in their brains to feel any emotion other than fear? Compassion, perhaps, for the boy's anguish? Or did the combat-trained major respond by fighting back against the enemy?

The image of Nora Bonesteel and her lost playmate, Nellie, sprang unbidden to her mind, and she forced herself to stop thinking of the Underhills' final moments. It was a form of prying, she thought. Suppose they could "overhear" her thoughts? That was nonsense, of course, but it was pointless for her to dwell on the horrors of their ordeal. She lowered her gaze to avoid the reminder of violence, and saw that she had nearly stepped in a rust-colored footprint on the beige carpeting. Stifling her cry of surprise with a deep intake of breath, she fixed her eyes firmly on the back of LeDonne's khaki uniform.

She must remember to pray for them, she was thinking as the deputy opened the door to the Underhill den.

Mark and Maggie Underhill sat together on the beige sofa, staring at the only splash of color in the room—a late-night television program on the screen in front of them. The rest of the room shrank away from the beholder in timid beiges and passive browns, offering no clue to the occupants' personality except to suggest that they had none.

On the wall above the sofa hung a family portrait of six people smiling self-consciously at the camera. Paul Underhill, stiff and formal in full military uniform, seemed unaware of the others' presence. Beside him, in a dress of straw-colored linen, his wife, Janet, simpered, her eyes upturned to gaze reverently at the major. The three older children stood restlessly behind their parents. Josh, a sallow and gangly adolescent in an ill-fitting navy blazer, glowered as if daring anyone to ridicule his awkwardness. His sandy hair glistened with oil, and his hands, just visible in the space between his parents, were twisted together, showing white knuckles.

The other two teenagers, Mark and Maggie, had inherited

their father's classic features and dark good looks, and were so alike that one could mistake them for twins. Maggie wore a white lace dress, with a gold cross at her throat. Her long dark hair was tied back with a ribbon of red satin, revealing tiny gold crosses in her earlobes. A solemn expression and the unnatural tilt of her chin gave her the appearance of someone in an old sepia photograph, holding the long and stilted pose of the daguerreotype. She stood directly behind her mother, forcing the viewer to see the unfortunate contrast between Maggie Underhill's youth and beauty and the dowdiness of the faded, negligible woman seated in front of her.

Mark Underhill might have been his father at seventeen, but his expression lacked the determination radiating from the older man. The boy was sleekly handsome, almost pretty. His dark hair was well groomed and fell across his forehead in a flattering side part, emphasizing his dark eyes and prominent cheekbones. Surely this young man's adolescence had been more pleasant than that of his older brother Josh. He wore a white shirt and red necktie, in harmony with his sister's attire, but instead of looking at her or at the camera, he was glancing apprehensively to the right, toward Josh and Major Underhill.

The youngest child, Simon, eight years old and still a cherubic blond, sat cross-legged at his parents' feet, looking sulky and impatient. One of Janet's hands was resting on the shoulder of his red blazer, as if to restrain him until the photo could be taken.

No one in the picture was smiling.

How odd that these ordinary, slightly dull people should die so suddenly, so dramatically. Laura realized that her detachment came from disbelief. The actuality of the Underhill murders had not hit her quite yet. She wondered if Mark and Maggie had realized the finality of it all. They were still staring at the television, oblivious to the presence of anyone else in the room.

Maggie Underhill's dark hair now hung in ringlets about her shoulders. A curling iron, Laura guessed. She wore a pink knit sweater and black jeans.

Mark Underhill looked Byronic in his oversized white shirt, his dark hair curling about the collar. Laura wondered if he had been asked to grow it longer for his role in the play. Major Underhill was not the sort of man who would have permitted his son to wear such an effete style otherwise.

The pair did not acknowledge the deputy or Laura. After an awkward moment of silence, she whispered to LeDonne. "Do you think they've gone into shock? Shouldn't they be seen by a doctor?"

"The rescue squad came out," LeDonne told her. "They checked their blood pressure, gave them something. The kids didn't want to go to the hospital. Before the rescue squad could argue about it, they had another call come in about a wreck on Route 11, so they had to leave. That's when Spencer called you."

Laura looked doubtful. "I'll do my best," she murmured, "but I don't have any experience in grief counseling."

"You're better than nothing."

The silent figures on the couch stared at the flickering screen. Laura picked up an oak straight chair and set it next to the sofa.

Suddenly, Maggie Underhill looked up at her with a curious smile. *"He is dead and gone, lady, He is dead and gone, At his head a grass-green turf, At his heels a stone."*

"Play's over now, Maggie!" said her brother, shaking her arm.

"It's been a great shock for her," said Laura. Sitting down next to Maggie, she leaned forward and said, "I don't know if you two remember me. I'm Laura Bruce, from the church, and I'm here to do whatever I can to help you get through this awful night."

Mark Underhill looked at her curiously. "Like what?"

"I don't know," said Laura. "Would you like to talk? Or perhaps I could make you some tea? Perhaps you'd like to go somewhere else for a while."

"No," said Maggie, who seemed to have come out of her reverie. "We're going to stay here. They're going to take away the bodies. Will they clean it all up?"

Laura glanced up at the deputy, whose shake of the head was almost imperceptible. "I'm afraid not," Laura stammered. "But I'm sure I can have that seen to tomorrow. Meanwhile, is there anyone who should be notified about this? Can I call anyone for you?"

Maggie Underhill shook her head. "Alone, alone, all all alone," she said dreamily. "Our grandparents are dead. And now Mom and Dad . . ."

"It isn't as if we're children, though," said her brother. "Could we plan the funeral, Mrs. Bruce? It will have to be done soon, won't it? My mother would want it to be nice."

"I suppose we could," said Laura, who had never planned a funeral before. The idea of doing so now did not strike her as an appropriate consolation, but the Underhills seemed to have mastered their grief. "Have you any idea of the sort of service you want?"

"We could bury them here on the farm," said Mark.

His sister shook her head. "Not here, Mark. They might not care for that. It isn't as if we had lived here very long. We never lived anywhere very long, did we?"

"Can you arrange to have their clothes taken away?" he asked.

"I expect so," said Laura. There were women in the church that she could ask about this. Surely some local custom existed for such necessities of death. "Would you like the church to give their clothes to needy families?"

"I'll be going back to the other side now, Mrs. Bruce," said LeDonne. "If you need anything . . ." His voice trailed off. No one was listening.

LeDonne closed the family-room door firmly behind him, and went back to join the others. The Underhill siblings weren't behaving like any bereaved relatives he'd ever seen, but that didn't prove anything. The few murderers he had seen in county cases were usually hysterical, with some combination of remorse and fear that was difficult to distinguish from genuine bereavement. Guilty people couldn't afford to take things calmly. Except in 'Nam, where you couldn't afford to take them otherwise. Still, their lack of emotion made him wonder. He followed the sound of voices into the kitchen.

Sheriff Spencer Arrowood was talking to the county coroner, Gerald Graybeal, the latest member of his family to run Graybeals Funeral Home in Hamelin. Beside them on the scarred wood floor lay three body bags, already sealed. Maj. Paul Underhill. Janet Underhill. Simon. And Josh. LeDonne looked around the room.

"We had only three body bags," said Spender Arrowood, anticipating his question. "I had to put the little boy in with his mother." Beneath the weariness in his voice there was an unmistakable strain of emotion.

"You taking the rabbit, too?" asked LeDonne.

Spencer nodded toward a green garbage bag folded next to the bodies. "Thought I would. I don't see how it fits in with anything, though. It was outside, and it hadn't been shot."

LeDonne's face darkened. "Be better if it had been. I hope the bastard that did that did get his head blown off."

The sheriff sighed. "I don't think there's much doubt of that. Wish he'd left a note."

"Why should he care what we think?"

Gerald Graybeal, a stout and hairy man with too red a face and too blue black hair, stifled a yawn. He glanced at his heavy gold watch, its band buried in the curl of hairs on his wrist. LeDonne wondered how the man could get it off without ripping out clumps of them. "Is that about it, Sheriff?" he asked. "There's not a whole lot I can do here, you know."

"I know," said Spencer. "But you know and I know that the law says there has to be a coroner present at a death scene to pronounce the victims dead."

"They're dead, all right, Sheriff. I've seen road-killed groundhogs that had a better chance of—"

"Yes, well, I appreciate your help getting them—" He nodded toward the zippered bags.

"Glad to help, boys." Graybeal hesitated. "Should I take them on to the funeral home, or do you need to run some tests?"

"Lab work," said Spencer. "They'll have to go to the medical examiner. I know it's an open-and-shut case, but we still have to do it by the book."

"You never know," said LeDonne unexpectedly.

Graybeal and the sheriff looked at him in surprise. "You don't think the oldest boy did it?"

The deputy shrugged. "I just don't like taking things for granted."

When the crime scene had been thoroughly photographed, measured, and tested and the dead had been sent away, Spencer Arrowood decided that he ought to go in and see the stranger he'd routed out of bed to tend to the living. Nominally, the Bruces' church was the one that Spencer himself attended, because a great-uncle of his had once been pastor there. In recent years he had scarcely set foot inside the sanctuary, but his mother still went regularly, and she had given favorable reports of the new preacher's wife. He had not been able to think of anyone else to call.

He made his way to the colorless sitting room on the other side of the house, where Laura Bruce was deep in conference with the two surviving Underhills, making funeral arrangements. She looked older than Pastor Bruce, the sheriff decided: he was still shy of thirty; she must be closer to forty, but still attractive. Her short dark hair curled about her face becomingly, and there was an earnest sincerity in her face that he found reassuring. She seemed to be coping well with tragedy.

When she saw him standing in the doorway, she excused herself to the Underhill children, who barely seemed to notice, and joined him in the doorway. "Sheriff Arrowood? I'm Laura Bruce," she said a little breathlessly. "Is everything all right?"

The tiredness seemed to hit him in the back of the neck and creep slowly forward to his eyes and mouth. "Well, it's as all right as it's going to get, I reckon. We've finished up here, and the bodies have been removed for autopsy. I just wanted to thank you for coming out here. Is anyone coming out to stay with the brother and sister?"

Laura's eyes clouded with concern. "They say there isn't anybody. I don't think they ought to be left alone, though, so I guess I'll stay."

Spencer Arrowood looked at his watch. It was a little past three o'clock, and he still had reports to write up, and a full day of bureaucratic details to attend to after sunup. He stifled a yawn. "Guess I could stay, too," he said. "Make sure everything's all right."

"Can I go out to the kitchen? I thought I'd make some tea. Would you like some?"

"I could use some, but are you sure you want to go traipsing through this house? We didn't clean it up, you know."

Laura closed her eyes wearily. "I know," she said. "As soon as we finish drinking that tea, I thought I'd start on it."

CHAPTER

3

The twelvemonth and a day being up,
  The dead began to speak:
"Oh, who sits weeping on my grave,
  And will not let me sleep?"

—"The Unquiet Grave"

The medical examiner's report and the inquest that followed were both perfunctory. The Underhills had all died of close-range wounds from the same weapon, a shotgun, and paraffin tests indicated that the gunman had been the deceased adolescent son, Joshua Underhill, who had subsequently committed suicide.

Representatives of the medical examiner's office had inspected the sheriff's diagrams of the crime scene, studying photographs of footprints and patterns of blood spatters on the walls of the farmhouse. As part of their final report on the case, they offered a reconstruction of the events that tallied with the first guess of the sheriff's department. Paul Underhill had died first, and judging from the front-entry shoulder wound, he had attempted to fight off his attacker. A horrifying chase through the house had ensued, leaving traces of blood in several rooms. Finally, another shotgun blast had slammed the retired major against the living-room wall, leaving gouts of blood that sent trickling arrows down to indicate his body, slumped against the baseboard.

Where was Janet during all this? Hiding? Attempting to go for help? She had died last. To the sheriff's surprise, the medical examiner's office insisted that the second victim had been eight-year-old Simon Underhill, the mischievous blond in the family photograph. His head still lay on the pillow, and the stain of blackened blood and gray matter on the wall behind him indicated that he had not raised his head when the killer approached him. Sleeping. There was some mercy in that. The bottom sheet was soaked to the waist level with blood from the head wound, but below that it was perfectly clean. How then to explain blood on the child's hand, curled under his right thigh? Serum testing proved that this blood belonged to an animal. The report offered no speculation regarding this fact. The rabbit outside, Spencer Arrowood thought. Was that a coincidence, or did it mean something? Since Simon Underhill had been shot while asleep in bed, the sheriff had assumed that the child had been an afterthought for the killer, caught by haphazard in the momentum of slaughter.

According to the medical examiner, Janet Underhill had been last. She was found a few feet from an open hall-closet door, lying facedown, shot in the back of the head at almost point-blank range. The killer had found her crouched in the closet, hiding behind the winter coats. He had dragged her out, throwing her facedown on the wooden floor of the hall. Putting his foot (bloodstained shoe print) on her shoulder blade, he had pointed the barrel of the gun at her head and fired. Not much of her cranial area was left: It had exited in one crimson swath straight in front of her.

But this was her son, Spencer kept telling himself. What would make a boy do that to his family? Drug use? Mental illness? There was no record of either. A tox screen on Josh Underhill's blood sample tested negative for drugs. In cold blood, then. What had made him do it? In order to keep that secret, Josh Underhill had gone upstairs, put the gun in his mouth, and pulled the trigger. He had gone to his own room to do it. That tallied with the suicide's pattern of behavior. In a murder-suicide you almost never found them beside their victim. Spencer pictured the gunman executing his victims in a raging frenzy, lasting ten minutes at

40

most. When the echoes of the last shots fade, there is a great silence, and the killer realizes that his act was irrevocable. More silence; more time passes. Finally, he goes away from the sight of his loved one, and in the privacy of his room, he sits down with the gun between his feet, barrel between his teeth, and reaches down for the trigger.

Four rooms befouled with blood and brain matter, the incidental selfishness of the madman. Why would Mark and Maggie Underhill want to keep living in that house of death?

Spencer had spent a futile morning questioning the two surviving siblings, learning very little about them or the relationships in their troubled family. Had there been any problems within the family? A drinking problem? Had Josh ever been treated for psychiatric problems? The brother and sister were courteous, but wooden in their replies. Spoken without emotion, their responses might have been comments regarding the deaths in *Hamlet*. They didn't know what happened, they told him. Perhaps an intruder? No? An accident, then. The sheriff did not even bother to argue with their indifferently proffered theories. The killer was dead; legally, the rest did not matter. It was only the frustration of the enigma that made him pursue it.

A second aspect of the case was his business, and he dreaded bringing it up to two new orphans, but he had no choice. "What are your plans?" he asked them when the crime-related questioning was out of the way.

"Plans?" they echoed, politely blank.

"You're both under eighteen. The law says that you have to have a guardian. You can't stay by yourselves on that remote farm."

"Why not?" asked Mark Underhill. "I can drive. There's the insurance money for us to live on. We can take care of ourselves."

"You don't want to live there. With those memories."

Mark shrugged. "It's an old house. We got used to the idea of people having died there."

"Besides," said Maggie, "we don't have any close relatives. And we don't want to have to go away. We want to finish school here." She was clenching and unclenching her fists in the folds of her skirt.

"We know how to cook and use the washing machine," Mark added.

Spencer sighed impatiently. "It isn't just a question of doing laundry and cooking your own meals. You'd have to see to taxes and house maintenance, and all the rest of the things that adults have to contend with."

The two dark-haired youngsters looked at each other for a moment. Finally, Maggie spoke. "What about Dad's lawyer?"

"Dallas Stuart? He can see to the settling of the estate, and probably to the money matters as well, but he's seventy-two. He can't be riding out to Dark Hollow to see if you need anything."

Mark scowled. "Like we don't have a phone! Okay, Sheriff, appoint us a guardian. Not someone that we have to go and live with but someone who would look in on us every now and then to make sure we were eating all right, and keeping the house in shape."

"The minister's wife, Mrs. Bruce," said Maggie. "She'd do it for us. She said she'd help us in any way that she could."

"I'll talk to her about it," said Spencer Arrowood, disliking the suggestion. Still, it made a certain amount of sense. Why should the kids be forced to leave their home and school just because they had no one to come and stay with them?

"I'm seventeen now," said the boy, sensing the sheriff's

weakening. "I'll be eighteen in May. It's just a formality, really. Just a couple of months."

"I'll talk this over with your lawyer and with Mrs. Bruce," Spencer told them. "It isn't settled yet, but I'll do what I can."

"Thank you, Sheriff," said Maggie Underhill with a dreamy smile. *"I hope all will be well. We must be patient: but I cannot choose but weep to think they would lay him i' th' cold ground. My brother shall know of it, and so I thank you for your good counsel. . . . Good night!"*

Spencer, recognizing the quotation, gave Mark Underhill a questioning look, but the young man only smiled and shook his head. Delayed shock, he thought. He made a mental note to talk to Laura Bruce about arranging counseling for both of them.

The Underhills were buried within the iron gates of Oakdale, the cemetery in Hamelin. There were many small cemeteries on the mountainsides in Dark Hollow, but they were all family plots, on land still owned by descendants of the deceased. Mark and Maggie Underhill hadn't wanted to start such a tradition on the farm. They were still strangers to the land and the community, and perhaps they wanted to remove the memories of the tragedy far from their own doorstep.

They huddled together now at the graveside, a little apart from the other mourners—mostly curiosity seekers drawn by the notoriety of the case. It was a cloudless autumn day. Buffalo Mountain's maple trees shone like a bloodstain against the shadows of the pines on its slopes, but the cemetery grass was still green.

Spencer Arrowood watched the two surviving Underhills with pity tinged with defensiveness. There wasn't anything he could have done, he told himself, but he felt obliged to come to the funeral. Now that he was in Oakdale, though, he found himself thinking about another graveside service, more than twenty years ago. He had been Mark Underhill's age then. He wondered if he had looked as pale and stupefied. He knew he had felt like that. The whole world had suddenly—randomly, it seemed—needed readjusting, and he had been given no advance notice to get accustomed to the change. He remembered staring at the flag-draped casket and feeling nothing but adolescent self-consciousness. Surely all these people were staring at him throughout the ceremony, waiting to report his every facial expression. He had resolved to have none, and that effort of will had made him oblivious to the words of the funeral service. He had never been able to remember what was said that day. Only that it seemed to last a long time in the summer heat and that it had ended with taps.

More than fifty people had turned up for the Underhill burial. Most of them had worn the traditional dark clothes, but because it was cold, they had been forced to add whatever coat they owned over their mourning outfits, so that the assembly was a curious mixture of reds and browns, with an occasional muffler of riotous plaid to break the solemnity. At the edge of the crowd he saw Laura Bruce, looking solemnly formal in a dark suit and hat. He almost raised his hand to wave to her, but he decided that it wouldn't show proper respect to the deceased to be glad-handing the mourners at the graveside. After the funeral he would approach her and relay the Underhills' request that she be appointed their nonresident guardian until Mark turned eighteen.

He noticed that Nora Bonesteel wasn't present. People said that she never did attend a funeral. Probably just visited with the deceased at her home up there on the mountain, he told himself sardonically. He had heard the legends about the old woman of Ashe Mountain without considering them one way or another. It didn't matter to him if she saw ghosts or not; such things had no place in his world of order and law and finding probable cause. His mother had been full of questions about the Underhill case. Did Nora Bonesteel really foresee the deaths? Had Spencer discussed it with her? (That would be the day.) He hoped none of the supernatural business found its way into the newspaper accounts of the case. The murders were sensational enough without bringing ghost stories into it. He wanted the Underhills to be left in peace.

The elderly lay preacher who was substituting for Will Bruce had balked at the task of delivering a graveside eulogy in such sensational circumstances, and after a short Sunday meeting, the deacons had decided to ask one of the other Hamelin ministers to officiate. The Reverend Charles W. Butcher, recently retired from Hamelin's Wesley Memorial United Methodist Church, had accepted the task. C. W. Butcher had seen it all in his forty years of ministry. He had buried boys shipped back in body bags from Korea and Vietnam; young people pried from the wreckage of their daddy's car after a joy ride; wives killed by estranged husbands mad with pain and rage. He had seen a world of sorrow, and it had left its mark in the deep lines of his face. He stood now in his good black suit, shiny with age, looking down at the four wooden caskets with an expression of serenity that suggested meditation rather than sorrow. No one in the crowd was crying. Earlier there had been murmurs of indignation that the murderer should be laid to rest side by side with his victims. Some even objected to Joshua Underhill being buried in consecrated ground at all.

C. W. Butcher turned to face those gathered at the graveside, friends and neighbors he'd known all his life. In Wake County you see the same faces and the same somber outfits at every funeral. Spencer, who went to more funerals than most people, knew that Dr. Butcher always started his eulogies with a verse of Scripture. He wondered which one he would choose this time. Thou shalt not kill?

With a gentle smile at Mark and Maggie Underhill, C. W. Butcher began. "Jesus said, 'Let not your hearts be troubled, you believe in God, believe also in me. In my Father's house are many rooms . . .''

Spencer saw Laura Bruce shiver in the wind. He wondered if she, too, had been thinking of the bloodstained floors of the Underhill house, and how she'd scrubbed them on her hands and knees with water and Clorox until first light. Many rooms.

". . . And when I go and prepare a place for you, I will come again and will take you to myself, that where I am you may be also. And you know the way where I am going."

A snicker that didn't quite get transformed into a cough erupted from deep in the crowd. Someone was thinking, *Maybe you all ain't going to the same place.*

C. W. Butcher paused for a moment and gazed out at the crowd, and all was still. "Because these words are in the Bible, few of us stop to think about the writer's experience. Tradition calls St. John the beloved disciple of Jesus. John writes of good times and bad. Jesus laughs at weddings, cries at funerals, and does violence to those who desecrate the Temple." He waited while the phrase "does violence" sank in. They were quiet now.

"So matter-of-fact does the story seem, we forget that historians believe John did not write it down until 95 A.D.—at least sixty-five years after the death, Resurrection, and ascension of the one we call Lord. Did it take John a lifetime to make sense of a homicide, a homicide set apart from all other homicides? Does anyone ever make sense of a killing?

"Remember, it was decades before John could record the

words he heard his old friend say, *'Let not your hearts be troubled . . .'* Indeed, we gather today with very troubled hearts, which may remain troubled for a long time to come."

Mark and Maggie seemed to huddle closer together under the collective stares of the crowd. Their impassive faces studied the ground in front of them, never once straying to take in the sight of the four coffins.

C. W. Butcher was ready to deliver his message now. People could feel it coming. He gave them a hard look, talking louder now. "There are some in these hills and hollers who will say and are saying, *'This is God's will.'* I've always felt ashamed of my colleagues in Christ who would suggest that God somehow wills tragedy, war, death, or destruction. God has not willed the deaths of Paul and Janet Underhill and their sons Joshua and Simon. God is not the author of chaos, but of order. God is not the mother of darkness but of light. God is not the sister or brother of violence, but of peace. So to those of us with troubled hearts, the patron saint of troubled hearts, St. John, calls us to the many rooms of healing our Lord prepares for us in his mansion.

"Today we are gathered with troubled hearts for two purposes. First, we gather with troubled hearts to bury and say good-bye to our family members and friends. We gather to say good-bye to Paul, Janet, Joshua, and Simon. And second, we gather with troubled hearts to say hello to one another. Just as John came together with his friends and family after Jesus' killing to offer and receive encouragement and comfort, so, too, we are gathered to remind Mark and Maggie that they are not alone. Troubled, yes, but not alone. God and the church and the members of this community are with you."

His stern eyes scanned the crowd, daring them to shirk

their duty. Will Bruce's wife looked as if she might cry, but he saw her nod her head in agreement with his words. Someone murmured, "Amen!"

"It took John a lifetime with friends and family to get over the death of his friend Jesus. So, too, we are all called to do whatever it takes to help Mark and Maggie Underhill know that they are loved."

Spencer Arrowood thought, They don't look loved. They look about as alone as anybody I've ever seen. With a stab of conscience, he resolved to look in on them every now and again. Because he was the sheriff, C. W. Butcher would expect no less of him. This was his flock, too.

"We are not called on to untrouble them, or to fix them," C. W. Butcher was saying. "We are called to love them. This is the place our Lord prepares for those whose hearts are troubled. It is not an easy place, but it is a place of love. You, the Church, the Body of Christ, know the way. I bid you follow it."

The crowd had begun to sing "Precious Lord, Take My Hand" in the faltering voices of a group without a leader. Spencer thought he could discern his mother's lilting alto above the straggling sopranos. It was her favorite hymn. She had come simply because the Underhills were fellow church members. He didn't want to talk to her now, though. She could always detect depression in him, but she mistook it for illness. He wasn't up to that conversation just yet.

After one verse the song trailed away, and after a brief silence, the lay preacher began to intone the final words of the funeral service. Spencer wasn't close enough to make out what he said. He saw Mark Underhill kneel down and pick up a clod of earth to throw down on one of the coffins, and then his view was blocked by a procession of onlookers who were heading for their cars. The wind had picked up a bit, and no one wanted to linger. He searched the crowd for Laura Bruce's navy coat and hurried after her.

At the sound of her name, she turned, and he saw that she looked as tired as he felt. There were dark circles under her eyes, and her cheekbones seemed more prominent than he remembered. She shivered in the wind, and pulled her coat closer around her, while he felt another pang of guilt about dragging her into the Underhills' tragedy.

"Hello, Sheriff," she said, summoning up a weak smile. "It was good of you to come today."

"We usually provide an escort for funerals," he said. "It's not like we have a whole lot of crimes to occupy us otherwise."

"I suppose not. Even this one involved more paperwork than detection, didn't it?"

He nodded. "They mostly do. I needed to speak to you so that I can finish up the last bit of paperwork on this one."

She looked bewildered. "You need to talk to me?"

"Yes." He saw her shiver again. "Look, you should get out of this wind. Would you like to go to the diner for coffee? If I'm not keeping you from anything else, that is."

It crossed her mind to wonder what the parishioners would think of a tête-à-tête in the diner with this earnest blond young man, but she scoffed at her own narrow-mindedness. He simply wanted to conduct police business somewhere warmer than a November cemetery. "I'll meet you there," she told him. "My car's just over the hill."

The rest of the mourners had left the cemetery. Spencer Arrowood watched the tottering figure in the navy coat until she disappeared from sight, and then he walked back to the graveside where the Underhills' oak coffins waited under the tent for the burial crew. He stood there in silence for a moment, remembering their faces as he'd seen them on that last night, and then he picked a white carnation from one of the standing wreaths. Twisting the flower absently in his fingers for a moment, he took a last look at the four caskets waiting to be lowered into the earth. On his way out of the cemetery he knelt at the grave of his brother—John Calvert Arrowood, killed in Vietnam in 1968—and placed the flower on the flat bronze marker.

CHAPTER

4

Shall we gather at the river,
Where bright angels' feet have trod . . .

When Sheriff Spencer Arrowood walked into his office behind the courthouse, Deputy Joe LeDonne and dispatcher Martha Ayers stopped their conversation in mid-sentence and turned to look at him with solemn faces.

He froze in the doorway, all thought of midmorning coffee gone from his mind as he waited for the news of whatever disaster was slated to ruin his day. "It's not a wreck, is it?" he asked wearily. He hated wrecks.

Martha took pity on him and went to pour the coffee herself. "Oh, sit down, Spencer," she told him. "There seems to be peace in the valley, like the old cowboy song says. We haven't had a call all morning. It's just something that we heard on the radio, that's all."

"All right," said Spencer. "What did you hear on the radio?"

"It's just show business news," said Martha, but she added, "It's still a damn shame."

When things weren't busy in the department, which was most of the time, Martha listened to WJCW in Johnson City, a progressive country station that could be relied upon to serve up Dwight Yoakum, Don Williams, and Reba McEntire without too much bluegrass in between.

Joe LeDonne came as close as he ever got to smiling. "Let me tell him, Martha. I had a workshop in dealing with the bereaved."

Martha glanced through the open doorway at Spencer's empty office, and shrugged. "We shouldn't be flip about it. It is a shock."

Spencer took a long swallow of coffee and waited for the latest mayor-of-Nashville joke, or a sensational story from the morning's national news. "Fire away," he said.

"We heard it on the radio this morning," said LeDonne. "The Judds are breaking up. Sorry. No joke."

"The Judds?" repeated Spencer, as if there weren't a two-foot poster of the mother-daughter duo above his desk.

"The deejay just said so. They held a press conference—in Nashville, I think—and announced it. Naomi has liver damage from hepatitis, and she has to quit show business. The doctors want her to take it easy. They think she's going home to Ashland."

"Naomi is the mother, isn't she?" asked LeDonne, peering through the doorway for a look at the sheriff's poster. "Damn! She's the pretty one, too!"

Spencer turned to look at the photograph, a gag birthday gift from the staff last April but one he secretly prized. Two women in sparkling country-and-western costumes stood onstage, sharing a microphone. Both were dark-haired and lovely, with a family resemblance that marked them as kin at first glance. But first glance said "sisters," which wasn't the case. The slender one on the right, the one with the darkest hair, the finest porcelain features, and a look of gentle sweetness that made you think of a doe—that was Naomi Judd. She was Wynonna's mother. "Well, they marry young in Ashland, Kentucky," people said philosophically, but the fact was that while Wynonna Judd was about twenty-three, Noami Judd didn't look much over twenty herself. And she was beautiful, with that kind of fine-boned beauty that would last a lifetime. Wynonna was pretty because she was twenty-something, but Naomi was something out of a Renaissance painting, a mountain Madonna.

"It's a damn shame," Martha said again.

Spencer felt an irrational urge to swear, out of all proportion to his interest in music. What, after all, did it matter to him whether a total stranger continued to make records or not? "How'd she get hepatitis?" he finally asked.

LeDonne shrugged. "The deejay didn't say. Probably all that bad food singers have to eat when they're on the road. I hear seafood can be dangerous."

"Well, how long will it take her to get over it?"

LeDonne and Martha looked at each other. "I don't think she will," said Martha. "Liver damage is permanent. It's the one organ that doesn't get better, and you can't do without it."

Spencer looked down at his rapidly cooling cup of coffee, trying to figure out who he was angry at—them for spoiling his morning with bad news, or Naomi Judd for her mortality. He walked into his office without another word.

Martha shrugged. " 'Mama, He's Crazy,' " she said to Joe.

He gave her half a smile to show that he recognized the title of the Judds' greatest hit.

After a few more minutes' silence, broken only by a Floyd Kramer oldie from the radio, Spencer called out, "Martha, can you get me the zip code for Ashland, Kentucky?"

Laura Bruce took a tentative sip of the tea-colored beverage in the earthenware mug. "What did you say this was?"

"Betony," said Nora Bonesteel. "Go on, drink it. It will do you good—in your condition."

She froze with the steaming mug inches from her lips. "My condition," she echoed. "You really do know things, don't you?"

"Some things." The old woman was not looking at her. She had turned to gaze out the big window at the meadow of brown stubble stretching down to the wood's edge. The lowering sky was gray with clouds, bleaching the color from the landscape. "When anybody says *November*, this is the image that always comes to my mind: bleak, as if the whole world was graveyard dead."

It had been a week since Laura's night ride through the holler in answer to the sheriff's summons. The color and animation had returned to the younger woman's face, and she no longer seemed so tired. The burgundy sweater she wore complemented her dark hair, making her seem less pale. She was curled up on Nora Bonesteel's sofa, enjoying another "parish visit." She had set out to visit the Underhills' farm, but a twinge of nausea—and perhaps dread at the memory of her last visit—had made her turn off before she reached their road, and head up Ashe Mountain to spend a comforting morning with Nora Bonesteel.

Laura looked about her for the pet groundhog. "Has Persey gone out to hibernate yet?"

"She left last week. Waddled out into the backyard and dug herself a hole under the grape arbor. Sometimes I envy her that little death of hers. The world is always warm and green when Persey's in it. She never sees the bleakness. Autumn can be pretty, too, I know, but it's a brittle kind of beauty. I'm always surprised to see blue skies and sunny days in November; seems like they never stick in my mind the way this does."

"We had a pretty day for the Underhills' funeral," Laura said. "But somehow it felt just as desolate as today looks." She shivered, and ventured another sip of herbal tea. "I was sad for Mark and Maggie, left with not a soul in the world but each other. There was even talk of putting them out of their home because they were under age."

Nora Bonesteel's face remained impassive. She busied herself with stirring a dollop of honey into her own tea. Laura studied the high cheekbones and angular features of the still-handsome old woman and wondered if she had Cherokee blood in her. The steel-blue eyes bespoke her Scots ancestry—and the Sight, of course. At last she spoke. "I'd have thought you had enough to keep you occupied without taking on grown young'uns to raise."

Laura squirmed under the tranquil gaze. "It didn't seem much to ask," she protested. "The sheriff came up to me after the funeral, and said that the Underhills had asked that I be appointed guardian. It's only until Mark turns eighteen in a few months' time. He said that all I have to do is check on them every now and then, and that he would do the same. He seemed so sincere and so worried about them that I couldn't very well refuse. How would it look if the minister's wife turned her back on two orphans?"

"You know best," said Nora Bonesteel in a tone that meant only that the discussion would end. She had finished her tea now and had taken out the workbasket of knitting that always sat by her chair. Her restless hands unraveled yarn as they talked.

"It's such a tragedy. They didn't talk about it, and of course I didn't ask them, but imagine! An insane older brother plotting to kill the family, and them escaping just because they had play practice at the high school. Living with him must have been a nightmare."

Nora shook her head. "Josh Underhill was a soft-spoken boy. Very earnest, though. I spoke with him up here a time or two. He liked to go out walking in the woods by himself. He wasn't fierce or what you'd call crazy. Just the opposite, I think."

"You're lucky *you* weren't killed," said Laura with a shiver of dread. "What did you talk about?"

"Legends. He had never lived long in any one place before, and I got the feeling that he was trying to get to know the land. I told him some of the old Cherokee stories about the Bear child and the Medicine Lake, where wounded animals go to heal, and about the Nunnehi."

"What are Nunnehi?"

"My Scots kinfolk called them the seelie court. Maybe all the mountain folk in the world have tales about them. They're said to live under the streams and deep inside the mountains, invisible most of the time, but sometimes you can come upon them dancing in a forest clearing. Sometimes they'd help a lost Cherokee find his way back to the village, and Nunnehi warriors appeared a time or two to fight alongside the Cherokee when they were losing a battle. You've seen fairystones, haven't you?"

Laura smiled. "Sure. They sell them in gift shops on the parkway. A dark crystalline formation in the shape of a cross. They look as if someone carved them."

The old woman drew out a chain from the folds of her dress, and held it out for Laura to see. "I've had this one sixty years and more," she said. "The old woman who gave it to me said it was formed from the Nunnehis' tears. Some say they cried when Jesus was nailed to the cross, and some say it was in sorrow over the Trail of Tears, when the Cherokee were force marched away to Oklahoma."

"Have you ever seen the Nunnehi?"

Nora shrugged. "It's not a Christian belief. It's just stories people tell to explain a thing they don't understand. Josh Underhill said he wished he could go off and find the Nunnehi dancing in a clearing and follow them home. No, you don't, I told him. They don't like people to know where they live. People who go there die soon after."

Laura gasped. "What did he say to that?"

"He said he didn't care." Nora stared for a moment at the tangle of crimson thread in her lap. "This was a good while back. I just thought it was the state of melancholy that teenage boys are so partial to. Sweetheart troubles, or grades and suchlike." Her eyes glittered in the lamplight. "I wasn't given to know."

"You know enough, Nora Bonesteel," said Laura. "Let's not talk about it anymore." With a complacent smile she placed her hand on the gentle rise of her belly. "I can't get over you knowing about the baby this early," she mused aloud. "I don't think I'm showing a bit. This skirt has an elastic waistband, but it still fits like it always did."

"You look all right," said Nora, looping the strands of wool over her knitting needle.

"I told Will when he called on Sunday evening. He's just over the moon about it. And worried about me, of course. I said I was fine."

"Did you tell him you'd been out gallivanting on country roads late at night visiting crime scenes?" asked Nora.

Laura grinned. "He worries enough as it is. Anyway, I didn't want to dampen the news about the baby. Will it be a boy or a girl?"

Nora Bonesteel shook her head. "I only see things in flashes every now and again. Most things aren't meant for us to know beforehand. Trust the Lord, girl."

"It's just that I'm thirty-eight, and I worry in case the baby isn't quite normal. . . . You're right. . . . It takes wonderful courage to care for a handicapped child, and I'm no saint. I'd go insane."

"Trust—"

"Trust the Lord. That's what Will would tell me, too, isn't it?" She tried to remember if she'd prayed about the baby, about its being all right when it was born.

"I hope Will Bruce would tell you not to dwell on it," Nora replied. "If you keep this up, you'll be mighty dull company for the next six months."

"Well, if I shut up about it, will you make me something for the baby? Booties or a little blanket or something? You make such beautiful things."

Nora Bonesteel seemed intent upon her knitting for a moment or two.

"It's due in April," Laura added. "No rush."

The old woman carefully untangled a knot of crimson wool. "I will make you something for the child you will have in April."

As boys, Tavy Annis and Taw McBryde had been fishing buddies. Now, half a century later, they had renewed the custom, still fishing at the same bend in the Little Dove River, five hundred feet downhill from the Clinchfield Railroad tracks that hugged the side of the wooded mountain. It was their favorite spot, not perhaps because the fishing was any better in the rock-studded depths of the river bend, but because the prospect of treasure lay in every cast of the fishing line.

The boys had grown up listening to tales from Taw's Uncle Henry, a railroad man from Pigeon Roost. That sharp curve on the tracks above the river bend had caused more train wrecks than you could shake a stick at, he told the boys. In the old days, when trains were the country's bloodstream, there'd be a wreck on that stretch of track every couple of years, sending a freight train full of coal and timber into the gravel-bottomed shallows of the Little Dove River. The train crews mostly survived, Uncle Henry assured them, but they had a struggle getting out, and they'd shed shoes and clothes to swim for it. That's where the treasure came in. The railroad salvaged the coal and timber, but what stayed at the bottom of the Little Dove were the heavy gold watches the railroad men used to wear. Why, there must be at least a dozen of them down there, Henry declared. And since gold didn't rust or rot, or do anything except get more valuable all the time, think what a fortune you'd have if you could get those watches up out of the river. For years Tavy Annis and Taw McBryde fished the river bend, hoping for gold instead of trout with every cast of the line. They had spent the treasure a thousand times in daydreams as adolescents, buying phantom Daisy air rifles and ten-speed bikes. But the Clinchfield gold stayed buried in sand and gravel under the currents of the river, and only the dreams dried up.

They were fishing again now; same spot, same river, but many things had changed since the old days. They were sixty-five now, with little in common except childhood memories. Nearly half a century ago, they had reached their own bend in the river, and from then on their lives had taken different paths.

Tavy had stayed on in Wake County to farm with his daddy in Dark Hollow, and he'd been there ever since. He was lean and leathery from a lifetime of outdoor work, and he wore overalls and work boots, the uniform of his trade. He was a widower now, deacon in the church, member of the local civic club, but somewhere in there still was the kid that had helped Taw McBryde chase the Everett sisters through the meadow waving a blacksnake over his head like a bullwhip. They were twelve then.

In a long-forgotten photo album in Tavy's attic, there was a faded black-and-white picture of Taw at sixteen, raw-boned in a shirt and tie and making sheep's eyes at a pretty dark-haired girl. It was the perfect picture of young love, except that if you looked closely at the bushes behind the courting couple, you could see an Indian in war paint and feathered headdress, brandishing a tomahawk, and ready to attack the oblivious lovers. Tavy Annis, renegade brave. He couldn't remember who had taken the picture, or whether Taw had been in on the joke. Taw was always the serious one, burning with ambition to get more than there was in little Wake County. If he couldn't find the gold in the Little Dove River, he would seek it elsewhere.

Taw had been pulled out of the hollers of east Tennessee by World War II, or maybe he had wanted to go, picturing his triumphant return with fame and fortune in his wake. But it had taken him forty years to find his way back home. He had ridden through the battlefields of France with Patton's Red Ball Express, seeing combat and learning more about the world than he'd dreamed of from the geography books of John Sevier High. How you gonna keep 'em down on the farm—indeed. After the war, he had headed north to the automobile factories in Detroit (where he learned that it was pronounced with the accent on the last syllable). Money was good in the car factories after the war. There was a waiting list a mile long for new cars, once they could start making them again, instead of turning out jeeps and tanks for the war effort. He wouldn't stay long, he told himself. Just until he earned enough money to go back to Wake County in style. But while he was in Detroit, he met Wanda, and when they got married, she had wanted to stay up there where her kinfolks were; they had bought a refrigerator on time, and he had to keep his job to make the monthly payments. A year later, the first baby was on the way, and it seemed foolish to think of giving up a good union job to go back to an uncertain future in Appalachia.

One year stretched into the next, always with some good reason not to go, until he had spent more than half his life in Michigan and his Tennessee accent had worn away into the flat, bland sounds of midwestern speech: y'all gave way to you guys in his need for a second-person plural. He was closing in on forty-five years in urban exile, his dreams still picturing Dark Hollow in 1941 simplicity, when Wanda died. By then the kids were grown and gone to jobs in the Sunbelt, and he was retired from the plant with a good pension for forty years' work. Suddenly, he had run out of family, installment payments, and excuses to keep him in Detroit. One night he was down at the bar with some old friends from work when the old Bobby Bare song came on the radio, the one about the homesick Southern boy being trapped in Dee-troit City. *"I wanna go home."* Taw had felt tears spring to his eyes when he heard those words, and he realized that he didn't want to see another skyscraper or sit through another traffic jam as long as he lived. He wanted to go home. His friends in Detroit kidded him about it at first. All you hillbillies go home, they said. Every time a redneck retires, he starts packing. You can get the boy out of the mountains . . .

The woman next door helped him run a yard sale, and he sent most of what was left after that to the Salvation Army. He told the realtor not to jack up the price on the house; he wanted a quick sale. Three weeks later, Taw McBryde was back in the east Tennessee mountains, looking for a place to live, and trying as hard as he could to go home again.

Hamelin hadn't changed all that much. Main Street still looked pretty much the way it always had, except that the movie theatre had closed, and a Laundromat had been installed in the building, so that the movie marquee was permanently set to read WASHARAMA. The old hotel was closed, too, but a neatly painted sign on its front door said that the historical society had plans to restore it as a local landmark. He didn't know too many of the people in Hamelin anymore. Most of his generation had died or moved away, and the youngsters—those under fifty—didn't interest him much. But when he drove out to Tavy Annis's place, he found that one piece of his past was still intact and visitable. There was Tavy, looking weather-beaten and gray, but still the same old buddy he always was, carrying around in his head all the same memories about the days before the war.

Even though it was bare November, it was still mild weather in midday, and Taw insisted that the pair of them go fishing, in celebration of their newly resurrected youth. Tavy didn't look too keen on the idea, but finally he shrugged and went along, as he always did in the old days.

With a trunkful of fishing rods and tackle pulled down from the smokehouse, they had set off in Taw's new Mercury, talking about old times as they headed through the valley toward their fishing hole.

"Houses look about the same," Taw said, watching the well-remembered landscape slip past him.

"New people in a lot of 'em, though," Tavy told him. "I reckon the Tilden place will be up for sale again soon. It sold last year to some folks called Underhill. He was retired military. Had a wife and a passel of teenagers. They kept to themselves, though."

"He's gonna farm the Tilden place? Cattle?"

"He's not going to be farming anything," said Tavy. "I'm surprised you haven't heard about it. A few weeks back, the Underhills' oldest boy took a rifle and killed his parents and little brother before he blew his own head off. The other two teenagers survived, but I doubt if they can make a go of the farm. Don't see why they'd want to live there, anyhow."

"There's no luck in that place," said Taw. "The Tildens never made much out of it, as I recall. Wore themselves out trying. Did these new people fix up the old farmhouse?"

"It's been done piecemeal through the years. You wouldn't know it from the old days. Don't reckon I'd want to live there, anyhow, not if it was a palace and they was giving it away."

Taw lost interest in the Underhills. "How's Wake High doing in football this year? Do we still play Johnson City?"

At a crossroads where a rusted Coca-Cola sign marked the ruins of an abandoned store, Taw slowed the car, and turned down the gravel road that led past the Tilden farm and onto their fishing spot by the river bend. They parked in a clearing under a grove of locust trees and followed the well-worn path to the river.

Taw took a deep breath of mountain air. "Some things don't change!" he sighed.

Tavy Annis looked at the ground. "Most things do." He stepped back and watched his friend step out of the brush to reacquaint himself with the waters of his youth.

Taw McBryde stood for a long time staring at the flow of earth-colored sludge that was the Little Dove River. It broke over the rocks in brown waves like tobacco spittle that trickled down the encrusted boulders. "I wouldn't a knowed it," he said, slipping back into the speech patterns of his youth.

Tavy sat down on a boulder near the water's edge, and began to rig up his fishing line. "It's that paper company over in North Carolina," he said. "They been dumping poison chemicals in that river for a lot of years now, and we're downstream from them."

Taw couldn't take his eyes off the river. "And there's still fish living in that?"

"Some." Tavy nodded. "If we catch any, we'd best throw them back, though. That's why I didn't bother about a fishing license when you said you wanted to come. Game warden says you can't eat 'em. Don't think anybody would, unless they was half-starved. I caught one once."

"Trout?"

Tavy Annis shrugged, staring out at the river. "Maybe. It had warts growing all over its head, and its eyes were white. I didn't even want to touch it to throw it back. I cut my line and kicked it back in the river, tackle and all."

"There's laws," said Taw McBryde. "Environmental protection. The government won't let you dump filth into rivers anymore."

"I believe they've cut back on the dumping some," Tavy agreed, "But it's been polluted a long time, and it's not getting any better. The people at the hospital swear some of the illness around here is caused by that damned river. But they say that since we're in Tennessee and the paper company is in North Carolina, there isn't a lot we can do to stop it."

Taw made no move to get out his fishing tackle. "I don't reckon even them gold railroad watches could'a lasted through this," he said.

Maggie Underhill slammed her schoolbooks down on the table in the front hall and thrust her fist into her mouth to stifle her cry. "I'm home!" It was an automatic gesture, hard to suspend now that there was no one to notify of her comings and goings. Mark was outside, putting the car in the garage. They had hardly spoken a word on the way home.

School seemed to last an eternity these days. They had decided to go back the day after the funeral, because there didn't seem to be much point in sitting around the house staring at nothing, contributing to the silence. At least school would offer a distraction, they had reasoned.

Maggie had foreseen the clumsy attempts at advice and consolation that would be thrust at them by teachers and well-meaning friends, and she felt nothing at all as she sat there, murmuring thanks for their concern. She had been less prepared for the cruelty flung at them by the thoughtless and the malicious. Purring sympathy, some of her former friends had pressed her for details about the deaths, insisting that it would do her good to talk about it. Others had jeered that maybe all the Underhills were crazy, and in heavy-handed lunchroom jests, they warned each other to steer clear of Mad Maggie.

When the teasing or the prying concern began, she would

excuse herself from the group with icy calmness, and then retreat to the bathroom, where she would huddle in the pink metal stall, weeping silently.

Mark seemed less affected by the reactions of his schoolmates to the family tragedy. He ignored the sympathizers just as steadfastly as he did the bullies, sailing past them with an unconcern that was more disinterest than disdain. In the week since the deaths he had said nothing of it to anyone. Not even to her. Both the sheriff and the school guidance counselor had suggested that they seek grief therapy in Johnson City, but Mark had politely refused for both of them. They could manage perfectly well, he insisted. He hadn't asked if she had wanted to go; hadn't cared. She had never really been close to Mark, despite—or perhaps because of—their closeness in age.

Maggie started up the stairway, past a gauntlet of family pictures hung in the stairwell, tracing the Underhill children from babyhood until the present. There was Josh in a cowboy hat, grinning toothlessly at a stuffed bear: Fort Sill, 1972, and Daddy was a first lieutenant. Above that was a framed wedding portrait of Mother and Daddy, 1969. Mother had long, straight hair that suited the era, but looked out of place with the beige suit she'd worn at her wedding. She looked very solemn, clutching her bouquet and staring slightly openmouthed at the camera. Beside her, 2d Lt. Paul Underhill, with a razored crew cut and crisp dress greens, eyed the camera with a winner's grin. Mark and Maggie were white-gowned infants in the first tier of pictures, gradually progressing to toddlers and well-groomed adolescents as one ascended the stairwell gallery. Simon appeared midway in the family history, a rosy blond baby in the same christening gown in 1983: Dad, a newly promoted major at Fort McPherson. Simon took up an increasing amount of space as a winsome toddler, much cuter than his sullen adolescent siblings. She tried to summon up an emotion that could be called missing Simon, but nothing would come.

Maggie stared for a moment at the progression of photographs, wondering if she could put out a finger, touch one, and say, "There. There is the time that things went wrong." But she couldn't. The good and bad times had a way of sliding in and out, so that you couldn't really separate them into two piles.

As she looked at the swirl of familiar faces, already receding to snapshots in her mind, one feeling came unbidden to the orphaned Maggie Underhill. Above everything else, she missed Josh.

CHAPTER

5

Ril Sams climbed Hanlon with his hounds last night,
but when they winded something below the top,
and wouldn't go beyond the lantern light,
and trembled on the lead, then he came home.
I trust the hounds; they know what made them stop,
what waits there in the mist on Hanlon's top.

—JIM WAYNE MILLER,
"Hanlon Mountain in Mist"

Taw McBryde remembered the Dixie Grill from his youth, and although the food did not equal his rapturous recollections of it, he continued to eat there a couple of times a week. Maybe nothing was as good as he'd remembered it being, he told himself. Memory is a selective thing, and an eighteen-year-old's appetite and lack of sophistication could account for much of the café's former glory.

He sat in the back booth, farthest from the jukebox, and studied the typed menu of "Today's Specials" while he waited for Tavy to show up. He had about decided on the $3.25 all-vegetable plate (mashed potatoes, green beans, stewed tomatoes, and fried apples) when a shadow fell across the page. Taw looked up over his reading glasses, and saw his dinner companion looming above him. He smiled and started to say hello when he saw Tavy's gray face and drawn features, staring at nothing. Taw's grin faded, and he gripped his friend's arm, pulling him into the booth.

"Tavy!" he whispered. "It's not your heart, is it? You look god-awful."

"Don't call the doctor, Taw. I already been today. And, no, it ain't my heart."

Taw set aside his menu, his appetite gone. "Tell me."

Tavy picked up the glass of water beside his place setting and poured it out across the polished pine tabletop, watching impassively as Taw grabbed napkins and tried to stem

71

the tide rolling toward his lap. "What the hell's wrong with you, Tavy?" he demanded, sopping water and ice cubes away from the table's edge.

"Cancer."

Taw stopped mopping, and stared openmouthed at his friend, oblivious to the trickle of water dripping onto his khaki work pants. "What?"

"Thought it was an ulcer," said Tavy, tracing circles in the wetness. "I'd been feeling poorly. Having some pains in my gut. So I went to the clinic in Johnson City to have it checked. They called me in today to tell me the results. They won't tell you news like that over the phone." He smiled bitterly. "Maybe they think you'll kill yourself. As if it mattered. It's in my liver, Taw, and spreading out from there. There ain't a damn thing they can do about it."

Taw heard all the words clear as day, but he couldn't seem to string them together to get any sense out of them. He looked at the gray man in the shiny blue suit who sat across from him, and thought that somewhere trapped inside that husk was little Tavy Annis, a towheaded kid with a possum-skin banjo and an unbroken yardage record for quarterbacks at Hamelin High. The boy mechanic who could fix any car with a wrench and a screwdriver. What was he on about now?

"You're sick?" Taw said stupidly.

"No. I reckon I'm dead. They laid it all out for me: the odds, the expense, and the methods of treatment, which they as good as said wouldn't do no good. And I told them they could keep their pills; I was going home. But that ain't the hell of it, Taw. You know what else the doctor said?"

"What?" The words spun past Taw's head, and before he could seize one topic, Tavy was on to the next one.

"The doctor—some kid in a white coat; couldn't have been more than twenty-eight, twenty-nine—looked at my chart, and he says, 'I see you're from Dark Hollow over in

72

Wake County. That's near the Little Dove River, isn't it?' I allowed as how it was, but so what?"

"The doctor asked you about the river?"

"Yeah. And then he starts talking about what a damned shame it is that the Titan Paper Company over in North Carolina isn't made to stop dumping pollutants into the Little Dove River. He said the cancer rate downstream from that plant—here in east Tennessee—is ten times the national average." Tavy let his hand fall limp in the pool of clear water on the table, and silent tears rolled down the furrows in his cheeks. "Taw, that damned river got me, just like it poisoned all the fish."

Taw stared at his friend, seizing on something to focus on besides the grief and horror. "Somebody better let those people at the factory know," he whispered.

Tavy Annis shook his head. "They already know all about it. Their lawyers have been fighting the cleanup orders for years."

Laura Bruce clutched the telephone receiver as if it were a human hand. "I can hear you fine, honey," she said again. "It's hard to believe you're half a world away. Are you getting my letters?"

Her eyes strayed to Will Bruce's clear blue eyes staring back at her from the photograph on her nightstand. She smiled at the image, as his voice flowed into her from another continent. She was propped up in bed on both pillows, cradling the headset against her neck, and resting her other hand on the small swollen mound beneath her cotton nightgown. "We're fine, Will. Both of us. I go back to the doctor in three weeks. How are things over there? Are you eating all right?"

Soon he would ask her about things in the parish. Should she tell him about the Underhills, or would that only add to his burden? She decided to listen to his news first, try to gauge his mood, before she told him about the tragedy.

Will Bruce's soft Southern voice rumbled through the phone lines. "I don't know, Laura. I'm stuck out here in the desert. I guess I feel like St. Augustine."

"That sounds good," said Laura, puzzled by the weariness in his voice.

He laughed. "Think again, pagan! Augustine had a major crisis out here in the desert. Wondered if his faith was worth a damn. This desolate country will do it to you. I sure wish I was back in the green hills of Tennessee."

"I wish you were, too, Will. But I guess the soldiers out there need you."

"Not so's you'd notice it. I'm not exactly in high demand. Every now and then somebody will drop by to try to scare up an argument on abortion, or ask me if I'm one of those crackpot kind of preachers who doesn't believe in evolution and who takes the last dimes from little old ladies' pension funds to buy myself a BMW. These kids think they're too young and too American to die. What do they need me for?"

Laura closed her eyes. *I don't need this*, she thought. *I'm doing your damned job here, Will. Don't make me minister to you as well.* She said, "You sound tired, honey. I bet you're pushing yourself too hard. What if I send you some iron tablets?"

"I'd rather have a box of Goo Goo clusters. And Doritos. How's everything back in Dark Hollow? I bet it's beautiful there with the leaves turning."

"Wonderful," said Laura. "Prettiest place on earth." The leaves had been on the ground for two weeks now. "Everything is fine, Will."

The headlights did not quite reach into the darkness. Maggie Underhill had to lean forward and strain to see the

74

curves in the road that always seemed just beyond the pool of light. She glanced at Mark, slumped in the seat beside her, and thought for a moment about waking him up and asking him to navigate, but she decided against it. If the alcohol was beginning to wear off, he might insist on driving, which might be worse to endure than the blinding dark. Play practice had been long and tedious, and Maggie was exhausted. Better to let Mark sleep and enjoy the silence.

Bare tree branches were thrust across the road like pitchforks, waving slowly in the wind.

In summer this country road was beautiful. She knew that because they had moved onto the farm in May, and she remembered seeing its green splendor in the months that followed, but now she could not call to mind the image of the tree-lined blacktop ringed by purple chicory flowers in the waist-high grass.

Now, in the headlights, there was no trace of color in the landscape. Did the grass have a tinge of green, or did she will it to look that way by knowing how grass was supposed to look? *There's rosemary, that's for remembrance.* Maggie had intended to practice her part on the way home, but it was late now, and the road was difficult. Perhaps Mark would rehearse with her tomorrow out in the barn. Laertes and Ophelia: brother and sister. She thought that was why she had been given the part, because Mark was such a strong character that he must be Laertes; she had been given Ophelia for poetic justice. Or because she was pretty, with her waist-long dark hair, and her big dark eyes. They didn't seem to mind that her voice was inaudible. . . .

Farther along, two red circles seemed to follow the slant of the road, taillights of a distant car—white and squarish, barely visible—an old car, Maggie thought. It seemed to pace itself, staying just beyond the flash of her lights, as if in light it would be no longer visible. *It is my parents,* Maggie thought. *They are driving this road before I was born. Father's hands will be fists around the steering wheel, and Mother will be very quiet, looking away into the distance.*

The old car stopped at an unmarked crossroad. Its taillights winked at her for a moment, and then it slid silently up the road and into the trees. It had nearly disappeared from sight before Maggie remembered that there was no need to practice in the barn tomorrow. They could shout from the housetop, and no one would hear. Mother and Daddy were under the earth in Oakdale. The house would be dark and silent when they reached it. Unless the red taillights in the distance were Mother and Daddy and Simon and Joshua coming back home from Oakdale. Coming back to see their little Markie and Maggie-May.

Maggie waited for long minutes at the crossroads, looking left and right into the darkness, until she thought it was safe to go on.

The sheriff's office was officially closed for the night. At the dispatcher's table, the telephone had been set to forward calls to the next county, where a full-time staff of law enforcement people answered any late-night emergencies in Wake County. They were seldom summoned. An occasional wreck or a domestic squabble was the most trouble anybody made in Hamelin after midnight. Spencer Arrowood could have gone home hours ago, but he had lingered long after LeDonne and Martha left the office, turning down their invitation to a spaghetti supper with the ever-plausible plea of paperwork to be finished. He didn't want to spend an evening with them talking shop, rehashing the Underhill case. LeDonne wanted to talk about the dead rabbit they had found at the scene, but what did it matter? Josh Underhill was as dead as his victims. They would never really know why.

Even with only part of his mind devoted to routine tasks, he had managed to finish all the pressing bureaucratic business by ten o'clock. Since then he had been attempting to write a letter.

He sat in his office before a glowing computer monitor, his brow furrowed with the effort of concentration. This was very different from report writing, wherein he was required to report facts without any taint of personal feeling. Now this long-denied process of feeling was the only message he had to impart.

Twice he had attempted to abandon the project, stomped around the office cursing his sensibilities, and twice he had gulped down a mug of half-life coffee and set to the task again.

Dear Ms. Judd, he had typed at the top of the page. To the right of that he had tapped out *Dear Mama Judd,* and farther along the same line was the simple salutation *Dear Naomi.* It was hard to decide what to call her, this total stranger that he knew so well. How odd that she should know nothing of him.

Hepatitis. He turned the word over in his mind, trying to find some justification for its presence in the life of a country singer. He had looked it up in one of the office reference books, and found a general definition that did little to satisfy his bewilderment. How do you offer sympathy to a total stranger facing the ultimate tragedy? Was he being impertinent to even try? Of course, the irony of it was that Naomi Judd didn't feel like a stranger at all to him. Why, he had blood kin cousins that were more strangers to him than Naomi was. He knew less about the cousins, and cared not at all. The country-music station announced her birthday each year, and a host of articles detailed her life, from her decor and favorite colors down to the mundane details of her Ashland, Kentucky, childhood. Naomi Judd was the embodiment of a fairy tale: a female Elvis, if you will.

77

She was still a teenager when her daughter was born, and for twenty years thereafter she'd lived in obscurity, training as a nurse, and raising her kids, with no more celebrity than he had. Then one day, when Wynonna was grown, they had taken a shot at the music business, singing together in a husky, melodious counterpoint. "Mama He's Crazy": That was the first hit, a perfect combination of song and publicity. People said, Here's a mother-daughter act singing this song, and *you can't tell which is which*. They had ridden that riddle to stardom, getting more beautiful and more polished as they went along.

And now it was over, because of some defect you couldn't even see, destroying the Judds from the inside out. She still looked perfect. He'd seen her on a Barbara Walters interview, and no one could look more likely to live forever.

Spencer looked up at the Judds poster above his desk. Was it Naomi's mortality that frightened him, or his own? He could remember when death was confined to old people that his parents were vaguely acquainted with. Then, as he grew older, death had begun to cut a swath through his parents' circle of friends, finally reaching Hank Arrowood himself. And interspersed through this steady attrition were the shocking accidents that claimed those his own age: his brother, Cal, killed in Vietnam; a football teammate lost in a car accident; a childhood playmate stricken with leukemia. These, though, he saw as random examples of bad luck, visiting his generation for form's sake; the majority of them, though, were going to live forever.

The illness of Naomi Judd said otherwise. Nothing will save you, it whispered. Not fame, or optimism, or wealth, or physical fitness, or other people's love. We can get you anytime we want, and you will be powerless against us. Contemplating the randomness of death made Spencer uneasy. He did not like to feel powerless. You shouldn't have to feel powerless if you wore a gun. That had been the whole point.

He set down his cup of coffee and bent over the keyboard once again: *Dear Naomi Judd: I cannot tell you how shocked and grieved I was to learn of your illness, and I hope . . .*

Mark Underhill twisted his gooseneck study lamp so that its light shone on the wall above Joshua's bed. The stains were still there, faint traces of pink against a surface scrubbed whiter than the rest of the wall. He supposed that he could scour the rest of the wall, or even repaint it a gleaming white, but there seemed little point in the exercise. He would always know that the stains were there, no matter what cosmetic effects were used to disguise them. Joshua had forever tainted this room with his blood and brains.

Mark slept in the other twin bed, under the window, with a red-and-blue Lone Star quilt, and a threadbare tiger saved from his infancy. The brothers had not so much shared a room as halved it. Mark's side was messy, plastered with rock-star posters and devoid of books, while Joshua's had been tidy and bare, except for his reading material, everything from *All Creatures Great and Small* to *Playboy*. Odd that he hadn't left a note, Mark thought, as hung up as he had been on words. Not that Mark would have wanted to read it. What did the immediate whys matter? It was done. It was finished. And now he and Maggie were left in twelve rooms of silence, four of them haunted with fading red stains and the indedible memory of bodies sprawled in death. *Thanks a lot, Josh. Where am I supposed to sleep now?*

It was all right for Maggie. He hadn't even entered her room. There were no bloody footprints to scrub away, no horrors to remember every time you looked at it. But the other three upstairs bedrooms . . . Well, Mom and Dad's bedroom wasn't exactly defiled. He'd got them downstairs, but Mark couldn't bring himself to move into their sanctuary. Even when their possessions had been removed, it still smelled of them; it was still their territory. Simon's little bedroom under the eaves—he would never set foot in there again. Let Simon haunt it to his heart's content, if his soul had ever awakened from that shotgun blast. Simon had been taken away, and buried miles from the farm, but as far as Mark was concerned, the little body still lay curled up in the pine sleigh bed, its blond curls spilling over the pillow, caked in gouts of red.

That left Mark's own room, the one he had shared with Joshua, where Joshua had come with a shotgun to sit down and consider the consequences of his killing spree before taking the easy way out, abandoning them without family to an indifferent community.

Mark wondered if any of that anguish still lingered, charging the air with despair. He dreaded going upstairs to sleep, afraid that if he opened his eyes in the darkness, he would find Josh standing over him, looking down with unutterable sadness. They had made a pact once, when he was ten and Josh was twelve. They had been hooked on horror movies at the time, and after watching a ghost story on television—had the ghost revealed the location of treasure to his living buddy?—the brothers had come to an agreement, shaking hands to seal the bargain. *Whichever one of us dies first will come back to tell the other what it's like to be dead.* That was the deal. It had seemed very daring and romantic back then, when neither of them really believed they were ever going to die at all. The pact had been casually made: sixty, seventy years from now, drop in, why doncha? Who knew that quiet, intense old Josh would kick open the Steppenwolf door before he even hit twenty?

Mark Underhill stared at the faint outline of the bloodstains on the bedroom wall and spoke aloud. "Look, Josh, the deal is off, okay? I know we made a pact, but I'm canceling it now. If you're here, go away, all right? I don't want to see you! I'm going to shut my eyes now, and I want you to get the hell out of here. You've done enough. If you wanted me to know what being dead was like, you sure as hell could have arranged it. Like you showed Mom and Dad and Simon. Just get the hell out of our lives!"

He buried his face in Joshua's pillow so that Maggie could not hear him sobbing.

Nora Bonesteel sat knitting in the firelight. Knitting was a skill that didn't require the use of sharp eyes, the way needlepoint does. Nora's eyes were good enough for her age—with reading glasses—but she needed a strong light to see the stitches, especially in dark cloth. Tonight she felt like sitting in shadows, letting the peacefulness of the night come over her while her thoughts wandered. She just needed something to busy her hands; her generation was not raised to be idle. Fifty years' experience had taught her to guide the yarn with her fingers, a little stiffer now with rheumatism, but still sure. The pile of crimson wool in her lap was beginning to take shape beneath the arc of her needles: A little sleeve protruded from one knitted side.

The flicker of firelight through the two front windows made her house shine out like a jack-o'-lantern above the dark valley, while across the ridge the Hangman glowered in a sliver of moonlight. She didn't want to think about the holler tonight. Her gaze lingered on a pile of *National Geographic*s stacked on the pine coffee table. She would like to have traveled. She'd done a little bit of "gallivanting" in her youth: a trip to Asheville to visit kinfolks in the forties, and once in 1956 an excursion to Myrtle Beach, chaperoning a church weekend, but the rest of her life had been spent within the shadow of the Tennessee mountains.

She would like to have seen how the Alps or the Andes measure up to them. She might have got away back in 1932, when a summer of blackberry picking and dressmaking had given her enough money to go to college at East Tennessee State in Johnson City. It was the depression then, so nobody had any money, and she didn't feel too much out of place with her country clothes and hill ways. The 1932 *Buccaneer*, a blue softcover yearbook of only a few dozen pages, shows a winsome girl with an oval face and black hair parted in the center and pulled back to the nape of her neck. She looks out of place among all the crimp-curled blondes, but there is a serenity to her features that almost transcends the sadness. She looks out from the page as if she knows something sorrowful about you, but she hasn't the heart to tell.

She had been studying to get her teaching certificate, but in late spring of her first year she took out her cardboard suitcase one night and starting putting all her belongings into it. The next day came word that Johnsie Bonesteel had died back in Dark Hollow. Nora was needed at home to see to her ailing mother.

She had never married. Occasionally, a teenager in calf love would ask her why, as if she'd missed out on the most marvelous experience imaginable, and she had a string of quick answers to reel off. *I didn't know the last man to ask me would be the last man to ask me. My sweetheart was killed at Chickamauga.* (She didn't use that one much these days. Young people had no sense of history and missed the joke.) *I put the last stitch in a Lone Star quilt and doomed myself to spinsterhood.* The real reasons were more complex. She was an only child who had learned early to live with solitude, and, finally, to like it. Her mother's illness kept her tied down for most of her twenties, and then she had inherited the house, so there was no great need to wed just for the sake of stability. She made a little money with her needlework, her goats, and her garden crops, but on a rural farm a little money was quite enough. So the urgency was lacking.

Lacking on both sides, truth to tell. The young bucks in Wake County knew well enough about black-haired Nora Bonesteel and her knowing. Hadn't she smelled that Watson fire two days before it happened? And didn't she stop working on Flossie Johnston's wedding dress the day Jack Sherrod was killed at the Battle of the Bulge, though it was weeks before the family was notified? People didn't have anything against Nora Bonesteel: She was a good Christian woman, and she couldn't help the Sight. Some folks said the midwife had forgotten to put the salt in her mouth when she was born, and that left her susceptible to the visions, but most folks felt it was just the Bonesteel way. Her grandmother had been the same; but still and all, they didn't want to get too close to her. It would be like having Death as an upstairs boarder, somebody said. People were always afraid of what she'd know about them; and they didn't want to be reminded of it.

Nora looked up from her knitting. The fire threw long shadows against the white walls, shapes that seemed to writhe and beckon in the dimness. She stared for a few minutes in the direction of the fire shadow. "Yes," she said gently, as if continuing a conversation. "I know why you felt you had to, and it isn't my place to call you right or wrong. We're not to pass judgment in this world. What's done is done." She hesitated for a moment in the silence, poised as if she were listening. "All the same, I'd let it go now. Go on now, just turn loose. Let the Lord work things out."

Nora Bonesteel went back to her knitting.

CHAPTER

6

I am but mad north-north-west; when the wind is southerly,
I know a hawk from a handsaw.

—*Hamlet*

It wasn't often that Sheriff Spencer Arrowood played taxi service for a human skull. Occasionally, it had been his grim duty to convey someone's mortal remains away in a body bag, but usually the rescue squad could be called to carry out that task. This skull, however, was so clean and anonymous, and so departmental, with the little metal hooks at its jaws, and its steel-hinged cranium, that it did not carry with it any of the ordinary pall of death. As far as the sheriff was concerned, this hunk of bones had never been mortal. Since he would never know its past or even its identity, to him it was merely a stage prop. At least it was going to be.

The student drama group at Hamelin High was doing *Hamlet* as its fall play, and as a favor to the drama teacher, an old friend of his mother, Spencer Arrowood had been coerced into borrowing a skull from the hospital in Unicoi County, and delivering it to the school so that "Yorick" would be present for play practice.

As he drove past the courthouse, he automatically looked at the park bench under the elms to see who Vernon Woolwine was today. Rain or shine, Vernon was always there, outfitted in an ingenious costume reflecting the condition of his psyche. "A welfare-funded exercise in street theatre," one of the county commissioners had called him, but it wasn't against the law to be crazy, and so instead of being sent to an institution, he had become one. By now the citizens of Hamelin were accustomed to the sight of Batman or Elvis lounging about in front of the courthouse, and they took a perverse pride in this civic peculiarity: Jonesborough might be a quaint little tourist trap, but it had nothing to compete with Vernon.

As he came level with the park bench, Spencer slowed the patrol car and gave an affable nod to the Teenage Mutant Ninja Turtle eating a doughnut. Vernon had scrounged up an adult-sized Halloween costume, maybe on sale in the week after the holiday, and he was perched in his usual spot, resplendent in a Styrofoam shell tunic, tight green pants, and a red kerchief, tied around his forehead. Idly, Spencer wondered which turtle he was. Maybe he'd ask at the high school; it would be a good icebreaker with the kids. Better than trying to discuss Shakespeare.

Spencer smiled, remembering his own days at Hamelin High in the mid-sixties. In his senior year the play had been *Macbeth*, and Spencer had strutted and fretted his hour upon the stage as the avenging thane of Fife. Martha, who was now the dispatcher at the sheriff's office, had played the waiting woman to Lady Macbeth, a cheerleader named Tyndall Johnson, suitably robed and wimpled for the role. But Spencer found that his most endearing memory of the school play was not his own theatrics, but James Jessup's discovery of Shakespeare.

Before the students began rehearsing the *Macbeth*, Mrs. Oakey had assigned them parts in English class and had them read it aloud, one act each day. Though none of them realized it at the time, it was a painless audition for the major roles. Those who read with the most expression and comprehension got the biggest parts.

James Jessup, as he recalled, ended up playing the cream-faced loon in the stage production, so that he hardly said anything at all, but Spencer believed that he had got more out of the play than anyone in the community. He was a wiry towhead from a farm family from way up the mountain in Pigeon Roost. He was probably the first person in his family to even get to the senior year in high school, and while his grades weren't outstanding, he was clever enough, and he could learn anything that captured his attention.

He had never heard of the play *Macbeth*, but the story of a murderous Scottish warrior in league with witches took his fancy as no algebra problem or French vocabulary list had ever managed to do. Once he grasped the story and the idea of the treacherous prophecy, he became consumed with the plot and with trying to figure out how it would end. Unlike the more cultured town students, Spencer among them, James Jessup had no idea how the play was going to turn out. Each day in class he would listen to the cadence of the dialogue with all the alertness of an attorney following the opponent's testimony. Oddly enough, he seemed to understand the language better than the town students. Every so often, when a word in the text was questioned, it was James, not Mrs. Oakey, who supplied the definition.

"*Palter*," he would say. "That means *fool around*, don't it? My grandma used to say that every now and again."

It turned out that he was going home to Pigeon Roost every evening and telling the story of *Macbeth* to his family, acting out all the parts himself and giving them updates on each new development as the acts were read out in English class. The Jessups were in the same suspense as he was, waiting for the outcome. In those days before television in the hills, the Jessup family had spent long hours in front of the hearth, debating how the prophecy "none of woman born" would come to pass.

On the night of the play, three generations of the Jessup family turned up in their ancient Ford truck and took front-row seats, not so much for James's acting debut as to see the thane of Glamis get his comeuppance from a tree-bearing rebel army.

Now Spencer knew that satellite dishes ringed the hills above Hamelin, and that the present generation of Jessups probably watched MTV and maybe even owned a video of Orson Welles's *Macbeth*. He wondered if, in the process of assimilation, they had lost all their magic. That would be a shame.

Now, more than twenty years after Spencer Arrowood's acting debut, the Hamelin High play was *Hamlet*. The students would be familiar with the play's plot. Some of them would have seen the Mel Gibson version at the mall in Johnson City, but the trade-off was that the thread of language would have been lost. He was willing to bet that no backwoods student had heard words like *bruited* and *boltered* from Granny at home. Today's granny was a depression-era baby whose stock in trade was the *Enquirer* and "All My Children," not folk ballads and mountain legends.

Spencer decided that as long as he was going there, anyway, he would spend some time at the high school. It was good to stay in touch with the county's young people, the largest source of potential troublemakers in any constituency. The sight of him chatting affably in the lunchroom—with his badge on his uniform and a pistol on his hip—might deter any amount of boredom-driven vandalism in days to come.

It wasn't as if he had any urgent business elsewhere. LeDonne was on duty now and could easily handle the lost-dog phone calls and the trespassing complaints. Hunting season was still two weeks away. The last real police business they'd had was the Underhill killings two weeks before.

Making an entrance with a skull under his arm wasn't a bad idea, either. Some of the girls in the hallway giggled, but there was a note of respect in their eyes as he strolled past them and into the principal's office.

"Special delivery," he said to Ora Hayes, who had been the school secretary back in his students days.

She sprang up from her desk just as he was setting the grinning death's-head on the counter. "Honestly, Spencer Arrowood! Showing off at your age. I'll call Mr. Gilchrist on the intercom. Do you want to wait?"

"Might as well, Ora. As long as I'm here, I'd like a word with Sam Rogers."

Ora Hayes paused with her finger on the intercom switch. "What do you want him for? Not more hubcap thefts?"

"No. The high school kids are behaving as well as can be expected at the moment."

The secretary nodded toward a closed door labeled MR. ROGERS—VICE-PRINCIPAL. "Go on in," she told him. "All he's doing in there is reading the paper."

Spender tapped on the door to give Rogers time to stow the comic page before he entered. "Don't get up. I was just delivering the skull for the drama class," he explained, settling down in the visitors' chair.

Sam Rogers, a thin, worried-looking man in horn-rimmed glasses, half-rose out of his seat to acknowledge his visitor and then sat down again, tapping his fingertips together in a gesture of nervous anticipation. "We hope you'll join us for a performance, Sheriff," he said at last.

"Well, I might do that," said Spencer, smiling. "Not that I hold with Hamlet being a hero, after killing Polonius in— what was it? Act three?"

The vice-principal, whose teaching specialty was vocational ed., inclined his head in cautious agreement.

"I wanted to check on the Underhill children. It's kind of an unusual situation, them living out there by themselves, and I just wanted to make sure they were doing okay."

Sam Rogers blinked. "They're living alone on that farm?"

"There weren't any relatives, and they didn't want to be sent away. The did inherit the land, you know. And they seemed to be pretty levelheaded kids."

The smaller man digested this information. "I haven't heard of any problems," he said cautiously. "Their attendance seems to be satisfactory. Of course, we're two weeks away from a grading period, so I can't give you any information about that."

The man had no idea how the Underhills were, Spencer realized. Maybe only a vague idea who they were. "Maybe I should talk to them."

Rogers looked at his watch. "We're doing some standardized testing this morning, and I'd hate to have to pull them out of class, mess up the results and all. If you could come back around one-thirty . . ."

Spencer Arrowood was on his way out the door. "It's not that important. It was just a thought. I think I'll drop by the cafeteria and take first lunch with the students—a little goodwill mission."

"Sure. Glad to have an extra monitor in there."

"If there are any problems with the Underhills, though. Depression, absenteeism, whatever, you call me, all right?"

"I'll do that, Sheriff," said Sam Rogers, turning away. His mind had already moved on to the next item on his schedule.

Joe LeDonne liked patrolling in the winter, when there wasn't an endless vista of green to make him uneasy, and no sound of rain on big leaves brought back a flood of unwelcome memories. The sight of bare oaks stretched out against a crisp blue sky reminded him of his boyhood in Gallipolis, Ohio, when hunting was an afternoon's pastime and not the yearlong exercise in weary terror that it became

in Southeast Asia. He slid his fingers across the butt of the
.45 he wore at his hip. Odd still to be carrying a gun after
all these years, he thought. There had been times in 'Nam,
standing over things he would not picture in his mind, when
he had sworn never to touch a firearm again. But a strange
thing had happened to him while he thought he was outliv-
ing that one-year tour: He didn't so much survive it as
mutate to accommodate its demands, and when he came
home, he was somebody else entirely. Somebody who enjoyed the rush of crisis situations, and who used danger as
a measure of being alive. Martha didn't understand this
intoxication with crisis that kept him on the edge; she kept
telling him to be careful, to drive slower. Lately he had been
talking about getting a motorcycle and taking up sky-diving
just to irritate her. It wasn't fair to her; she was loving him
in the only way she knew how, but she had missed the
whole point. Joe LeDonne didn't want to be safe: The only
safe people are the dead ones.

Late autumn was a good time to patrol the outlying
reaches of the county. Stripped of foliage, the woods were
less able to conceal evidence of wrongdoing: The copper
sheathing of a moonshine still might flash from the side of
a mountain clearing, or a hunter's brake on national forest
land would stand revealed in the barren woods.

As he drove deeper into the wilderness on the deserted
road, he felt the thrill of expectation that came from being
alone and waiting. It tensed the muscles in his thighs and
made his breath come in short bursts. It was a kind of
intuition he had developed long ago, in the jungle. The feeling was so strong that he wasn't even surprised when he
saw the man with the rifle walking up the road.

LeDonne slowed the patrol car, looking hard at the
stranger in camouflage. He was tall and muscular, early
forties, sandy hair thinning out on top. He was close enough
to hear the motor of the car, but he didn't turn around to

see who was behind him. The deputy pulled the patrol car sideways in front of the hiking man, forcing him to stop. Spencer Arrowood would never have engineered such a deliberate confrontation; LeDonne, however, wasn't interested in public relations but in the rush of courting danger. This dude didn't look like a local voter, anyway.

He didn't look scared, either. LeDonne had to give him that. When the fender of the patrol car came to rest a few feet in front of him, he had stopped in no particular hurry, and now he stood patiently waiting for the deputy to make the first move. It wasn't as if it were illegal to carry a rifle in plain sight outside the city limits.

LeDonne took his time getting out of the car. Hurrying was for rookie officers; it meant they were nervous, and wanted to get the confrontation over with. Sometimes it got them shot. Much better to take your time and let the other fellow build up a case of nerves anticipating your approach. He let a good two minutes pass before he eased himself out of the car.

"Afternoon," LeDonne said, closing the car door behind him. He didn't smile. His eyes never left the stranger's face.

The man raised his eyebrows, quizzical but polite. "So it is."

"Could I see some ID, please?" LeDonne's left hand rested casually near his holster.

Shrugging, the man set the stock of the rifle on the ground and with his free hand dug in his hip pocket for his wallet. "Here you go, sport."

The frown deepened as LeDonne examined the license photo and the printed description. The man's name was Justin Warren; he was forty-three, and the address listed for him was Nashville. The deputy took a long look at the expressionless man. "This isn't hunting season," he said, nodding toward the firearm.

"I wasn't hunting."

"And this is national forest land, so hunting is illegal, anyhow."

"Uh-huh."

LeDonne was careful to conceal his annoyance. "So, sir, do you want to tell me what a resident of Nashville is doing all the way over here in Wake County carrying a rifle in a national forest?"

"I own some land adjoining the federal tract. I was out walking and decided to take the road back."

"Are you always armed when you go for a walk?"

"I hear there are bears in these parts," said the man with an air of innocence that heightened the sarcasm.

LeDonne glowered. "Sir, it is against the law to carry a loaded weapon on a public road. I could give you a ticket for a firearms offense, but since you are a legitimate property owner on this road, I will let you off with a warning. Remember what I said about hunting, though. The season starts the week before Thanksgiving."

"Thank you, Deputy. I'll commit it to memory." With a grave smile, Warren picked up his rifle and strolled past the fender of the patrol car without a backward glance.

Joe LeDonne watched the man saunter down the road. He shifted his weight from one foot to the other as he walked. Another veteran of the war in Southeast Asia. The deputy made a mental note to ask around in Hamelin: realtors, registrar of deeds. He wanted to know what a Nashville vet was doing buying forest land in the back of beyond. He had a good hunch about it.

She set the hot cookie sheet on two trivets on the countertop, and lifted the cookies off one by one with a wooden spatula of hand-carved poplar. It had been made a century ago by Will's grandfather, as had the applewood spoons and the rolling pin of polished cherry. When Laura had first come to the Bruces' mountain kitchen with its blue willow china and the claw-footed oak table and chairs, she had been uneasy about using these heirlooms for fear of spoiling them, but Will wouldn't hear of her buying plastic replacements at Kroger's in Johnson City. It was family tradition, he'd insisted, and so to please him she had gingerly employed the ancient utensils as she learned her way about her new life. She was not yet comfortable with them, but today it seemed fitting to use them. She was baking Christmas cookies for Will. It seemed odd to be thinking of Christmas so early in November, but the postal service was advising everyone to mail early, because long delays in delivery were inevitable. She didn't know what Will's favorite cookies were; he hadn't been especially keen on sweets, but she decided to make a batch of chocolate chip cookies, because the newspaper said that those were everyone's favorite. They would go into a foil-lined cookie tin she'd found in the pantry, with a picture of deer on the lid.

She had puzzled a long while over what else to send. Socks? Golf balls? Finally, she had settled on a stack of paperback westerns, a crossword-puzzle magazine, and a cassette of the Statler Brothers' greatest hits. The last present to go in the box, wrapped in candy-cane paper, bore a tag that said, "To Daddy from Baby Bruce"; it was a book on fatherhood.

Laura smiled to herself as she put it in beside the stack of Louis L'Amours. Will had sounded so despondent the last time he phoned, saying that no one out there seemed to need him. She thought that a reminder of the baby to come would assure him that he was needed and wanted back home. Absently, she reached for one of the warm cookies. She seemed to be hungry all the time now, but worse than that was the fatigue. She wanted to sleep sixteen hours a day, and now that the mornings were dark until well past seven, she found it harder to resist the urge to lie in bed half the day. So much for burning up any of those extra calories that she was taking in. She was beginning to show now—a gentle but obstinate curve had replaced her flat stomach—and no matter how much rest she got, the dark circles stayed beneath her eyes.

She supposed that she'd look like a cow by Christmas, and she'd probably have to sew new clothes for the holidays. Oh, God, Christmas! Laura sank down in the ladder-back chair, the half-eaten cookie forgotten in her hand. There were church decorations to be seen to, a Christmas pageant for the children, caroling to organize, and arrangements to be made for helping the needy. How could she possibly manage all of it alone? The very thought of the chaotic season to come made her want to crawl back into bed and sleep until spring like Nora Bonesteel's groundhog.

"I have quite enough to contend with these days without having to cater a birthday party for *you*," she said aloud. It was as close as she had come to prayer all day.

Taw McBryde hadn't used a typewriter more than ten times in his life, but he'd kept an old secondhand portable for writing the odd complaint letter to the mail-order people or pecking out a Christmas letter for mimeographing. Now he sat stiffly in front of the worn keyboard, staring at the blank sheet of paper, as white as Tavy's face. They didn't talk much about the cancer, and Taw resolved not to notice the physical signs of his friend's encroaching illness. Tavy tired more easily now, and there was a closed look about him that indicated his growing disinterest with the world.

They were sitting in the kitchen of Taw's five-room thirties-style house, which he had furnished from the Goodwill in Johnson City. In forty years of marriage, he had endured enough coasters to protect the tabletops and plastic to protect the upholstery. Now that the missus was gone, he would do as he pleased. He bought tables already ringed with water spots and a sofa scoured by cat claws. Such damage as he inflicted thereafter would scarcely show. A sweating beer bottle sat on the scarred maple dining-room table next to the typewriter, its moisture pooling on the unwaxed surface. Neither man noticed or cared.

"You reckon we ought to send this to Nashville?" asked Taw, indicating the still-blank sheet of paper.

"I don't know," said Tavy softly. "You got any other ideas?"

"What if we send a letter to our senator, and one to our U.S. Senator, and then one to North Carolina's senators."

"Saying what?"

"Hell, saying *this river kills people and we want you to put a stop to the pollution. Clean the damn thing up.* That's what we pay taxes for, isn't it?"

"I bet our tax money is a drop in the bucket compared to what that factory kicks in. They probably keep a pack of lawyers at their beck and call, too. Whatcha call it? Lobbyists."

Taw sighed in exasperation. "You can't lobby for permission to kill people," he declared. "Those people in the government mean well. They want to look out for the honest citizens. It's just that they're so far away and busy that every now and again they need the wrongs pointed out to them, so they can right them. So we'll call the situation to everyone's attention, and ask them to pass a law and make the polluters quit." He didn't look like much of a match for the lobbyists, an overweight, elderly man in a Ban-Lon shirt and paint-stained work pants. But behind the steel-rimmed spectacles his eyes flamed with indignation.

"Well, I reckon we can try," said Tavy in tones of polite disinterest.

"We have to do more than try," Taw insisted. "We have

to put a stop to this damned poisoned river. There's kids living all along it, Tavy. I say we go to the library in Jonesborough and see what we can find out about the whole business. Or maybe we could get the senator to send us some information."

Tavy nodded. "Just don't tell him I'm dying."

"Why not?"

" 'Cause why should he bother with somebody who won't be around next year to vote for him?"

Maggie lay in bed looking up at her hand. What did it feel like to be mad? How would it change one's perceptions? In drama class Mrs. Purdy had said that real actors thought themselves into the roles they played. She said that you could not act a thing convincingly unless you could feel what it was like within yourself. Old Purdy hadn't meant anything personal by it; she probably said it to all her drama classes, but this time everyone turned and stared at Maggie just the same. *She must be able to feel her part,* their eyes said. *Hasn't her father been killed by someone she loved? Just like Ophelia.*

Maggie had felt her face grow red, and she looked away from her classmates' stares. She would not let them see any emotion in her. Let them see her play Ophelia and make what they could of that. She would not respond to their coy invitations to talk about it—"not keep things bottled up inside." She would confide in none of her new acquaintances, nor in the teachers who offered consolation; their solicitude seemed to her more morbid curiosity than genuine concern.

What did it feel like to be mad? It was already dark outside, but play practice did not begin for another hour. Perhaps she could find out by then. Maggie stretched out her fingers against the background of the cracked plaster ceiling, willing it to turn into a starfish. Crazy people saw things that weren't there, didn't they? The hand remained a hand: Her fingers were stubby; the nails ragged and bitten. She held up a strand of dark hair, curling it slowly around her fingers. It is a snake, she thought. It will move on its own, and its forked tongue will dart out at me, she thought. She closed her eyes, trying to picture the snake, willing the wiry coil of hair to turn into rough, dry snakeskin, telling herself that she could feel it pulsing between her fingers, but despite her efforts, she could not coax her mind into delusion.

When she stood on the stage, she mouthed the speeches of Ophelia, but she could not summon up any real sorrow over the sham death of Polonius (greasy fullback Carlyle Watts with cornstarched hair and granny glasses). She would not let herself think of Joshua and the others. Actually it was easier to become Ophelia lying here on her bed than it was on the stage at the high school. There she was hemmed in by painted sets and Carlyle Watts's tendency to forget his lines. Here in her rose-patterned bedroom under the eaves, she could imagine Ophelia's father and the others in the play as they ought to look. She could be transported with grief over a poor silly old man in over his head in statecraft.

But just now she could not manage an escape to Elsinore; she remained Maggie despite all her efforts at concentration. Too bad, because Maggie ought to see about fixing some dinner for herself and Mark before play practice, and Maggie needed to put a load of clothes in the washing machine downstairs. Maggie had algebra homework and a French test on Friday. And Maggie had to live in the silence of this old house, walking past closed doors with her eyes averted because she remembered what had been in them.

How did Mark stand it, sleeping in the room he had

shared with Josh? How could he play Laertes with so much emotion, and show so little at home? They barely spoke. He slept a lot. Otherwise, he stared at the television, seeming not to care what was on. She did not tell him about her nightmares, and he did not break his silence. Sometimes she thought of asking someone for help, but the thought of all those faces cloyed with sympathy dissuaded her.

With a sigh, Maggie swung her feet onto the floor and willed herself to go downstairs and make some sandwiches. She wasn't hungry, but someone might ask if they had eaten, and fixing the food was easier than having to confer with Mark to agree on a lie. As she reached the head of the stairs, she heard the phone ringing in the kitchen. She ran down the stairs and through the front hall as two more rings pealed, but when she reached the kitchen and gasped a breathless hello into the mouthpiece, there was no one on the line.

As she walked toward the refrigerator to get the makings of the sandwiches, it rang again. This time she snatched it up after the first ring, "Hello?"

"Maggie? This is Laura Bruce."

Maggie turned her back on the sinkful of dirty dishes, shielding the receiver with the crook of her arm as if the caller could see the kitchen's dishevelment through the telephone. "Yes, Mrs. Bruce? How are you? We're fine." She had not quite managed to keep a note of defiance out of her voice.

"Well, Maggie, I wondered, because I hadn't seen you lately. I've meant to get out there, but with this old car of ours . . . and I've got morning sickness so much these days."

"Do you?" said Maggie, examining her fingernails. "Congratulations."

"I wondered if you'd like to come to church again, Maggie. I know it's been hard for you, but—" She thought she heard the girl's sharp intake of breath. "Well, let's not talk about that. I really wanted to know if you wanted to do a solo with the choir for our Christmas service. There's a lovely old mountain carol that seems just suited for a clear alto voice like yours."

Maggie shifted from one foot to the other as she glanced about her mother's kitchen. The floor was dull now, with bits of dust and straw lying here and there on the unswept linoleum. On the table, among scraps of crusted food, sat a tin can of Spaghetti Os with a spoon in it; so Mark had already eaten his dinner. Out of the corner of her eye, she thought she saw her mother standing at the sink, twisting her burlap apron, watching her. Maggie whirled around, but there was no one there.

"Maggie?" said the faraway voice on the phone. "Are you there?"

"Yeah. Sure. I guess I'll come. But Mark won't. He only went to church whenever Dad made us, but I'd like to sing."

"That's good, Maggie. Shall I come and pick you up?"

Maggie took a long deep breath before she said no. "I'll drive myself, Mrs. Bruce."

"If you're sure . . ."

"Mrs. Bruce, did you call me before? Just a minute ago? You didn't? Oh, no reason. Just thought I heard it ring, that's all."

Joe LeDonne always came back from patrol looking like day-old coffee, but this time Martha saw such a deepening of his glower that she asked him what was wrong. He shrugged and sat down on the front end of his desk, staring at the county map above her head. The can of Diet Pepsi, which he drank summer and winter without fail, rested between his knees as he considered the problem.

Martha tried to jolly him out of his mood. "What did you find? Moonshiners?" she asked, grinning.

"I don't think so," LeDonne murmured, not really listening.

"Did you ever read about that fifty-two pounds of radioactive material that went missing over at the Erwin Naval Facility? They never did say what had become of it, did they? Although how the government could lose fifty-two *pounds* of something is beyond me. Anyway, I've figured out what happened to it."

"Have you?"

Martha's smile broadened. "I figure some of those old boys back up in the hollers have made themselves an *atomic still*. No more getting caught by the woodsmoke, and it'll run forever."

Joe LeDonne laughed in spite of himself. "Well, if they've got one, Martha, I'm sure as hell not going to take an ax to it. I ain't glowing in the dark for no damn moonshiners."

Martha waited. He would tell her now what was troubling him. They had been together for several years now, through tough therapy and Joe's bouts of depression over a war that wouldn't turn him loose, but at least she knew him better now. She knew how to deal with the nightmares that still came sometimes, and she knew the look in his eyes that said he needed to be left alone. It hadn't been an easy adjustment to this relationship, but after two failed marriages, Martha had about decided that anything that came too easy wasn't worth having. She didn't want to give up on LeDonne; not until he chased her away, and so far he hadn't. She gave him an encouraging smile.

The crease between his eyes went away as he smiled back, and he held up the Pepsi can to her in a mock toast. "Okay," he said. "I ran into a new landowner this afternoon, and I want to find out a little more about him, that's all. I think I'll check the realtors, and maybe the registrar of deeds, and see if I can turn up anything on Wake County's new citizen."

"Why?" asked Martha. "Does he look like a bank robber?"

"No. I'd say he looks like a mercenary. And I want to know what he's doing in a county that's more than half national forest. It sure as hell ain't bird-watching."

CHAPTER

7

And He walks with me, and He talks with me,
And He tells me I am His own . . .

For one shocked moment Spencer Arrowood wondered where Vernon Woolwine had gotten the skull. Vernon stood apart from the crowd in the foyer of the Hamelin High auditorium, returning grins with a dignified nod, as befitting a prince of Denmark. Spencer thought he detected in Vernon's costume a strong influence of the Olivier photograph on the local video store's cassette of *Hamlet*. From somewhere he had scrounged up a blond pageboy wig that looked mortally foolish with Vernon's quasi-Cherokee features, and his black tights and velvet tunic could have stood being a size larger if the Johnson City Goodwill offered more of a selection. The sword at his belt was a curved plastic one, apparently borrowed from his Ninja impersonation. Spencer recognized the impressive metal decor around the top of the tunic: Coke-can tabs bent into an overlapping chain. Vernon was nothing if not resourceful.

The skull almost threw him, though. Even after years of telling everybody in sight that Vernon was as harmless as a fruit bat (and the similarities didn't end there, either), the sheriff felt a stab of dread when he saw the smoothly polished bone cradled in "Hamlet" Woolwine's beefy hand. When Spencer edged through the crowd for a closer look, he recognized the calf skull and broke into a grin of relief. Vernon bowed. In contrition for his moment of doubt, Spencer returned the bow.

The high school play was hardly the social event of the season, even in tiny Hamelin, but since nearly everyone in the community had children or kinfolks in the production, most people went along to the production anyhow. You had to encourage young people in something besides sports.

For Spencer Arrowood, attending the play was an exercise in diplomacy. It gave him a chance to exchange pleasantries with the citizenry. Here he could smile. He didn't want the people of Wake County to remember him always as a sidekick of disaster: the man who stands in the ruins of your burgled living room, or fires questions at you as you stand beside your crumpled Chevrolet. He wore his uniform for recognition, not comfort. As he studied the crowd, he saw Jeff McCullough, the one-man newspaper staff, whose only requirements tonight as drama critic would be to mention everybody and to spell their names right. Some friends of Spencer's mother were there, in attendance now as proud grandparents of cast members. He found it hard to believe that he was old enough to be the father of one of these hulking adolescents. Stranger still was the realization that here was a generation that never had an innocence to lose; Vietnam was as remote to them as the Boer War. For them the word *war* would forever mean Desert Storm, a six-week miniseries sponsored by Hallmark.

Spencer's mother was probably in the audience somewhere, sitting with the ladies of her garden club. He wondered if she minded not having a grandchild to watch on stage. He knew she'd had hopes of it when he married Jenny, but when that ended, the subject of children became an unspoken taboo in their conversation.

The doors to the auditorium opened, and the crowd surged forward. There was no admission; no assigned seating. Just grab a mimeographed program and try not to sit too near a proud daddy with a flash attachment.

He stared at the red velvet curtains, thinking not of his

own days before the footlights but of Naomi Judd. What
did it feel like to stand poised behind a curtain with a thousand fans holding their breath, straining for that first
glimpse of you? He supposed that for the first few months
or maybe even years, it must be like opening night in the
high school play: all glamour and personal glory. But surely
the splendor would spiral down into routine. He wondered
if she ever felt bad on the stage, if she worried about her
taxes, or if new shoes hurt her feet. Or now, with incurable
hepatitis sapping her strength, did she tell herself at each
performance, *It's coming to an end.*

The houselights dimmed, and the play began. The curtain
rose on cardboard battlements, where two burly linemen in
homemade tunics and Styrofoam armor paced out the watch
at Elsinore. Maybe they should consult Vernon Woolwine
on custom design for the next production, thought Spencer,
unable to suppress a smile. The ghost, when he appeared,
was certainly wooden enough to be dead, but the young
actor was fortunate in the size of his family, and his share
of the applause was generous.

Laertes appeared in scene 2. Mark Underhill's dark good
looks carried across the footlights, and his voice, lacking
a Tennessee accent, seemed more fitting for Shakespearean
dialogue than those of his local-born comrades. Spencer
thought that might be a twentieth-century prejudice: the
assumption that sixteenth-century Londoners spoke like the
BBC. The Underhill boy was a better actor than the others,
too. He said his lines with conviction, while his fellow
actors struggled to spit out each syllable of a memorized
piece.

Mark's sister appeared in scene 3, accompanied by a murmur from the audience. Maggie Underhill was too heavily
rouged to be really pretty under the stage lights, but you
could see the fineness of the bones beneath the makeup. She
looked regal. She also looked terrified. Spencer wondered

whether this was stage fright or good acting. In the row behind him, he heard a woman mutter, "Poor kid. She's lived this part, hasn't she?"

The gentle Ophelia seemed properly submissive to her father and brother in the scene in which they caution her about Hamlet's flirtation. With downcast eyes, she spoke her lines in a barely audible voice. Spencer wondered what things had really been like for Maggie Underhill with her father and brother. Was all that fear left over from the family tragedy, or had she escaped into the mind of a medieval Danish girl?

The sheriff's attention wandered after that to the department reports that needed to be written and a list of errands that had to be run on his day off, but Maggie Underhill's voice drew him back to the play. She was talking to Polonius about her encounter with Hamlet, but as she spoke, she wandered toward the footlights, her voice rising as if she had forgotten where she was. "My lord, as I was sewing in my closet, Lord Hamlet with his doublet all unbraced, No hat upon his head, his stockings fouled, Ungart'red, and down-gyved to his ankle, Pale as his shirt, his knees knocking each other, And with a look so piteous in purport As if he had been loosed out of hell To speak of horrors—he comes before me."

Tears streamed down her face, but the sound of applause drowned out any cries she might have made. Spencer thought there was more to the scene than that speech, but perhaps he was mistaken. Polonius helped his "daughter" offstage, and the play resumed with another scene.

The remainder of *Hamlet* was uneventful. Maggie played Ophelia's mad scene without any of her former presence. After that one outburst, she had muted her performance to an imitation of the rest of the troupe, intent upon getting her speeches out by rote. Act 4 was her last appearance. The only point of interest after that was the intensity of her

brother's hatred toward Hamlet. It seemed so real that the
sheriff found himself wondering if Mark Underhill and
Carlyle Watts had offstage scores to settle with each other,
but Watts seemed bewildered, as if he were unable to manage both emotion and memorization all in one go.

Spencer wished that LeDonne had come to the play. Not
that the deputy gave a rat's ass for local politics or classical
drama, but he was a shrewd judge of character. No, not
character. He was a reader of emotions. LeDonne seemed to
have a knack for knowing what people were really feeling,
regardless of whatever image they wanted to project. He'd
seen a kid with the face of a choirboy cut loose with a
string of obscenities—and, incidentally, an admission of
guilt—after five minutes' conversation with the impassive
LeDonne.

After the play was over, he joined the crowd of well-
wishers who surged toward the stage to congratulate the
actors, dodging the doting parents with cameras. Mark and
Maggie Underhill had come onstage for a curtain call with
the rest of the cast, but as soon as the applause died down,
they had dropped the hands of Gertrude and Polonius and
headed toward the wings. Spencer, determined to assuage
his guilt for not checking on them sooner, ducked behind
the curtain in search of them. Instead, he met Florence
Purdy, the drama teacher, still holding the obligatory director's bouquet.

"I suppose you're here to collect the skull?" she said.

Spencer had forgotten all about it. "I guess I could take
it along tonight. Enjoyed the play, though." Miss Purdy, a
persimmon-faced redhead, was entirely too optimistic about
the cosmetic benefits of rouge. Tonight, in her ruffled black
evening dress, she looked like a rooster's grandmother.
Spencer knew it would cost him two more minutes of small
talk to get rid of her with any tact at all. Fortunately, he
got to spend most of the two minutes listening instead of

having to think up more compliments. In the middle of her discourse on the difficulties of obtaining costumes when students' mothers don't sew anymore, he decided that the minimum time he had allotted her for socializing had expired. "Tell you what!" he said, as if he had just thought of it. "Why don't you find that skull for me while I tell some of your actors what a great job they did. If I don't hurry, they might get away."

Before she could protest, he hurried off in search of the Underhills. He found them coming out of the dressing room, looking considerably less medieval in jeans, with the stage makeup already scrubbed off their pale faces. Maggie's hair was pulled back in a ponytail, and in the absence of makeup, dark circles had appeared under her eyes, making her look older than fifteen. Mark wore a black leather jacket and a blue ski cap jammed over his dark curls. They stopped when they saw him, glancing at each other and then down at the floor.

Spencer was used to that reaction. It was one of the depressing parts of his job. There were people to whom he would forever be a reminder of a speeding ticket, a domestic quarrel, or a nightmare best forgotten. Since Wake was a small county, and had always been his home, most people's tension upon seeing him was fleeting, a response to the uniform more than to him personally, and then they remembered him as the guy from high school, or the softball team, or the Ruritan Club. Others never got over their association of him with tragedy. He had stood on too many doorsteps bearing bad tidings. He wasn't Death, but he was most often his messenger. *Nora Bonesteel probably gets this look, too*, he thought.

"You both did a fine job of acting tonight," the sheriff said to them, exaggerating his Southern accent, as he did when he wanted to put people at ease. "I think your parents would have been proud of you."

"Thank you, sir," said Mark Underhill. "We thought about dropping out of the play because we are in mourning, but we didn't want to disappoint the rest of the cast."

"Or Miss Purdy," said Spencer solemnly.

Mark Underhill's smirk was fleeting. "Oh, fer sure."

"Well," said Spencer. "You were both excellent. I wanted to come back and tell you how much I enjoyed the play. And I thought I'd see how you two were getting along. I've been meaning to stop by, but something always comes up."

Maggie Underhill said nothing. Her fingers plucked at the ends of her dark hair.

After a short silence, her brother said, "Stop in anytime you like, Sheriff, but don't go to any trouble on our account. We're doing all right, aren't we, Maggie?"

Her voice was a monotone. "Yes."

Spencer couldn't think of any way to prolong the conversation. "Well, if you ever need anything, you give me a call."

"Sure," said Mark, who was already heading for the door, with Maggie at his heels. "If we run into any problems, we'll let you know, sir."

I'll check on them in a week or so, Spencer told himself. Just to make sure.

Jeff McCullough, the one-man staff and editor of the *Hamelin Record*, wished the high school would consult him before they scheduled their extracurricular events. Take the play tonight. Because the children of so many subscribers were featured prominently in the cast, *Hamlet* would be one of the major news stories featured in the next edition of the weekly newspaper. In fact, a three-column photo of the actors anchored his front-page layout; the other newsworthy item, the school board budget meeting, did not lend itself to photo opportunities.

His problem was that the play had been scheduled for the night before the *Record*'s Thursday noon deadline. Was that any way to cooperate with a well-meaning journalist? To accommodate this late-breaking story, Jeff McCullough had to take his photos at the dress rehearsal, and then he'd had to attend the play the next night as well, for as sure as he got lazy and skipped the real performance, somebody would get sick and use a stand-in, or some fiasco would happen onstage, and if his story came out in the paper without those details, everybody would know he'd fudged his review. So he went to the play, and of course nothing out of the ordinary did happen, so here he was, at eleven o'clock at night, hunched over his keyboard, finishing up the play review, and trying to get the front page laid out, so he could drive to the Johnson City print shop tomorrow and put the newspaper together.

It was a lot of trouble for a feature; a daily would have been able to handle the rush with all their staff, but he had to do the best he could with his own efforts on unpaid overtime. He couldn't do without the article on *Hamlet*. His readers cared about activities at the high school, and he had a solemn responsibility to keep them informed. At twenty-eight, Jeff McCullough was a serious and dedicated journalist, hoping for better things. He loosened his tie and yawned, wondering how long he could live on hot dogs and Twinkies.

McCullough was going through the mimeographed program, double-checking his spelling of cast names, when he heard the knock at the door. "We're closed!" he yelled. Why couldn't people turn in their "Free Kitten" ads during regular business hours?

The knock this time was louder.

The editor threw down his pencil, and stalked to the door. The shade had been pulled down to cover the glass, and in front of it dangled a sign that said Closed.

McCullough peered past these obstructions, and saw two old men peering back at him. Maybe it's a fire or something, he thought, flipping back the brass lock. He pulled open the door, motioning for them to come inside.

"We're actually closed," Jeff McCullough told the men as he ushered them in. "Is this some sort of emergency?"

"We think so," said the thinner of the two. He looked about seventy, but his face had a pale, pinched look that didn't bode well for his health. His red flannel shirt looked at least a size too big for him. "I'm Tavy Annis," he said, "And this is my friend Taw McBryde. We got to talking tonight at the café about what we ought to do, and when we saw your lights on, we figured we'd come over here and see what you thought."

"Yeah, we think you ought to publicize the situation," said the heavyset man beside him.

Jeff McCullough glanced at his watch. He still had a good hour's work to do. He looked again at the two visitors. They were waiting patiently, unsmiling, and as far as he could tell, neither of them was drunk. Oh, what the hell, he thought. It's never too early to start working on next week's edition. "Why don't you have a seat over here, and tell me what this is all about," he said aloud.

He offered them coffee, and they thanked him politely and said no. When he'd got a fresh cup for himself, and settled in his swivel chair, facing them, the thin one, Tavy, began to speak. "I've lived here in Wake County all my life, right by the Little Dove River for over fifty years. A few weeks ago, I went to the doctor because I was feeling poorly, and he said I got cancer. There's not much hope."

Jeff McCullough blinked. "I'm really sorry."

"Tell him the rest, Tavy," the other man said. He took out a cigarette, looked at it, and tossed it into a nearby wastebasket. "Force of habit," he muttered to no one in particular.

115

"The doctor at the clinic said there have been a lot of cancer deaths among people who live near the Little Dove River on account of that paper company in North Carolina dumping pollutants in the water. I could give you his name if you wanted to interview him."

"Maybe you ought to drive over to the paper company, too. Interview them," Taw McBryde suggested. "We need to put a stop to this polluting right now."

McCullough looked from one man to the other. "That's a big story," he said at last.

Tavy Annis looked pleased. "We figured the people in this county had a right to know about it."

"They probably do," said the editor. "But ... I'm not sure how to explain this. It's not a story the *Record* could really handle."

"Why not?" snapped Taw. "It's sure as hell local interest."

Tavy Annis twisted his hands. "We're not cranks, you know. I didn't believe it myself at first, but what we're telling you is the truth."

McCullough nodded. "Yes, sir, I know, but it's a very complicated issue. I'm a one-man newspaper staff putting out one paper a week. Now, to do a complex environmental story, you'd need reporters talking to government officials, paper-company people, cancer researchers. I don't think my budget would even cover the phone bills on this story, even supposing I had the time to devote to it, which I'm afraid I don't. And then there's the possibility of a lawsuit from the paper company for libel."

"Libel! It's the truth! They're poisoning people!"

"Yeah, but that paper company is rich. And they probably have a whole stable full of lawyers on retainer just to fight cases like this, whereas we would have to hire one to defend us, and in a lawsuit, being right can be just as expensive as being wrong. Even if we won, they'd appeal until

116

we ran out of money." He shook his head. "*That* wouldn't take long!"

They sat in silence while the two men digested this information. Finally, with a look of disgust, Taw said, "So you won't help us fight them?"

McCullough let out a weary sigh. "Look, you don't want me. I have very little power and damn few resources. How much trouble can you stir up with a podunk weekly newspaper in rural Tennessee? You have the right idea about using publicity, but you need to aim higher."

Tavy looked thoughtful. "The *Johnson City Press-Chronicle*?"

The editor stopped himself from laughing just in time. "A little higher than that, guys. How about *60 Minutes*, or the Donahue show? What you need is national exposure on this thing so that public opinion will force the company to clean up its act. Have you written to your congressman?"

Tavy nodded sullenly. "Yep. Haven't heard anything yet."

"That's a good first step, though. At least you've put your concern on the record, so to speak." He frowned, tapping the end of his pencil against his thigh. "I wish I could think of somebody to put you in touch with. There must be some environmental groups in the state. I can ask around. Before you go public with this crusade, you really need some hard evidence."

Taw McBryde scowled. "My buddy is dying. Isn't that proof enough?"

"No. Who's to say how he got cancer? Maybe he ate apples soaked in weed killer. What *doesn't* cause cancer these days? Do you know exactly what chemicals are in the river water?"

"Have you seen that river?" asked Tavy. "It looks like tobacco spit. The fish are deformed."

"I know." McCullough shuddered. "There's no question

about the pollution. I wouldn't even go out on the Little Dove in a boat, but saying that it looks bad isn't evidence of cancer-causing chemicals. You should try to get somebody to test the water. To analyze it, so you can say for sure what chemicals it contains, and then find out if any of those chemicals are used by the paper company."

Tavy Annis shifted in his chair. "That's a lot of work to ask of a dying man."

"Yes, sir," said McCullough. "But it's the only way you're going to accomplish anything. Trying to stop that paper company by putting an article in the *Hamelin Record* would be like trying to shoot down a B-52 with a slingshot."

Taw McBryde stood up, signaling that the meeting was over. "Thank you for your time, son," he said. "You've given us a lot to think about. Sorry to bother you so late."

"I only wish there were more I could do," said Jeff McCullough. He showed the two men to the door and then went back to his article on the Hamelin High production of *Hamlet*. Suddenly, his job seemed ridiculously trivial.

On the lamp table beside the couch his mug of coffee grew cold, but Joe LeDonne didn't care. He had forgotten that it was there. He stared into the fireplace, watching the flames make fire music on wood and following his memories back to other, less contained conflagrations. In his present state of mind, it would have been safer to watch Letterman or even to call Martha and spend the night at her place, but LeDonne seldom took the safe route. Besides, there was no point in disturbing anyone else at this hour just because he couldn't sleep. Martha had to be at work at eight, same as he did, but she required more sleep to do it. Better for him to commune with the flames. He was used to being alone.

He had chosen this two-bedroom frame house because it

had a fireplace in its small living room. And because the fifties bungalow came cheap. He'd given it a coat of paint, and hauled in some secondhand furniture he'd picked up in Johnson City, and he was satisfied. Martha was always after him to hang some pictures, or to get the couch reupholstered, but somehow, without actually arguing with her about it, he never did. He didn't want the place to start looking like home to him. He didn't have a home. The people in the veterans' support group over in Knoxville had a lot to say about that, and the word *martyr* figured heavily in their comments, but what they thought or said didn't change anything. This was who he was, and Martha could either take that or leave it.

He had spent about half an hour now with his ghosts, reliving the old battles, watching the old deaths as helplessly as ever. Remembering was sort of like saying a rosary: Mike, Bajo, Simmons, Sweet Sam, Parnell. Now he had gone into his memories and come out on the other side, and the pain it brought was so familiar that it was comforting. Comforting to feel anything at all. Now he could consider new things. LeDonne was thinking about a man on a dirt road with a rifle and the rolling walk of an infantryman in a jungle war.

After his encounter with the cocksure Justin Warren, LeDonne had made some inquiries about the property on the national forest road. Sure enough, the man owned property back there: 200 acres, mostly wooded, adjoining the national forest. The deed listed a 1,200-square-foot cabin and some outbuildings on the land. It had a stream, a right of way to the road, and a well, but no electricity. The power lines didn't go out that far, and apparently Warren hadn't requested that they extend the service to include him. That figured. It told LeDonne what he was there for.

There were only two things that would bring a man like Warren out of Nashville to buy property in the east

Tennessee mountains. The first possibility was drugs. Marijuana was a big cash crop these days, and Appalachia was a prime place to grow it. Smart felons grew the stuff on national forest land, because if the law caught you growing illegal substances on your own land, they could confiscate the property. Grow it on government land and all you stand to lose is the crop—and maybe a few years of your life. But Warren wasn't a marijuana planter, because he didn't have any electricity. These days the feds caught big-time growers by checking electric bills in rural counties. The high-tech tools of drug farming—high-wattage sodium halide lights, big coolers, and ventilation fans attached to barns—used a lot more power than the average home consumed. Some growers tried to evade detection by bypassing the electric meter, but Warren couldn't do that because no wires went close to his land.

Besides, when LeDonne encountered Warren on the road, the man had been too calm to have felonies on his conscience. He didn't look like a Sierra Club bird-watcher, either, though. Warren was up to something.

The deputy would bet anything that Justin Warren had bought a little place in the backwoods so he could keep playing soldier. Maybe he was the kind of moron who thought that World War III was right around the corner, and that the Appalachians would keep him safe by blocking the fallout when they nuked Washington and Oak Ridge. If that was the case, Warren would be stocking up on canned goods, batteries, and bottled water, waiting for civilization to go boom! so that he and his lost boys could enjoy their never-never land together.

If he wasn't a survivalist, then he was running a training camp for mercenaries. Every weekend a dozen cars would go into the forest road, and stay parked there until Sunday night, while their gung-ho owners scurried around through the woods with greasepaint on their faces, pretending to be in boot camp. These would-be Rambos would run obstacle courses through the woods, climb ropes, scramble over log walls, and take turns tracking each other in the forest at night, just for the hell of it. LeDonne doubted if many of them would be veterans. Just Warren, their fearless leader. The others were usually Wannabes, playing army. Most people who had done it for real wouldn't be caught dead out there.

Survivalist or mercenary camp counselor. Neither of those exercises in absurdity was strictly illegal, but they both had the potential for trouble. Strangers with guns are not a good thing in any county. Let those assholes accidentally shoot a couple of Appalachian Trail hikers, and the shit would really fly, LeDonne thought. Besides, they could frighten the locals, disrupt legitimate hunters, and make generally less than desirable neighbors.

LeDonne decided that he ought to pay Justin Warren a visit some weekend, just to remind him of some of the local ordinances concerning firearms, trespassing, and controlled substances. But first he'd tell Spencer where he was going, in case any of the Wannabes got trigger-happy.

Maggie Underhill wished they had remembered to leave some lights on at the farm when they went to the play. How could we have forgotten? she thought. It was dark when we left. The house, a white shape in the darkness, loomed ominously ahead of them. Just as it had that night in October when their brother Joshua had turned out all the lights and then . . . turned out all the lights. She shuddered.

In the darkness beside her, Mark spoke for the first time since they had left the school. "Damn! It's going to be so cold in there. I hate a cold house, but there's no way the wood stove could have kept burning for all these hours, so I didn't bother to light it. I wish Dad had put central heating in this mausoleum."

"It was too expensive," Maggie said. "Remember? When Mom and Dad first looked at the house, they talked about it, but the contractor's estimates were very high, and they decided not to."

"Sure. Dad couldn't have afforded it on his military pension, and trust Mom not to get off her butt and get a job, but he could have used the other money, couldn't he?"

"What other money, Mark?"

He pulled the car up past the lilac bush, close to the open woodshed. As he opened the car door, his face was illuminated for a moment in the cab light. His smile was secretive and sly. "You know about the other money, don't you, Maggie?" he whispered. "We shouldn't talk about it, though."

Maggie pulled her coat close about her, and followed her brother up the stone path to the side porch, where they had left the kitchen door unlocked. As she reached the steps, Mark flipped on the kitchen light, and then the hall light, and the living-room light, as he made his way about the house. He wouldn't admit it, but the darkness of the house frightened him, too. It was impossible to enter the house without remembering the night they had found the bodies. But all the lights had been on then, hadn't they?

She hoped Mark was going to light the fire, and that the house would be warm by morning. Otherwise, she would skip breakfast, or maybe school altogether. She hated the cold. It was like being dead. She wasn't particularly interested in going back to school, now that the play was over, anyway. All the lessons seemed so pointless. Algebra. Who cared?

She had just stepped into the kitchen when the wall telephone began to ring. The suddenness of the blast of noise close beside her made her gasp, letting out a little cloud of warm breath in the chilled room. She looked around at the sinkful of dirty dishes, the dingy floor, and the cluttered kitchen table, holding her breath, waiting. The phone pealed again, and Mark did not appear in the doorway to answer it, so, to stop the noise in her ears, Maggie picked it up. "Hello?"

"Maggie? It's good to hear your voice. You did all right in the play tonight. You remembered all your lines, and you looked beautiful. I'm real proud."

"Thank you." The cold in the kitchen seemed to penetrate Maggie's brown wool coat, and travel up her arm into the receiver, and finally into her brain. The words took several heartbeats to register after she heard them, and by the time she had recognized the voice and realized all the implications of hearing it, she realized that they had been talking such a long time, and so amicably, that it would be pointless to scream, so she kept listening, and watching her breath make clouds in front of her. The voice was saying kind things, soothing words.

"I've missed you, Maggie, and I thought you might be sort of lonely, too. So I thought I'd just tell you that everything is all right, and you did fine tonight. Now why don't you clean up the kitchen, all right? It's an awful mess. Why don't you clean it up before you go to bed?"

Her voice was scarcely more than a whisper. "All right, Josh. Good-bye."

Maggie hung up the phone, and slid off her coat, heedless of the cold. She cleared the stack of food-encrusted dishes out of the sink, and filled it with hot water and dish soap. Humming tunelessly in the freezing kitchen, Maggie Underhill began to clean up the mess.

CHAPTER

8

Little girl, tell me where did you get that
    dress,
  And the shoes that are so new?
—I got the dress from a railroad man,
  And the shoes from a man in the mines.
In the pines, in the pines, where the sun never
    shines,
  And I shiver when the cold wind blows.

—"In the Pines"

"I have been doing some research," said Tavy Annis, taking a sip of his iced tea. He still looked thin and haggard, but there was an animation in his face that had been absent for many weeks. He sat in their usual booth at the grill with a plate of uneaten meat loaf pushed away from him, a manila folder filled with papers in its place.

Taw McBryde picked at his own helping of country-style steak. "Well, that's good, Tavy," he said. "You look better." He supposed he'd be doing research, too, if he had been given a death sentence. Second opinions; experimental treatments; hell, faith healers. But the words of encouragement he wanted to utter stuck in his throat. He hoped Tavy wasn't going to be bilked out of his life savings by some quack who couldn't give him an extra hour of life. "What kind of new treatment is it?"

"It isn't about me," said Tavy, shaking his head. "There's not much point in fretting over that. But I've got a little time left, and I figured I'd spend it on something worthwhile. Leave a mark, you know."

"Yeah."

"Get the bastards who did this to me."

Taw speared a forkful of fried apples, avoiding his friend's eyes. "You're still going to the doctor, aren't you?"

"Of course I am. I need all the time he can give me, and I sure as hell don't need any pain. He says if it comes to

127

the worst, he can fix me up with a black box on my side that'll pump morphine directly into me any time day or night, if I need it for the pain."

"I thought that stuff was illegal."

Tavy's smile was grim. "Well, Taw, do you reckon I might get hooked?"

"You're a hell of a dinner companion these days, I tell you that," said Taw, reddening. "You don't eat enough to choke a cat, and your idea of small talk makes me want to hang myself."

Tavy grinned. "If you ever start being polite to me, I'll know my time is up. But that's okay. I don't want you to humor me, but I might need some help getting even. If I run out of steam, I want you to keep up the fight."

His friend looked uneasy. He speared a chunk of fried steak, looked at the congealing gravy dripping from it, and put down the fork. After a moment, he said, "You heard from the congressman yet?"

"Yeah. I got the letter right here." Tavy waved an official-looking envelope postmarked Nashville. "Looks like a form job to me. *Share your concern ... blah blah ... Have no jurisdiction in North Carolina ... These things take time ... Making every effort.*" He sighed. "I bet if we sent that joker a complaint about sighting a UFO on the top of Lookout Mountain, we'd get the same damn letter."

"But at least you let the congressman know about the problem," said Taw. "That's what the newspaperman told you to do. Did you write any of the bigger papers?"

Tavy nodded. "*Knoxville Journal.* Not that it'll do much good. And I called the Environmental Protection Agency, and got the runaround. So I decided to get the facts for myself."

"So what's in the rest of the folder?"

"Photocopies of articles. I've been spending time in the library in Johnson City, doing some research on this pollution business. I figure the next letter we write ought to contain less bitching and more facts."

Taw grunted. "Facts like what?"

"I got hold of a book called *Green Index: A State-by-State Guide to the Nation's Environmental Health*. And according to it, the South ranks in last place."

"Meaning?"

Tavy ran a bony finger down the page. "Out of seventeen states with the highest toxic chemical emissions, nine of them are in the South. Out of twelve states producing the most hazardous waste, same nine Southern states."

"Including Tennessee?"

"It's North Carolina we have to worry about, buddy. The good old Tarheels sending some of that tar down the river toward the Volunteer State. And we just volunteered for cancer. Speaking of which, it says here that out of 179 plants constituting the greatest risk of cancer, more than a hundred of them are in the South."

Taw frowned. "That don't seem right. I thought we lost the Civil War 'cause we weren't industrialized. How come all of a sudden we have all these killer factories?"

"Well, we're not the only states in trouble. The fat cats who run the industries got their own way for a long time without having to clean up diddly squat. Oh, yeah, it's a mess in the Great Lakes region: bad air, polluted water, toxic waste. And out West they got permanent smog, but those folks got smart faster than we did. They started passing tougher laws to stop all that shit. All we seem to be doing is trying to lure new factories into locating down here." He sneered. "God forbid we should discourage them with a few environmental restrictions."

Taw reached for the paper, and skimmed the list of statistics, his lips moving as he read. Finally, he looked up at his friend. "Tavy, you don't have time to run for Congress, and I sure can't do it."

Tavy let the manila folder fall shut. He closed his eyes. "No. But we have to do something with this. Something."

At the sheriff's office Martha Ayers had strung a ribbon from the bulletin board to the calendar nail, and now she was balanced on a chair, slipping Christmas cards over the ribbon to form a line of colorful greetings. Joe LeDonne, reared back in his swivel chair with his feet up on his desk, watched her in bemused silence.

"Well, we need a little festivity around here," Martha declared. "It's going to be Christmas pretty soon, for God's sake! And it's not like we have any prisoners around so that we have to act all strict in front of anybody. I just wish we had a better class of cards."

"What do you mean?" asked LeDonne. "They look all right to me."

"They're just impersonal, Joe. Look at this one: *We Wish Our Customers Happy Holidays*, from your friends at the Power and Light Company. Big whoop. And *Have Yourself a Sober Little Christmas*, from the Tennessee Highway Patrol. You'd think some of the people in this town could send us a Christmas card, considering all we do for them!"

"Arresting their kids for vandalism?" Joe was grinning, but Martha refused to abandon her cause.

"Like watching their houses day and night every time they take off for Myrtle Beach. And going out and helping to get their cows off the road every time the fence breaks! I'd just like to see a little more appreciation from the citizens, that's all."

"They can keep their Christmas cards," grunted

LeDonne. "All I want for Christmas is not to see the inside of the emergency room, so if the people of Wake County would just stay off the damn road on Christmas Eve, and not shoot their in-laws at the Christmas party, I'll be happy."

"You'll get part of your wish, Joe. Spencer's on patrol Christmas Eve. No ER for you." Martha balanced a red-and-white Noel card on the end of the ribbon. "That one is from Mrs. Arrowood," she said. "It was nice of her to send us one. That reminds me, I've got the best present for Spencer. It's perfect! Do you want it to be from both of us?"

"That depends," said LeDonne. "If it's candy-cane underwear, then I'll pass."

The dispatcher made a face at him. "Very funny. I don't know his size—just yours! This is just perfect for Spencer. I mean, it's kind of a gag, but I think he'll really like it, anyhow, even if he pretends he doesn't."

"What'd you get him?"

Martha reached into her desk and pulled out a small envelope marked *Ticketron*. "I'm going to put these in a great big box and make him dig through a mess of tissue paper to find them. It's a ticket to the Judds' farewell concert in March!"

LeDonne raised his eyebrows. "Just one ticket?"

"Well, it was eighteen dollars, Joe. I'm not made of money. Besides, as gone as he is on Naomi Judd, I didn't think he'd want to take another woman along to distract him. This way he can see her one last time before she retires from show business. I think he'll like it, don't you?"

"Yeah, probably." LeDonne reached for his wallet. "Here's a ten, Martha. Put my name on the card, too."

Martha sighed. "Well, that's most of my Christmas shopping done. I just wish you were that easy to buy for."

The deputy smiled. "Why, just tie a bow around your waist, Martha." He ducked as a paper clip came flying in his direction.

The Shiloh Church Ladies' Circle (and formerly Sewing Society) was meeting on a small farm outside Hamelin, at the carefully decorated home of Barbara Givens. Because her husband worked in Johnson City, Barbara Givens was able to afford a nicer house than many of her rural neighbors, and she had lavished time and energy embellishing the place with country decor. At the Ladies' Circle Christmas party, Laura Bruce devoted much of her attention to surreptitiously observing the Givens's furnishings. If Will hadn't been a minister, Laura would have written a catty but hilarious letter detailing the more virulent excesses of Barbara Givens's country mania. . . . *The bathroom is definitely not for claustrophobics. This overwrought room, the size of a broom closet, is completely shrouded in dark brown wallpaper with little tiny pineapples all over it. The facial tissue is disguised as a crocheted country cottage, and the bathtub is lurking behind ruffled curtains of brown satin. The toilet evidently has delusions of being an art gallery, because it is surrounded by about a dozen little archly precious pictures of flowers and childlike animals.* . . . Laura realized that the Givens's rustic splendor was the envy of half the church Circle, but that knowledge did not help her fight off the urge to smirk when her gaze encountered a duck decoy. Laura had no doubt that Will would find the house equally silly, but she knew that he would not approve of any ridicule on her part. *The house is immaculate, and Barbara is terribly proud of it*, Laura told herself, as a concession to her husband's generosity of spirit. *Surely kitsch is in the eye of the beholder.*

The truth was that she found the entire event tacky, but

she refused to acknowledge this fact, even to herself, because she felt that such superficial judgments would be a great failing in a minister's wife. So Laura smiled and tasted bizarre desert recipes, and maintained an expression of rapt interest through discussions of the fabric store's monthly sale, applesauce cake recipes, and the minor ailments of everyone they knew. She parried questions about Will's experiences overseas, her age, and she resisted all efforts to make her take sides in local squabbles.

They almost got her, though, with the childbirth horror stories. Laura's "condition" seemed to remind every woman of some tale of protracted labor or agonizing complication, and every time Laura changed the subject, someone else would begin a new reminiscence.

"I'm sure you have nothing to worry about, dear," Mrs. Hoskins assured her. "Although you did wait a bit late to have a first baby."

"I wanted to be married first," said Laura, unable to resist the quip.

The others laughed merrily. In old ladies and pregnant women, displays of temper passed for wit. "Is Reverend Bruce going to get to come home for the birth?" someone else wanted to know.

Laura felt a sting in her eyes, but she swallowed air until it went away. "No. The Red Cross will get the word to him as soon as they can. Unless he gets sent home before April. We could always pray for that."

"Is it due that soon?" asked Amy Jessup. "You aren't showing very much."

Laura was saved from another tart reply by the hostess's announcement that it was time to open the gifts. The Ladies' Circle observed an old-fashioned custom of choosing *prayer partners* each September. Each Circle member drew the name of someone else in the group to be her *prayer partner*; the information was a secret: each woman knew whose name she had drawn from the box, but she did not know who had drawn hers. For the next three months, Circle members prayed for their prayer partners, but they might also send encouraging notes in the mail or do favors, like leaving a jar of preserves at the door. The prayer partner's identity was revealed at the Ladies' Circle Christmas party. Under Barbara Givens's beribboned chintz-and-bunny- "country" Christmas tree lay packages, one for each member of the Circle. Each gift was from a prayer partner, and her name was revealed on the card inside.

Laura's prayer partner had been Sarah Nevells, a fourth-grade teacher at Hamelin Elementary. Laura had been too busy to do much in the way of thoughtful kindnesses over the past few months, but she did send a greeting card to the school once, saying *Teachers are a National Treasure*, which Laura sort of believed, but mainly she had sent it because she thought Sarah Nevells would appreciate the sentiment. She had signed it *Your Prayer Partner*, which seemed very silly to her.

Choosing a gift for a stranger (under five dollars, the rules specified) was more of a challenge. After wandering around the mall for an hour, debating every possible purchase, Laura decided that the task was impossible. *Scented soap*: Would she take that as an implication that she needs to wash? *A book*: What if she doesn't like it or thinks I intended some message in choosing it? *Earrings*: Are her ears pierced; does she even wear earrings? Finally, in a last-minute panic, Laura bought her prayer partner a box of flowered stationery. It wasn't exciting, but at least she couldn't think of any way for it to be offensive.

Laura wondered who had drawn her name. She had come to church one Saturday to find an arrangement of flowers on the altar, with a note saying, *Arranged by Laura's Prayer Partner*, but other than that, there had been no sign of a benevolent hand at work on her behalf.

At least it would make a good story to tell Will, she thought. It proved that she was attempting to observe the parish customs. As the others tore into their packages of scented soaps and paperback romance novels, Laura carefully unwrapped the small box in her lap. Inside was a homemade baby bib, appliquéd with a scene of black sheep grazing beneath an apple tree.

"That must be from Barbara!" cried Lois Hoskins. "A country bib! Isn't it precious?"

"It is," said Laura, holding up the needlework for everyone to admire. "It's wonderful." Oddly enough, she meant it. Country didn't seem silly at all on baby things, she told herself.

Sarah Nevells thanked Laura profusely for the floral stationery. Her gift to her own prayer partner had been a note saying: "*As your Christmas gift, I rescued a kitten from the Johnson City Animal Shelter. You may have it, or I will keep it for you, but it owes you its life.*"

"I wish I'd thought of doing that," said Laura wistfully. It was just what Donna Reed would have given a prayer partner.

"Well, Anne Louise, you didn't get a present!" Barbara Givens remarked, seeing one member of the group without a package.

"No. My prayer partner was Janet Underhill. I guess she must have drawn my name as well."

Everyone fell silent for a moment, thinking about the murdered woman.

"Well, it's a great pity what happened to her," Millie Fortnum declared. "I just shudder every time I think about it."

Lois Hoskins nodded. "I wouldn't have believed it, though. Josh Underhill used to come to Sunday school every now and then, and he was always such a nice boy."

"They say you can't tell about murderers," said Millie

135

Fortnum. "Or maybe he was drunk. Being in the rescue squad, I can't tell you all the awful things I've seen happen on account of drunk people."

"He didn't drink, Millie," said Mrs. Hoskins with a steely expression.

Anne Louise Barker was still staring at the tabletop Christmas tree, shining with tartan ribbons. "I felt like I ought to get her something," she said at last. "It isn't as if I forgot her."

"What did you do, Anne Louise?" asked Laura Bruce. She had been thinking how glad she was that she hadn't drawn the name of the murdered woman. Even having to choose floral stationery was better than that.

"Well, I baked some Christmas cookies, and I took them to her children. I thought if it was me, I'd want someone to look after my young'uns." She sighed. "I hope they'll be all right out there alone on that dreadful farm."

"What are they doing for Christmas?" asked Lois Hoskins.

"Well, I asked them, and the boy said they had plans. Going to relatives, I guess."

But Maggie is singing at the Christmas Eve service, thought Laura. *And they don't have any close relatives.* She made a mental note to check on them when the weather was better.

Dallas Stuart had just purchased a new desk calendar of lawyer quotations for the coming year, and he was busy entering his court dates and other commitments on its pristine pages. He liked to get his duties taken care of before the chaos of the holidays was upon him. Soon grandchildren would be arriving, and his wife would start accepting party invitations from here to Knoxville, and his schedule would be shot until after New Year's. He always left spaces between his appointments during the early part of January to accommodate all the divorce cases that would spring up during the Christmas season. He must remember to advise his young partner, who handled the criminal cases, to leave open spaces on his schedule, too, for the assault cases and the shoplifters. 'Tis the season, Stuart thought sardonically.

He missed the old days, the holidays of his boyhood. Depression-era Christmases may have seemed spartan at the time, with some hard candy, an orange, and a baseball being the sum total of his gifts, but as the years passed, those days took on a luster in his mind unequaled by the affluence of later holidays. Modern holidays emphasized material things at the expense of real joy. Take his grandkids, for instance; a darling pair of children, but between his wife and his daughter-in-law, spoiled rotten. Why, at the end of Christmas day, those young'uns probably couldn't tell you all the presents they'd received, and they wouldn't play with half of them ever again. They wouldn't know what it was like to try to make one pair of shoes last until June. Times had changed in the mountains.

On his desk, the intercom buzzed, and Alva's voice interrupted his thoughts. "The Underhill boy is calling, Dallas. He wants to talk to you. Line one."

Dallas Stuart looked a little shamefaced as he picked up the phone. He reckoned affluence wasn't everybody's problem, after all. "Is that you, Mark?" he said genially into the receiver. "I was just thinking about you and your sister. How are you?"

"We're fine, Mr. Stuart," said Mark Underhill. "I wanted—"

"Glad to hear it," the attorney replied. "Because I'd been meaning to give you a call myself. A couple of days ago, my wife asked me to find out if you young people had any plans for Christmas. We've got the family coming in this year, and we thought a couple more youngsters would just add to the merriment." Eleanor would give him a piece of her mind for inviting strangers home for Christmas without consulting her, but he'd get around her. He'd simply explain that the thought of those two orphans alone in that tragic house had hit him all of a sudden with more guilt than he cared to bear during the Yuletide season. She wouldn't mind really; she just didn't like domestic surprises when she'd already planned her menus.

Mark Underhill's voice broke through his reverie. "It's very kind of you to ask us, Mr. Stuart," he was saying, "But my sister and I already have plans. I was calling you about something else."

"All right." Dallas Stuart disguised his sigh of relief with a discreet cough. "What can I do for you?"

"Did my father say anything in his will about another bank account?"

Whatever the attorney had been expecting to hear, it was not that. "I don't think so," he murmured. "Let me just go to the filing cabinet and get the papers. Can you hold on?" When he put the phone down, Stuart shuffled to the oak-veneer cabinet, still trying to figure out what the Underhill boy was getting at. There wasn't a lot of money in that account, but the life insurance money had been added to it by now, hadn't it? He found the file in the back of the second drawer, and went back to the phone.

"What do you mean by another account, Mark?" he asked, skimming the documents. "You mean savings bonds, or something like that?"

On the other end of the line he heard the boy take a deep breath. "My father had acquired a good deal of money in various ways while he was overseas, and that money was not reflected in the bank statements from the local branch. I wondered if there was anything in his papers about a safety deposit box or a key or anything like that?"

"Your father never mentioned anything like that to me, Mark. Are you sure you understood him correctly?"

"What about an address of a foreign bank or an account number?"

"Nothing. It's all perfectly straightforward, and there's no indication that your dad had any more money to leave than you'd expect of a retired military man. Can you tell me why you think there ought to be more?"

Mark Underhill laughed. "If you can't help me, there doesn't seem to be any point in going into it, does there? I guess I'll have to find out for myself."

Dallas Stuart found himself listening to a dial tone. By the time he put the folder back in its proper place, he had forgotten about the Underhills, and was busy reviewing his party obligations at the end of this year's calendar.

It was a strange way to spend the Saturday before Christmas—standing on a grassy hillside next to the railroad tracks with fifty other people, most of them with kids in tow. Strictly speaking, Spencer Arrowood wasn't on duty, but he wore his uniform, anyway, under the sheepskin jacket that was keeping him warm, and he'd driven the patrol car to make his presence official. He'd never seen a fight break out at this event, but it was just as well to be prepared.

The day was as fine as you could ask for in December. The high white clouds didn't obscure the sun, and the breeze was mild, with the temperature in the low fifties. Anybody with a decent coat on would be comfortable enough. Of course, quite a few of these people wore no coats at all; that's why they were here.

One wiry old man in a red plaid jacket left the group of women and children on the hill, and sauntered down to the railroad track. He put his ear to the steel rail for a moment, then stood up, shaking his head. Not yet. The crowd let out a collective groan, but it was good-natured.

They were a little tired of waiting, but they weren't going anywhere.

Spencer adjusted his brown Stetson, and strolled down to the track. The steel rails stretched away between the cuts in the mountain pastureland, curving out of sight at the bend where the forest began. Spencer's boots crunched on the gravel siding as he leaned out to look along the length of track facing east. All was still. He turned and waved to the crowd camped out on the hill. Some of them had brought blankets to sit on; others stood and talked, cigarettes dangling from their fingers, as shrieking blond children chased each other through the clumps of people and into the weeds.

There was a sameness to them, he thought, scanning the faces. Many of the women were overweight from a lifetime on the diet of the poor. The deep-fried and starchy foods that are both filling and cheap make pasty complexions and lumpish bodies. The men were short and gaunt, a combination of ancestral genetics and poor nutrition. Beer and cigarettes in lieu of vegetables and jogging didn't help any, either. But they were honest people, and if there was work to be had, they'd put in long hours without a murmur.

People he knew from Knoxville and from the flatlands were always saying how great the house prices were in east Tennessee, and how cheap it was to live in the mountains, but Spencer reckoned that living in the mountains cost most of those people on the hillside ten years of their lives. And maybe a future for their children. But they wouldn't leave— not for jobs or love. Those that did leave sickened in exile in the ugly cities of the Midwest, pining for the hills of home. Even people who weren't poor, like himself or Dallas Stuart's young law partner, J. W. Lyon, could make more money and advance in their careers by moving elsewhere, but they continued to stay in the shadows of the mountains. Why can't we just get out of these hills? he wondered for the thousandth time. Why are we willing to sacrifice so much to live in this beautiful place? If this were the Garden of Eden, God couldn't drive us out of here with a flaming sword; we'd sneak back when the angel wasn't looking.

The sad thing was that the poverty wasn't natural to the region. The livestock business had thrived before the chestnut blight, and just to the north of Hamelin lay land that bore the richest deposits of anthracite coal in the world. You could stand by this railroad track any hour of any day you chose and watch a mile-long coal train hauling the natural resources away. The coal mines weren't locally owned, and they didn't put much back into local taxes, either. The mine owners could afford lawyers and lobbyists to see to that. Spencer had read once that 90 percent of the state of West Virginia was owned by absentee landlords.

The coal companies would be running the train today; the only one of the year that didn't haul coal. At least they made this gesture; offered a little money to the people. But maybe if things had been different politically, there wouldn't have to be a train like this one.

Somebody up on the hill called out to him. "Merry Christmas, Sheriff!"

Spencer grinned and waved back. "Merry Christmas, y'all!"

Most of them echoed his greeting, but a few of the men scowled and turned away. He recognized them. They were regulars in his line of work: the ones who got in more than their share of car wrecks and brawls. People who had frequent run-ins with the law were the type who held grudges; it was convenient to blame the sheriff for their misfortunes.

"The train should be along soon," Spencer called out, cupping his hands around his mouth to make himself heard. "When it does come in sight, I want all you mamas and daddies to keep the children behind this rock. He pointed to a boulder sticking out of the base of the hill, five feet back from the rails. "Those trains are big and dangerous, and I don't want any accidents spoiling everybody's holidays. Okay?"

There were solemn nods from many of the women. The children stared at him, big-eyed and silent.

"I'll stay down here to make sure everybody remembers to keep back. If anything falls in front of this boulder, you can come down and pick it up after the train is past. Understood? And remember not to be greedy. Let everybody get something. Especially the little fellers." He looked sternly at a pack of teenage boys hovering on the edge of the crowd. They pretended not to hear him.

Spencer sat down on the boulder and joined the wait. Above the trees on the other side of the tracks a hawk circled lazily, eyeing the intruders. Somebody in the crowd on the hill tried to get some carol singing started, but the response was ragged, and soon died away. People wanted to be able to hear the train when it came.

A tow-headed three-year-old in a Kmart fighter pilot jacket peered up at Spencer with an expression of round-eyed solemnity. "Is that your gun?" he asked.

"Sure is, son," said Spencer with equal gravity. "I'd take it out and let you have a look at it, but guns aren't to be played with. I bet you have a toy one at home, though, don't you?" He wondered if the child was cold in that plastic jacket with the air force patches on the shoulders.

"Well, I have a wooden one. I got a labor sword, too."

"A *labor sword*?"

"It lights up, and makes a noise when you shoot." The little boy demonstrated the appropriate sound effect.

"A *laser* sword," said Spencer, sorting out the child's meaning.

"Morgan, get on back up here and quit pestering the sheriff!" Waving her arm for balance, the boy's mother perched on the side of the hill, just out of arm's reach.

"Come on back up here, Morgan! Do you want that train to get you?"

She didn't look more than twenty herself. Her hair was naturally blond and her fine-boned face was much too fair for the black eyeliner and mascara she used. It gave her features a hardness that did not belong there; underneath the cheap makeup she was probably quite pretty. She wore a fake-fur jacket and tight jeans, but she still managed to look maternal in her concern for her straying child.

Spencer smiled up at her. "He's a handful, isn't he? I'll keep an eye on him, if he wants to stay down here. See that the big kids don't get it all."

She blushed and looked away. "This is my first time coming to this," she said softly. "If my momma and daddy were alive, they'd have a fit seeing me here. They didn't believe in taking charity. It's just because of him." She nodded toward the blond boy, staring at the bend in the tracks. "My husband is overseas, see, and the money he sends back doesn't go too far."

Spencer felt himself blushing as he listened to the shame in her voice. "What do you reckon little Morgan wants for Christmas?" he asked her.

She squinted off into the sun. "Oh, some old weapon, I reckon. He just loves those Ninja Turtles on the television. He's been talking about getting a plastic Turtle sword. And a Ghostbusters Proton Pack, whatever that is. He sees all these commercials with his cartoons every afternoon, and he remembers every one of them. He's a smart boy."

"Well, that's good." Spencer was trying to think of some way to find out where she lived without being too obvious about it. He'd seen Ninja Turtle swords at the Kmart in Johnson City; they cost less than ten bucks—not much to pay to keep from being haunted by a solemn-faced ghost of Christmas present. Before he could resume the conversation, though, someone on the hill jumped up and yelled, "It's a-

143

coming!" and the crowd surged forward, craning their necks as if they could see around the bend.

The sound was a low rumble at first, indistinguishable from distant thunder or an eighteen-wheeler half a mile away, but a few seconds later the sound sharpened to a rhythmic churning that seemed to shake the air itself, and then the scream of a whistle clinched the matter. "Here comes the train!"

Mothers grabbed the wrists of their toddlers, and walked down the length of track, until the whole group formed a line almost as long as the train itself. Spencer stayed where he was, keeping an eye on the little blond boy, who was dancing with excitement. "Will I see Santa Claus?"

"I wouldn't be surprised," said Spencer. "Why don't you wave at the train?"

The black locomotive rounded the bend, and blew its whistle again, this time in greeting to the people along the tracks. Young and old, they shouted and waved back. The train slowed down as it passed the first group of children standing in the weeds. Instead of the usual complement of coal cars, the locomotive pulled a couple of excursion cars and a caboose. Men in overcoats were standing on the platforms of the excursion cars, with large canvas sacks at their feet. When their platform drew alongside the row of waving people, the men began to throw things onto the hillside, well away from the path of the train. Wrapped boxes. Red net stockings filled with hard candy and small toys. Footballs. Boxes of dolls and plastic tea sets. On the hill, the squealing children scrambled for the prizes.

"Let the little ones get some!" shouted the grown-ups.

Spencer put his hand on the little boy's shoulder. "Get ready!"

The men on the excursion car smiled and waved, then dipped into their sacks for new boxes to pitch. "Merry

Christmas!" they shouted, tossing out a rainbow of brightly wrapped candy.

A box landed with a plop at the sheriff's feet. Inside the cellophane-wrapped cardboard lay a toy gun and holster, a pair of plastic handcuffs, and a tin sheriff's badge. The well-dressed man on the platform tossed Spencer a mock salute before he went back to waving at the shouting children. The train picked up speed now, hurrying on to another trackside rendezvous in the next little community, a donation from area businesses, the railroad, and the coal companies, bringing Christmas to the rural poor. On the porch of the red caboose, Santa Claus shouted Christmas greetings above the clatter of steel wheels.

The sheriff knelt down and picked up the cardboard box out of the dust. "There you are, fella," he said, handing the box to the blond child. "Now you can have my job."

"Oh, boy! It's a gun!"

"Tell the man thank you," he heard Morgan's mother say as he walked away.

CHAPTER

9

I wonder as I wander out under the sky
How poor Baby Jesus was born for to die,
For poor wretched sinners like you and like I,
I wonder as I wander out under the sky.

—traditional Appalachian carol

Winter had come to the Tennessee mountains two weeks shy of the solstice marking its official advent. The glorious curtain of leaves fell to the valley in mid-November, so that hunting season took place on brown hillsides devoid of cover. The Hangman, barren as a skull, towered over Dark Hollow, and Nora Bonesteel's house looked as blank as a sleeping child, with only a breath of chimney smoke to indicate life. With a sigh of relief at having finished another summer, the people gave up their outdoor pastimes for another season. Gardens lay neglected in the wind, and fishing poles went into the hall closet until spring. Now was the time for quilting, watching football on television, and hunkering down to wait on spring.

The cycle of the seasons had been going on a long time for the mountain people. Not just in the Appalachians, with descendants of Germans, Scots, Irish, Welshmen, and all the other settlers, but long before that, when an ancient tribe, the Celtic hearth culture in Switzerland, had observed the changing year with similar customs, the ancestors of these people had been together. In the centuries since their time, the descendants of that Celtic hearth culture migrated west to Brittany, to Germany, Scotland, Ireland, Wales, and Cornwall, taking with them fragments of the old beliefs. Taking along the Sight, they'll tell you. And the habit of lighting signal fires to pass along a piece of news from ridge to ridge over miles of open country. When they met up again in the great American culture stew on the eighteenth-century frontier, they didn't know they were long-lost kin, but it showed in their way of doing things. A folktale here, a superstition there, or a snatch of an old fiddle tune would be just recognizable enough for folks to see the family resemblance that traced their lineage back to the hearth culture of the ancient Celts, those mountain dwellers whose Appalachia was the Alps.

"Don't shoot the Scotsmen," George Washington had told his troops in the Revolution. "After the war is over, they'll stay."

Stay they did. But they didn't want anything to do with the flat coastal land where the English had settled, where the folks crowded their houses together in little villages and then went outside its boundaries to work the land. The Scots, the Irish, the Germans, the Welsh, all wanted land of their own surrounding the house, and space between neighbors. They especially didn't want a lot of well-to-do folks running their lives, and making laws right and left. So mostly the English stayed in flatland that could pass for Hampshire, where they could have big farms, needing many workers to run them. The others settled for hilly land more suited to livestock and orchards than field crops, and they did the work themselves. They brought their fiddle tunes from Ireland, their knowledge of whiskey making from Scotland, and their quilt patterns from a time before history began.

The mountain and flatlander ways of life would clash head-on in 1861, when the Southern mountaineers couldn't see any reason to leave the Union, but no one saw that coming. Nor did the Sight apprise them of the coming of railroads, riverboat navigation, and the industrialization of the flatlands that would leave the settlers' descendants high and dry in their mountain paradise, with no jobs and no political power. As Nora Bonesteel often said, "The Sight never tells me anything I want to know."

Right now she wanted to know when her ride would come to take her to church, but the view from the front parlor window was blocked by the uphill slope of the meadow. She waited in her armchair by the fire, listening for a car horn on the road above. A silly red knitted tam and brown woolen gloves lay in her lap beneath the spine of the Bible. Nora Bonesteel was reading Jeremiah. On the table beside her sat a square package wrapped in slightly rumpled Christmas paper; it seemed sinful to waste such pretty decorations by using them only once. That and a few cards set up on the mantelpiece were the only indications that Christmas was near. She was getting too old to fool with an indoor Christmas tree; so she strung popcorn on the blue spruce in the side yard, so that her holiday tree was decorated with the colors of feasting birds.

When the knock came, she almost missed it, so intent had she been upon hearing the sound of a car horn. She snatched up the package, and hurried to the door, pulling on her gloves as she went, and found Jane Arrowood standing in the doorway making clouds with her breath. The cold had turned her cheeks as red as her woolen coat, and her carefully waved white hair sparkled with snowflakes.

"I've come to take you to church," Jane announced. "Though why we're fool enough to go out on a night like this is beyond me."

Anybody else might have said, "I'm sure we'll be all right," but Nora Bonesteel never said things like that. People were likely to take it as a guarantee. "Well, I like to hear the singing of the carols," she said at last. "Were the roads slick?"

"They're tolerable. Half an inch fell, but it's stopped for now. My son Spencer put snow tires on my car last week, though, so I didn't have any trouble. I know you were expecting Laura Bruce to pick you up, but I told her she had no business being out driving tonight in her condition. She said she'll see you at church, though."

Nora Bonesteel closed the door behind her.

"Aren't you going to lock it?" asked Jane.

"No."

Although Jane Arrowood couldn't have been more than a dozen years younger than Nora herself, she held the older woman's arm in a protective grasp and guided her down the porch steps to the yard, where the brown grass drooped beneath a dusting of snow. Up the hill in front of them, Jane Arrowood's gray car sat with its engine idling, and above it, just visible in the twilight, the pines on the mountain crest were wreathed in snow garlands. A few feet from the porch, Nora suddenly halted. She put out her hand to touch the bark of a sapling, its bare limbs silted white.

"Is that your chestnut tree?" asked Jane.

"One of them. I reckon it'll be all right. It's so hard to tell if things will make it through the winter." She wiped a line of snow from one of the slender branches and walked on up the hill.

Will Bruce's church was a white spiral in the darkness, illuminated only by the lights over the gravel parking lot. It had been built by the church members themselves in the 1890s, with solid oak floors and hand-carved pews. The builders had been craftsmen, but not wealthy people, so they had constructed a steeple to make the church look "fitten," but there was no bell to toll within its wooden frame. The church had two stained-glass windows; the rest were simple glazing. The picture of an angel hovering over two children on a bridge had been given by the local doctor in the thirties in memory of his wife; and the congregation had raised money for the other one in 1945, Jesus in Gethsemane, in memory of the boys killed in the two world wars. The stone walkway between the yew hedges was crowded with latecomers, packing into the sanctuary in ever-tightening rows.

Jane Arrowood pulled into one of the few vacant spaces left, at the end of the lot farthest away from the church. "I'm afraid we're going to have to walk a bit," she told her passenger. "I must speak to the grounds committee about reserving some handicapped spaces."

"I wouldn't want you to take one on my account," said Nora. "I used to walk the whole way here not too many years back." She pushed open her door and stamped her feet into the thin crust of snow. "Ready if you are, Jane."

"I am, but I warn you, Miz Bonesteel, if there's standing room only in there, I'm going to pull age and rank on some of these young pups and get us seats. You see if I don't!"

In the darkness Nora Bonesteel smiled. "We-elll."

The last strains of "The Holly and the Ivy" were just dying away as the two women entered the darkened sanctuary. Two candelabra on either side of the pulpit provided the light for the evening service, illuminating the decorations of ribbon-trimmed pine boughs. The youth choir, a dozen adolescents in white robes, stood in their accustomed place behind the pulpit. Above them hung a red velvet curtain that covered only the white wall of the back of the church, the mystery being that there was no mystery.

True to her word, Jane Arrowood had marched up to two young men in the back row and gestured furiously until they relinquished their seats. The sight of Nora Bonesteel just behind her may have speeded up the process. As the two women slid out of their coats and settled into the pew, Laura Bruce caught sight of them and smiled. Then she motioned for the congregation to stand to share a hymn with her choir.

" 'What Child Is This?' " whispered Jane Arrowood. "It's my favorite of all the carols."

"I heard it sung at a wedding once," Nora Bonesteel whispered back.

In one dazed moment Jane Arrowood realized that old Miz Bonesteel had made a joke, and then she had to hold her breath to keep from giggling out loud. Behind them, the two young men, now standing, exchanged disgusted looks and wondered why old ladies couldn't behave in church.

Farther toward the front Joe LeDonne stood beside Martha, balancing a hymnbook in one hand, but not singing. He looked uncomfortable in his dark suit, with the blue silk tie she'd given him knotted at his throat like a noose. You'd think he had been dressed by a taxidermist, Martha thought when she saw him, but wisely she had kept this remark to herself. They didn't go to church very often; for LeDonne, changing patrol schedules made a convenient excuse to be absent, and Martha, who had hardly missed a Sunday as a teenager, discovered that the demands on a working woman's time consumed most of her weekends. By the time she did the laundry (and *his* laundry), cleaned the apartment, and cooked a few casserole suppers to freeze for the week ahead, she barely had time to read the paper, much less think about getting dressed up and going anywhere. Once in a while she discussed this privately with God; ten years of reading Billy Graham's daily advice column had convinced her that it would be useless to discuss the matter with him.

The Christmas service was special, though. She wouldn't have missed that for anything. Hearing all the old songs took her back to the days when she was a little girl, with her wish list down like a litany: A BIKE-anda-BRIDE DOLL-anda-PAINT SET-anda-CARPET SWEEPER. What had she been that year, five? That Christmas was the one she framed in her mind, defining the word forever after. The year the tree had been a blur of icicles and colored lights and all the things she'd asked for had really turned up under its branches on Christmas morning. Daddy had been working then. She'd always fast-forward through the other Christmases, especially the married ones, still anticipating the one to come. But it wasn't so easy getting heart's desire after you stopped being a kid.

She stole a glance at LeDonne's solemn features, and smiled a little. They had bought a little white pine tree and decorated it together with ornaments she'd saved from home. Joe had even bought a cassette of country-music stars singing Christmas carols for them to play as they trimmed the tree. At home, the turkey was in the oven, with another three hours to go, and there was a little gold box with her name on it hidden behind the cable box on top of the television. It wasn't a bad Christmas.

Joe LeDonne was watching Maggie Underhill. She was standing in the choir loft next to a chubby redhead, looking as oblivious to the congregation as a plaster angel. When she looked up, which was seldom, her dark eyes fixed on a spot high and to the back right of the sanctuary. Her brother wasn't in the pews; LeDonne had spent a couple of hymns looking furtively about for Mark Underhill, a scrutiny that had forced him to exchange smiles with half a dozen beaming strangers. The only thing that seemed to be in her line of sight was the stained-glass window with the angel. The craftsman who made it must have copied the design from a Victorian print; LeDonne remembered seeing the picture in the home of a great-aunt when he was a child. It was the sort of picture country people liked to hang in children's bedrooms: the pink-robed angel, with the face of a chorus girl and eagle's wings, bending tenderly over two toddlers, brother and sister, as they crossed the river on a swaying footbridge. Such sentimentality had gone out of fashion. You wouldn't find that picture in any modern church. He wondered why Maggie Underhill kept looking at it. The angel didn't look like her mother.

Maggie Underhill herself looked more like an angel than her mother had; more like an angel than the stained-glass kewpie did, for that matter. Her dark hair curled around a perfect oval face, still young enough not to need enhancing with makeup. LeDonne wondered what she was like beneath the demure exterior. "What Child Is This?" indeed.

He hadn't talked to her very much. Spencer questioned the two of them on the night of the killings, but LeDonne remembered the Underhills sitting silently in their colorless family room, watching television, and he'd wondered what emotion they were holding back. It was hard to tell: All strong emotions can look alike; sometimes even the person who has them can't tell which one he's feeling, love or hate, fear or rage. He'd bet against love, though, in the Underhills' case. Not that it mattered. Whatever the survivors felt toward any of the rest of the family, Joshua Underhill had done the shooting, and he was dead. LeDonne ought to be able to dismiss it from his mind, but he couldn't. The Underhill deaths still bothered Spencer, of course, but that was because the sheriff felt sorry for the two beautiful orphans; he was always meaning to drive out to the farm and check on them. LeDonne wondered if he had. He knew that his own preoccupation had nothing to do with concern for the welfare of Mark and Maggie Underhill. He kept replaying the scene in his mind: the dead rabbit that didn't look like any normal butchering for meat, the placement of the four bodies, the spatter patterns— he kept wondering if there was something they'd missed. Something that would make sense of the case.

On the front pew beside her, Laura Bruce had set her cassette tape recorder, capturing the sounds of the Christmas service for Will Bruce, who was present in spirit. Deacon Guthrie, in his Tex Ritter voice, was reading Scripture. The passage he had chosen was the second chapter of Luke, of course—"And there were in the same country . . ." Laura winced as he began it, remembering the handmade Christmas card she had just received from Will. On the card, a sheet of typing paper folded in half, Will had drawn the rounded white village of Bethlehem as it is shown in Christmas illustrations, but above it, on two opposing cliffs, he had sketched two modern tanks, their cannons aimed at each other. One was marked with a Star of David, the other with the Arab's symbol, a star and crescent. Beneath the drawing, Will had written, "And there were in the same country . . ."

Laura hoped that the tape of the service might cheer him up, although he would receive it weeks too late for Christmas. She had asked the choir to sing the one carol that she knew he was fond of, "I Wonder As I Wander," and she'd included "What Child Is This?" as her own special reminder of their child to come. After the service was over, she'd add a private message of her own, telling him who was there, describing the church decorations, and assuring him that everyone in Dark Hollow missed him very much. Perhaps she ought to make an announcement to the congregation that anybody who wanted to wish Will a Merry Christmas could record a brief message after the service.

She needed to make announcements at the end of the service, anyway. The church was taking up a collection of food, toys, and clothing to take to Tammy Robsart, who lived in the trailer park. Tammy had quit high school to get married, and her twenty-year-old husband was off in the Gulf as well, leaving his wife and three-year-old son to get by on whatever he sent them, which didn't seem to be much. Laura had visited her once early in the fall, but she couldn't think of any way to help the girl. Tammy had no parents to move in with in order to save money, and her father-in-law had been sent to jail for killing his wife in an argument. There didn't seem to be much point in trying to find a job for Tammy. Since she had no skills and no education, she wouldn't earn as much in salary as she would pay in day care. Tammy Robsart was nineteen and her son, Morgan, was three, but Laura Bruce could see not one ray of hope for either of them, regardless of the efforts of "the system." Still, she organized the Christmas drive, because she felt that a charity project would be good for the parish and because she wanted Morgan Robsart to have some kind of Christmas.

Will would like that. She must remember to tell him about that on the tape, too. He worried about Dark Hollow so much more than he did about himself. She knew he missed his home. His letters still spoke of the frustration of exile in the desert, and his feeling that God could better use him somewhere else. Laura tried to reply with cheerful, newsy letters, debating on baby names and color schemes for the nursery, but she said little about Will's depression. She felt that she was hardly the person to offer spiritual counseling to an ordained minister.

Deacon Guthrie finished the reading with a jovial "Merry Christmas—Amen!" and closed the lectern Bible with a thump. Recognizing her cue, Maggie Underhill stood up and walked to the front of the choir loft to begin her solo. The organist turned around on her bench; she would not be accompanying this solo. Instead, Tavy Annis, looking like a bag of bones rattling around in his blue suit, stepped forward and opened his battered violin case. Mostly, when Tavy played square-dance reels and bluegrass train songs like "The Orange Blossom Special," the instrument in the case was a fiddle, but tonight, for Maggie Underhill's solo, it would be a violin.

He rosined the bow, and drew from the strings the first mournful notes of the old song, one of the few Christmas carols written in a minor key. Maggie, her eyes still fixed on the stained-glass angel, took up the melody in her husky contralto. "I wonder as I wander out under the sky, how poor Baby Jesus was born for to die . . ."

Taw McBryde felt his eyes smart with tears as he watched his old friend play. Surely this was the strangest of all the songs of Christmas. He hadn't heard it in years. Up north in Detroit they never sang it in church. Christmas was a happy time—"Joy to the World"—and nobody wanted to be reminded of the sorrow that was present the other 364 days of the year. Easter was the time for dirges. But these strange fey people, seeking out mountains wherever they found themselves, could not forget in their joy of Christ's beginning that they knew how the story would end. The minor-key melody of the song was as sad as any funeral requiem, but it was beautiful, and probably very old. It didn't sound like the other tunes people sang. Taw knew nothing at all about music theory, but he tried to puzzle out how this song was different. The best he could come up with was that the tune didn't go where you thought it would. It went up at the ends of lines, where tunes usually go down, and the end of the verse didn't sound like an ending at all; the notes just hung there in the air, as if the singer had forgotten what came next. It was a strange carol altogether, words and music. It sounded like whoever wrote it had remembered all the things Christmas is supposed to make you forget: that it's the dead of winter and a long time till spring; that peace on earth never did come to pass; and that the Christ Child and every other little baby, so beautiful and full of promise, was born for to die. The dark-haired girl singer in the choir loft couldn't be more than sixteen. She sang the words sweetly, as if they didn't apply to her, but all you had to do was look at the parchment face of Tavy Annis to see the truth of it: It's coming to us all, sooner rather than later. Taw felt the winter in his bones. He looked away from the singer, staring instead at the flickering candles beside the altar, while he waited for them to sing something else.

After the benediction, Laura Bruce thanked the congregation for all their hard work in making the service a success. She was careful to mention each participant: flower arrangers, musicians, even the ladies who cleaned the sanctuary. "I just have one or two announcements," she said to the rows of restless faces. "I wish Will were here to do this, and I guess y'all do, too, but I'll do my best. First, there's a collection box in the front of the sanctuary here; if anybody has brought anything for Tammy Robsart and her little boy, please put it there." Several people stood up, with parcels in their arms, and made as if to head for the collection box. Laura signaled for them to wait. "There's just one more thing. I have a tape recorder up here, and I've taped the service to send to Will in the Gulf. If anybody wants to come up and say Merry Christmas to him on the tape, please do. I know he'd love to hear from you."

Freed at last from an hour's confinement, people struggled into their coats and gloves and surged past her, collecting choir members or dropping their donations into the charity box. As Laura finished thanking Deacon Guthrie for the fine Scripture reading, Nora Bonesteel appeared at her side. Laura's face lit up as she saw her. "I'm so glad you came!" she cried. "Mrs. Arrowood absolutely refused to let me come and get you!"

"It can be a treacherous road for those that don't know it," said Nora, "but I'm right glad I came. The singing did my heart good."

Laura saw that the old woman was carrying a wrapped

present. "Is that for the Robsarts?" she asked. "Shall I go and put it in the box for you?"

"I brought this for you," said Nora. "Don't put it in the box. A while back you asked me to make you something for your child, and so I have."

"Oh, how wonderful of you!" cried Laura. "Can I open it?" Without waiting for a reply, she tore at the taped ends of the red paper. "Oh, this is so sweet of you ... and it's such a good baby. I hardly ever feel it kick around in there ... Oh!" Her voice died away as she opened the box and took out Nora Bonesteel's gift. The red sweater was beautifully hand-knitted, embroidered at the neck with a design of green coiled circles, but it was much too large for an infant. Laura thought that it looked large enough for a four-year-old. She faltered in her thanks, determined not to let her disappointment show. "It's just beautiful," she said at last. She wondered if Nora Bonesteel were getting perhaps a little senile, or if she didn't remember how tiny newborn babies were.

"It's all right," said Nora. "I believe I'll go over and say hello to Will on the tape."

As she turned away, Laura remembered that she hadn't yet told Maggie Underhill how beautifully she had sung her solo, but when she looked about the emptying sanctuary, the girl was gone.

Spencer Arrowood spent Christmas Eve on the Johnson City highway, where the holiday lights were red flares and the flashing sign of the rescue-squad ambulance. A family in a green Toyota, hurrying to get to Grandma's house for dinner, lost traction on an icy curve and slid into the oncoming lane of traffic. They hit a pickup truck driven by an old man.

A passing trucker used his CB to summon help and then stopped to direct traffic until help arrived. Spencer got there minutes before the ambulance. The trucker and some other witnesses had got the family out of their car. "I seen a wreck catch fire once't," the trucker later said to explain why he hadn't waited for the ambulance. The old man in the truck hadn't been wearing a seat belt. They could see that they might as well leave him where he was.

Spencer took blankets out of the trunk of the patrol car and wrapped up the two kids, who looked about four and six years old. The little girl had a bloody nose, but they looked okay. He told them that everything was going to be all right, and put them in the backseat of the patrol car, out of the wind.

"Our presents is in the trunk," the little boy said.

"They'll be okay," Spencer told him. "You'll get them."

"If anybody tries to steal 'em, will you arrest him?"

"I sure will," the sheriff promised.

The driver, their father, lay on the side of the road, covered by the trucker's overcoat. His wife stood nearby in that silent daze that meant shock was coming on. "Come on," Spencer pleaded silently to the ambulance. He hated wrecks; the awful wastefulness of death and destruction to no purpose whatsoever. He also hated the fact that being on the scene made him feel helpless. His medical training was minimal; except in extreme emergencies, everyone was better off if he left things to the rescue squad that followed close on his heels. He was supposed to talk to witnesses, look at skid marks, photograph the scene, determine blame. Sometimes the pointlessness of it sickened him more than the carnage.

When the rescue squad arrived, he left them to tend to the living, while he went about his own tasks of preparing for the aftermath, when the insurance companies, if no one else, would care about what happened and why. As he walked toward the twisted car, he slid on a patch of ice and nearly fell. This time Allstate would have to sue God.

"We're leaving now," said Millie Fortnum, one of the rescue-squad members, as he was kneeling to measure a skid mark. "I wish I could have wished you a Merry Christmas somewhere other than this, Sheriff."

"Same here, Millie," he said. The fog from their breath made a little cloud in the glow of the flashlight. "The other fellow didn't make it, did he?"

"The one in the pickup? No? The others will, though."

"He wasn't from this county."

"No. From Sullivan." Suddenly, Millie understood. "Oh, I see. You don't have to be the one to tell his family."

Spencer nodded. "Right. All I have to do is the phone calls, the paperwork, and then—say, by midnight—I'll be all through."

Someone on the squad yelled for Millie. Patting his arm, she loped off toward the van. "Merry Christmas, Sheriff!"

His estimate had been just about right. He finished up the last of his paperwork at 11:40, usually too late to stop by his mother's house, but tonight being Christmas Eve, she would wait up for him. She would want to tell him about the church service he'd missed, and they'd have the traditional cup of eggnog to commemorate the occasion. He thought he might sleep over in his old room, since it was so late. No point in going home, when he was going back over in the morning, anyway.

Just on midnight as he drove down Hamelin's deserted Main Street, he looked at the snow-covered park bench in front of the courthouse, half-expecting to see Vernon Woolwine in Christmas regalia. "Don we now our gay apparel," Spencer thought, smiling. As he slowed the car, he caught sight of an unmoving form on the bench, and for one stricken moment, he thought Vernon had frozen to death, but when he looked again, he saw that the figure perched there under the streetlight was a plaster garden gnome, sprinkled with snow. Vernon had left a deputy.

CHAPTER

10

A sad tale's best for winter: I have one
Of sprites and goblins.

—*The Winter's Tale*

Nora Bonesteel always gathered her balm of Gilead buds on Epiphany, if the day was fine. January and February were the months for harvesting the plants, but Nora liked to harvest hers early in the new year, in case the coming winter turned out to be a harsh one. This year the signs were mixed: There had been six thunderstorms in the late fall, sending ripples of low thunder across the valley—a sign that the coming winter would be harsh. But the woolly worms' coats weren't as thick as she'd seen them in years past, and the pinecones had not opened any earlier than usual. Still, she thought it was best to get the task of harvesting done first thing and then not have to worry about it anymore. Human frailty was less predictable than winter weather.

She cinched the belt on her black wool coat and shoved the knitted tam over her silver hair. She wore two pairs of wool socks under heavy work boots. Across her left shoulder she slung a burlap bag to collect the buds in. When she left the house, she stood on her front porch for a moment, savoring the crisp winter air, and the cold sunshine that made sharp shadows on the grass, but brought no warmth to the day. The meadow was a field of brown stubble, studded with the glistening black shapes of leafless trees; spring was far away. Across the valley the Hangman shone white above his collar of pines.

As she crossed the yard, Nora thought about walking over to the pile of loose earth that marked Persey the groundhog's winter burrow, but instead she walked past it and stumped down the hill to the creek bank to inspect the balm of Gilead plants. This was not a season for reunions. It was no time for excursions, either, so she kept her mind fixed on the task before her, shutting her mind firmly to old songs, and to the lure of the mountain itself. It was too cold today for one of the Nunnehi's excursions; an hour lost on the hillside and she could catch her death of cold. Fifty paces downhill to the bank of the stream, to the balm of Gilead trees. It is January sixth, she told herself, George Bush is president.

The excursions used to happen more frequently when she was a child, but she still got a drift of one now and again. She wouldn't have minded, but for the cold. The first time it happened she couldn't have been more than six. She was walking through the cane brake on the ridge, headed for her aunt's house, trailed by a hound pup, and thinking of nothing in particular, when she looked at where she was, and found that the cane was gone. She was surrounded by tall brown grasses, swaying slowly in the breeze, and the trees at the edge of the field looked somehow different. She stopped walking and listened for sounds from her aunt's yard, children calling or dogs barking, but all was silent. Finally in the distance she heard the drone of human song, like nothing she had heard before. It was a rhythmic sing-song, a chant in words that she could not make out, but she knew not to go toward that sound. Beside her, the brown puppy whined and huddled against her leg. Not knowing what else to do, she had walked on down the hill, in the direction that her aunt's house should have been. She squinted up at the August sun, brushed gnats out of the pools of sweat on her face, and pushed the tall plants aside with a sturdy forearm. In the heat and aggravation her mind forgot to worry about the strangeness of the field, and when she noticed again, the leaves in her face were cane plants, and in the distance she could see a row of Esther's white sheets on the clothesline, flapping in the breeze. She told her grandmother about that excursion, for she'd heard folks in the family say that Grandma Flossie had the Sight. The old woman had listened to little Nora's halting account of being on the ridge and yet somewhere else. She nodded thoughtfully as the tale unfolded, and twice she asked Nora to make the sounds of chanting that she'd heard on the hill.

"Was I lost, Grandma?" the little girl asked.

"In a way you was, Nora," Grandma Flossie replied. "You had the place right, but the time was wrong. I judge from the sounds you heard that you was back in a field of buffalo grass in the days when the Indians owned this land. You just strayed a little from the path of time, that's all."

Nora's eyes were round in the firelight. "What if it happens again and I can't find my way back?"

"Why, I don't think that's likely," said her grandmother with a sad smile. "But if it was to happen, I reckon the Nunnehi in the hollow hill would come out and fetch you home."

For a long time after that, Nora would try to get off the path of time whenever she went out rambling, but she found that you couldn't stray on purpose. It happened when you weren't thinking about it, and never for very long. Once when her Aunt Esther was in the front porch swing singing an old ballad, it happened. Ten-year-old Nora was sitting on the stone steps of the porch, with her back to Esther's singing, when suddenly, in the verse about the dead soldier who'd come no more, she saw that the mountains had changed. They weren't the familiar rounded mountains surrounding Dark Hollow, green with oak and pine trees; these dark and angular peaks were taller and treeless, brooding under storm clouds that weren't there before. Nora kept silent and looked at the strange mountains that seemed somehow to go with Esther's singing. When the last verse laid to rest the Scottish soldier, Nora turned to ask Esther what was wrong with the mountains, but when she looked again, they were Tennessee hills once again, as green and wooded as ever.

The excursions happened less frequently as Nora grew older, perhaps because she never gave her whole mind to anything, as one does as a child; a grown-up's mind has at the back of it a steady drumbeat of obligations, no matter what the circumstances, and perhaps that kept her on the time path, marching steadily along to the place where it would end for her. Sometimes she missed the excursions, but not today. Today was January sixth, and George Bush was president. It was a day too cold to get lost in. When she found herself among the balm of Gilead trees, she glanced back up the hill to make sure that her little house was there unchanged, and it was.

Years ago, people in the mountains used to harvest balm of Gilead buds to sell at the little country stores. When home remedies were still a popular form of medicine, the buds might sell for a dollar a pound, a good return for a day's work, since one large tree might yield several pounds of buds. Now the making of the salve was almost a lost art, and since lack of demand had driven the prices down, few people bothered to brave the cold to pick the buds.

Nora Bonesteel kept up the tradition. She made the salve herself, and stored it in mason jars on the cool shelves of her concrete cellar, alongside the canned tomatoes and homemade watermelon pickles. The clear salve would keep for years.

When Nora was a girl, a few of the old women had claimed that balm of Gilead ought to be harvested at dawn or dusk, but these days she dispensed with that part of the ritual. Early morning and evening were colder than midday, and she was too old to brave a chill for the sake of rough magic. She understood the logic behind the stricture, though. There was a power in the borders of things: in the twilight hours that separated day from night; in rivers that divided lands; in the caves and wells that lay suspended between the earth and the underworld. The ancient holy days had been the divisions between summer and winter, and that border in time created a threshold for other things; that was why ghosts and goblins were thought to roam on Halloween and Beltane. The mountains themselves were a border, Nora thought. They separated the placid coastal plain from the flatlands to the west, and there was magic in them.

The balm of Gilead trees on Nora's land grew at the edge of the creek, so perhaps there was enchantment enough in that border, without their needing to be picked at the threshold of day to strengthen the charm. Some people whacked the whole tree down to a stump when they harvested the buds, because the tree is fast growing and will renew itself in three years. Nora didn't need as many buds as that, though; she wasn't going to sell them. She would pick the buds from the branches the way she would pick apples in October from the trees farther up the hill. A pound or two would make enough salve to last until next year, with some extra jars to give away, if need be. She might cut a couple of small limbs from the tree, and stick them into the ground by the creek. They would take root there in the damp earth and make new trees for years to come.

She turned her back to the bright afternoon sun, and began to strip the buds from the sturdiest branches. Modern medicine probably had treatments just as good as her homemade salve, but she knew that she could rely on this one for burns and sores on man or beast. When she finished harvesting the buds, she would take them back up the hill to the house and heat a dozen buds in the cast-iron skillet with a quarter cup of mutton tallow. When the mixture cooled she would mash up the buds, and then strain off the clear liquid into jars to use for home doctoring. Nora's people had used this medicine for centuries, and while she seldom needed it these days, she was loath to let go of the ritual.

Lately she had been dreaming about fire.

Spencer Arrowood was staring up at the Judds poster above his desk, but he wasn't really thinking about them. He had eaten chicken and dumplings for lunch at Dent's, and he was wishing he could take an afternoon nap without catching hell about it from somebody, probably Martha. As if in answer to this prediction, Martha appeared in the doorway looking virtuously wide awake after a brown-bag feast of raw carrots, peanut-butter celery, and black coffee. Either Martha would live forever, or it would seem like it.

"Naomi is not her real name," Martha announced, waving the magazine that had been her lunchtime diversion.

"What?" Spencer groped for continuity.

Martha tapped the poster with pink-taloned impatience. "Naomi Judd. It's not her real name. Well, the Judd part is, but they made up Naomi and Wynonna when they went into show business. Her name is Diana, like the princess of Wales."

"So it would have been okay for show business," said Spencer, taking the easy shot at one of Martha's favorite celebrities.

Martha ignored him. "It wouldn't have fit her image. She was Mama Judd, and Naomi is one of those pioneer-type names that suggests old-fashioned values and country ways. She was a nurse. She lived in Los Angeles for years." Her tone of voice left no doubt as to what she thought about people who put on country airs.

Spencer waited. This didn't seem to be about Naomi Judd. Martha's lips were pursed into a tight line as she gazed up at the smiling woman on the poster. "She's the same age we are," she murmured. "Isn't it strange to think we're old enough to have a grown daughter like Wynonna?"

"It's strange to think we're old enough to be dying of degenerative diseases," said Spencer.

"And nothing to show for it," said Martha, sitting down uninvited in the straight chair in front of his desk. "What have we got, Spencer? Jobs that aren't terribly high in pay or prestige. No kids. No mark made on the world."

"We've got our health."

Martha was not appeased. "What's the point of living another uneventful forty years?" She followed his gaze upward to the poster. "Don't feel sorry for *her*, Spencer Arrowood! She's had it all, even if she goes tomorrow. She's beautiful, rich, famous, and she's got a daughter to carry it on. I'd trade places with her in a New York minute, liver and all. Why, look at you, Spencer. I do believe you're about half in love with her, and so is pretty near every other fan of country music. And she's got a husband. I'd give a whole lot more than a vital organ for some of that love. I don't know why some women get so much of it without even trying, and others don't get so much as a flicker no matter what they do. I think—I think if I could trade places with Naomi Judd and die, the whole world's vote would be unanimous to let me do it. Unanimous."

He saw the sparkle of tears in her eyes, and he wanted to run. Why didn't the phone ring? "Where's LeDonne?"

Martha sniffled. "On patrol. It's my job to know that, because I'm the dispatcher. But when his shift is over, you'd be asking the wrong person."

He didn't want to get involved in their private lives, didn't want to hear her side of it behind his deputy's back. Joe

LeDonne couldn't be easy to live with, though, with all his moodiness. But that was Martha's lookout; she'd known it all going in.

"I don't know what's the matter with him, Spencer," she said as if he'd asked. "He's so withdrawn these days. I rack my brain trying to think up topics of conversation, and he answers me with this world-weary voice, like as not saying, *Whatever you want to do*. Like he's a prisoner of war. Like I'm a goddamned Vietcong. And sometimes he just disappears, and I don't know where he's off to. He's in a daze, seems like."

"Have you brought it up in the veterans' support group?"

"We couldn't go last week. He *forgot*. I didn't see him till the next morning here at the office. He said he was just off by himself, thinking. I don't know what to believe, Spencer. Sometimes I halfway wish it was another woman, so I could be sure he wasn't having a breakdown." She hit the desk with her clenched fist. "I don't deserve this! I've loved him, dammit, when it wasn't the easiest thing in the world to do!"

"Look, I'll try to talk to him. If I can do it without prying, I'll see if anything is bothering him. Okay?" He stood up, about to invent an urgent errand.

Martha nodded mistily. His promise of intercession seemed to solve all the problems of life's meaning for her, but for the life of him Spencer couldn't see why Joe LeDonne's love should make any difference at all in the pointlessness of her next forty years of living.

"Oh, and Spencer? Sam Rogers called from the high school."

He sighed. "What did *he* want?"

"He said to tell you that the Underhill kids didn't come back to school after the Christmas holidays. Thought you would want to be told. It's not illegal. The girl turns sixteen this month, but he thought he ought to report it."

Spencer nodded wearily. "I'm going to have to drive out there when I get a chance. Anything else?"

"Yeah. You're due to testify in court in twenty minutes. You'd forgotten, hadn't you?"

"Why, no, Martha," he lied. "I've been looking forward to it. It'll be the high point of my day."

There was a print of a Monet painting on the ceiling. Laura lay on her back on the steel table and stared up at the pastel blur of flowers above her head. She supposed that it was better than looking at the ceiling, since Dr. Jessup did keep his patients waiting quite a while in the examination room. Perhaps he thought that the combination of piped-in music and French art would make the wait less tedious, but Laura didn't feel that she needed any such distractions. This was only a routine monthly examination to check on the baby's progress, and she had a hundred things to think about while she waited. On her way into the Medical Arts Building, she had seen another patient from Hamelin. Tavy Annis, the old gentleman who had played the violin for Maggie Underhill's solo, had nodded solemnly to her as they passed in the hallway. He had stopped at the door of Dr. Atef, the cancer specialist. Laura felt a pang of guilt that she should be visiting a doctor for such a joyous reason, while old Mr. Annis was facing death. He looked thinner than he had at Christmas, and his skin was almost transparent.

She pulled the paper sheet closer around her swollen belly, thinking a quick, silent prayer on behalf of the poor dying man. At least he was old; it would have been even sadder if some young person were facing such a death. Her thoughts returned to her own health. Her weight gain wasn't too terrible—she would worry about losing it again next summer—and her blood pressure was normal. So was the urine sample she'd had to bring them in a paper cup;

that was good: It meant that she wasn't developing edema. The nurses took all the preliminary measurements before they ushered her into the examining room. Beside the steel table stood the ultrasound machine that Dr. Jessup used to take pictures of the child inside her. He had given her the first picture, and she had sent it off in a letter to Will, labeled "Our First Baby Picture." Will wrote back that the ultrasound photo looked like a weather satellite picture of a hurricane. He had teased her, saying maybe they ought to name the baby Hugo or Camille.

Laura's thoughts had strayed from baby names to a grocery list for homemade soup by the time Dr. Brian Jessup bustled in, whistling between his teeth. He was about Laura's age; still looked like a tennis player, and his manner with his patients was one of jovial optimism, which Laura found comforting. "How are you feeling?" he asked as he adjusted his stethoscope.

"Like a beached whale," said Laura, looking up at him over the curve of her belly.

"That's fine," he said. "Whales are beautiful."

She was quiet then so that he could listen, first to her heartbeat, and then, farther down on her abdomen, for the sound of the baby's heart. He moved the stethoscope several times on her side. "He's hiding out in there," he muttered, shaking his head. "Let's see what we get on ultrasound."

He squirted a cold fluid on her swollen belly, and set the machine's receiver in place above the womb.

"I sent my husband the first photo you took," Laura said, trying not to squirm. "He's in the Gulf, you know, and—"

But Dr. Jessup wasn't listening. He was frowning at the pattern of white specks on the small screen. He moved the receiver in sweeping circles across her abdomen.

"I read somewhere that ultrasound can sometimes tell if the baby is a boy or a girl," said Laura. "You know, if it's turned the right way, and I wondered . . ." The coldness had crept into her heart now, but she was determined to keep up bright chatter until Brian Jessup said something like "Oh, there it is!" or "This machine is acting up again."

But Jessup said nothing. His frown deepened until a furrow appeared in his forehead. He sighed and looked away.

"What is it?" asked Laura.

"Mrs. Bruce, I'm afraid I can't find the baby's heartbeat. I'm going to send you to the hospital for some further tests, but I'm afraid they'll only confirm what the ultrasound is telling me now. The baby has died."

Laura sat up. "No," she said. "The machine must be broken. I can feel it move. When I walk, the baby moves."

Jessup sat down on the stool beside the steel table. "I know it must feel like it's moving of its own accord," he said softly. "But it's gravity. Your movements cause the fetus to move in the amniotic fluid, but . . . that's all."

"But how could it die?"

"It happens. Sometimes the umbilical cord gets wrapped around the throat, cutting off the child's oxygen supply, but sometimes the death occurs for no reason that we can detect. It wasn't anything you did. Please believe that."

Laura felt nothing yet. She was having a conversation that had no personal meaning yet. "Maybe your machine is broken."

"Maybe." The weariness in his voice belied that hope. "I'll ask the nurse to call the hospital, and we'll make sure. I'm really sorry."

Laura nodded. Later, she would have to think about telling Will, about living through all the questions in the months to come, about her own sense of loss, which had not yet hit her. She must keep her mind on the immediate consequences. In her throat she could taste tears. "And then? I suppose you'll have to schedule an operation?"

Jessup looked away for a moment, and then, reluctantly, back at her. "No. That isn't the procedure. It's better for the mother if labor is allowed to occur naturally so that the hormones readjust naturally, and so on. Artificially terminating the pregnancy is not good for the system. Your body will take care of it on its own."

Laura swallowed hard. "When?"

"We can't tell," he mumbled. "It varies."

"Tomorrow? Next week?"

"No. Probably longer than that. If you were farther along, it would occur more quickly, but as it is . . ." His voice trailed away into a mumble.

"As it is—what?"

"It could be two months."

"But the baby is dead."

"Yes. But your body doesn't quite know that yet. It will take it a while to catch on, and then you'll have a normal labor and delivery, but with an unhappy ending. At least, though, you're prepared for it."

"It will all be for nothing."

Jessup switched off the ultrasound machine. "I'll tell the hospital that you're on your way, Mrs. Bruce."

Later, when she left the Medical Arts Building, she looked around for Tavy Annis, but he was gone. She pictured herself telling him, "I'm not sorry for you anymore. We both have death inside us."

It was past two in the afternoon, but Mark Underhill was still asleep. This had become normal routine for him now. He awoke in the late afternoon and prowled the house in the hours of darkness, finally falling asleep around seven in the morning. It was like living alone, Maggie thought. Their paths seldom crossed, except in the early evening hours, when he would blaze into the colorless den, switch off her television program, and talk to her with an urgency that made him oblivious to any response she made.

"We need the money, Maggie. You see that, don't you?" he would say, pacing up and down as he spoke. "It's rightfully ours, after all, now that Dad is dead."

"Yes, Mark." She had tried to discuss the matter at first, saying that she had never heard any stories about Dad having any fortune hidden away, but Mark always dismissed her objections with a sneer. "Of course there was a hidden stash of money," he would insist. "We all knew about it."

Now she simply agreed with his premise, and let him talk. He never seemed to mind her silence. Sometimes he said people in the Pentagon had given the money to Major Underhill for an arms deal that never took place, and sometimes the fortune was a cache of gold from the treasury of South Vietnam, or drug money from a Saigon heroin deal. It was half a million, two million—he was never quite sure, but it was a lot. Enough to keep them in comfort for the rest of their lives. Sometimes he would offer Maggie a trip to Paris or a sports car for her sixteenth birthday.

Mostly, though, he seemed more concerned with getting the money than with spending it. He was angry that the money was being kept from them when it was rightfully theirs. At first he thought that Mr. Stuart, the attorney, was trying to swindle them out of their inheritance, but later he decided that Mr. Stuart didn't know anything about the money. It was up to them to discover where it was hidden, Mark insisted.

While Maggie slept in the hours after midnight, Mark searched his father's belongings for information about the money. He studied the bank statements, turned drawers out looking for safety-deposit-box keys, and sifted through the paperwork in Paul Underhill's desk, seeking some clue about the missing fortune. Night after night, he looked in the same places, always saying that he must have missed it when he looked before. Maggie was never asked to help in the search, and she was glad. She didn't want to touch her parents' belongings. But if Mark had told her to, she would have had no choice.

She'd had no choice about school. One day just after Christmas, Mark had announced that they weren't going back to school when the holidays were over. All the people there were phonies who hated them, anyway, he said.

"But what about graduating?' asked Maggie. "What about college?"

"We'll finish school," Mark promised. "When we get Dad's money, we'll enroll in the best private school in the country. You can buy your college wardrobe from designers in Paris, if you want to."

"But suppose there isn't any money?" she persisted.

Mark gave her a pitying smile. "Of course there is, Maggie," he said gently. "Look around you. You don't think they sank it all into this place, do you?"

His logic was ironclad, impervious to her diffident arguments. In the end it was easier to acquiesce, but perhaps it had not been wise of her to do so. After she ceased to debate with him about the existence of a family fortune, Mark began to speculate on more immediate ways to retrieve the money. His searches became more determined, and his belief in the fortune was unshakable.

Maggie was sitting in the shadows of the family room, watching a game show with the sound turned down to a level that was almost inaudible. She was wearing her jeans and one of Josh's old wool sweaters, because it was cold. There was a small electric heater that her mother had used in the upstairs bathroom, and Maggie had brought it down and set it in front of the sofa, but it added very little heat to the larger room. She brought down an old bedspread and covered her legs with it to hold in her body heat. She wore lipstick only to keep her lips from chapping, and her dull hair was caught up in a ponytail at the nape of her neck. It needed washing, but because she hated the feel of wet hair in the chill of the old house, she limited shampooing to once a week, hoping each day that the next would be warmer. She was afraid of becoming ill in the cold. Mark was too absorbed in his own obsessions to care for her. If she took to her bed with a fever, he might even forget that she existed at all.

She watched the gyrations of the game-show contestants with drowsy indifference. The muted ding of a bell sent them into muffled squeals of delight, so low was the volume on the set. Slender, cheerful housewives with bobbed hair and pastel dresses clapped their hands and smiled triumphantly when their answers tallied with those on the announcer's card. Maggie tried to imagine what their families were like, what homes they lived in. Surely none of these well-groomed, complacent women actually needed the money.

To Maggie they looked like the officers' wives she had seen on the military bases where her father had been stationed. They would roll shopping carts through the PX with blond toddlers in tow, smiling that same vapid smile, complacent in their security and their status. Their husbands had come into the army via ROTC programs in college, so perhaps they had been cheerleaders or sorority girls in their youth. Maggie's mother had not fit in with these tanned and supple aristocrats. Her husband had joined the ranks of officers through a field promotion in Vietnam, and he had never quite made it to gentleman. She was a high school graduate with an indifferent average on the business track, neither pretty nor popular.

Janet Underhill shied away from the pretty, vivid women who formed the social organizations for wives, feeling that her existence of generic brands and polyester, her ignorance of fashion and current events, and her tongue-tied awkwardness in the presence of their sparkling emptiness irrevocably barred her from their society. Paul Underhill called them the "club soda" women, all fizz and no substance.

Maggie suspected that he, too, was uneasy around them. She supposed that she caught her own shyness from her parents' distrust of these pretty, outgoing people. They always made her feel shabby and slow-witted, and when she encountered such people, she always wanted to shut her eyes until they went away. Sometimes she wished she could become one of them, safe in the approval of a pack of identically pretty people, but she knew that it would never happen. She was always different, and the club soda people could sense that, smell it. Nothing, not beauty or money or wit, could fool them into accepting an outsider.

Mark appeared in the doorway; his eyes were narrowed with sleep, and his chin was a stubble of beard, indifferently grown, and shaved off when he thought of it. He yawned and stretched, peering at the clock on top of the television. He wore an army sweatshirt and jeans, but he was barefoot. Maggie didn't know why he never seemed to be cold.

"Jesus, I'm tired!" he moaned, flopping down on the sofa beside her. "I've been up for an hour, going through Dad's papers. He wasn't exactly organized."

"Are you hungry?" asked Maggie, glad of a chance for companionship. "I could fry some hamburgers."

"Whatever," shrugged Mark. "Although we really ought to go out and celebrate. I guess that can wait, though, until we have the money."

Maggie looked up. "The money?"

"Yeah. I found it." He dug in the front pocket of his jeans and pulled out a folded slip of paper. "At least I know where it is, and how to find it. Look at this."

Maggie took the paper from her brother's outstretched hand. "It's a dentist's bill," she said. "Dad went to the dentist in Johnson City the week before he died."

Mark nodded gleefully. "Exactly. Don't you see, Maggie? He had to leave a clue that no one could find but us."

"But what is it?"

"The number of his Swiss bank account. He had it engraved on his tooth!"

Maggie nodded. "Yes, Mark, I see." She did not say, But we buried him, Mark. She knew that it would not matter. She must talk it over with Josh when he called. Josh would know what to do. "I'll go and start the hamburgers," she told Mark, handing back the dentist's bill. She was almost always in the kitchen when Josh called.

CHAPTER

11

Many people are confused about hillbilly vampires.
They think: A hillbilly vampire should look like
   George Jones in a cape
   Or Ricky Skaggs with fangs
   Or Lyle Lovett, period.
They think
   the hillbilly part comes first
   the feeder, not the fed upon
They do not understand that this is another outside industry
   Come down to the hills in the dark
   For raw material.

> —AMY TIPTON GRAY,
> "The Hillbilly Vampire"

Winter settled into the Tennessee mountains in mid-January, fulfilling the dread that had lingered in people's minds since the October leaf fall. Winter's coming, people would say each autumn, looking for signs from nature to tell them how bad it would get: thick-furred squirrels, or crickets in the chimney, or hoot owls calling in late autumn. Christmas weather was seldom below freezing, but when the new year dawned, you'd best have your firewood stacked to the beams of the woodshed, and your pantry stocked, because the freeze was coming, sweeping down off the mountains like a bird of prey. *The hawk is flying low*, people said. That meant it was cold, with a bitter wind driving the chill into the bone. The snow would come later, sometimes not until March.

Laura Bruce had always hated the cold. Flagging temperatures seemed to leaden her brain, and made her body curl in upon itself with an irresistible desire for sleep. Cold made an invisible wall between the house and the outside world, so that every attempt to venture past the threshold was a small skirmish to be endured. Now she felt that Will Bruce's small, warm house had itself become a womb and that she was dead in it. She was numbed by winter into a state of half-dreaming, so that the days passed in a blur, and whether she woke at all was of no consequence. She would look at her scrubbed, colorless face in the mirror, and at the shapeless body, pendular beneath sweatshirt and sweater, and she felt no sense of connection with that reflected being. Laura Bruce was ready for a long siege against the cold, and the stagnant coldness within her body, and she wasn't coming out until spring.

Dr. Jessup's pronouncement, declaring the end of her pregnancy, had come two weeks ago. The hospital confirmed it with bureaucratic solemnity and offers of tranquilizers. She refused the drugs. Winter was sedative enough. She had gone home to the empty house—the empty woman to the empty house—and shut the cold behind her. She ate when she remembered to and tried to believe the doctor's verdict enough to shed tears over it, but although intellectually she accepted the medical evidence, emotionally she was numb to its effect. It might be happening to someone else, for all she felt. The child was, after all, still there, still a part of her. He had not been taken away from her—yet.

She had told no one, least of all Will, whose complaints were all of airless heat and insects. His battles were against boredom, discomfort, and the threat of his own faith by the indifference around him. He made his plight sound very important; or rather, he made it clear that his difficulties constituted a deep crisis in himself. To her, the complaints, so carefully enumerated in his letters, seemed melodramatic and trivial. They were always listed first, before any afterthoughts of endearments for her. Sometimes Laura, in her newfound coldness, thought her husband sounded like a spoiled child who is not enjoying his outing. What struck her most was his naive innocence in the magnitude of his suffering, as if things could not be worse. She wished she could exchange her solitary deathwatch for the luxury of theological bickering in the bright sunshine with people who were alive. She would not tell him how it was at home, the child's death, because she sensed that whatever sympathy he proffered would be insignificant compared to the fact that he would add this grievance of vicarious loss to his other woes, and that she would become yet another of his burdens, spiritual merit badges in his quest for holy martyrdom.

She found an old copy of Andersen's fairy tales on the bookshelf in the back bedroom and began to read them, wanting nothing more challenging to stir her thoughts. After a few pleasantly inconsequential stories, she began to read "The Snow Queen," and there she found messages and symbolism that she sought but never found in the Christian gospel. She saw herself not as Gerda, the loyal little girl who braves cold and danger to rescue her kidnapped friend, but as the Snow Queen, a being of cold itself.

Little Kay, with the splinter of troll-glass stuck in his heart, hitches his sled to the Snow Queen's sleigh and is carried away to her palace of ice at the top of the world. In his fright at being captured by this beautiful but inhuman creature, Kay tries to pray, but he finds that instead of the Lord's Prayer, he can only remember the multiplication tables. That was Will Bruce, Laura thought. Stuck through the heart with his captain's bars, he tries to pray, but can only utter the articles of army regulations.

The Snow Queen wraps Kay in her ermine robe, and kisses him twice. But she tells him that he must have no more kisses from her, for if he does, he will freeze to death in her embrace. At the top of the world, she sets him down on the ice floor of her palace and tells him to try to spell *Eternity* with shards of icicles. If he succeeds, the Snow Queen tells him, she will give him "the whole world and a new pair of skates." Laura wondered how Will was doing, trying to spell Eternity with grains of sand. She was past making the effort. The petty demands of the congregation and the polite convention of writing cheering letters to her man-at-arms seemed strange and remote to her now, like quaint customs remembered from a guidebook to a place she had never been. Now she would have solitude, and a spiritual hibernation, before she could wake up to any other concerns but this. She must sit in the chill of the empty house and wait for her own "thawing," the stillbirth. It would be weeks, Jessup had warned her; perhaps months. That one fact, and the weight of it inside her, was all that she could manage right now. Everything else would have to go on without her.

Laura closed the book before she got to the part of the story where Gerda rescued Kay from the Snow Queen's palace with her tears. That chapter wasn't relevant. It was going to be winter for a long while yet, and she was its sovereign, the Snow Queen, with a human child trapped inside the ice palace of her womb who would never be able to spell *Eternity*.

Tavy Annis smiled to reassure the young girl behind the counter. Her stricken expression suggested that she thought he had come to die in her reception room. His face was the white color of skin under a Band-Aid, and his gray suit seemed to hang on bones. She glanced at Taw standing resolutely beside him as if to inquire what he meant by allowing this specter to be out and about, but Taw refused to be deferred to by a clerk; it was his friend's crusade. He went back to studying the rainbow-trout picture on the office calendar.

"Is this the place that does chemical analysis?" Tavy asked. "Our county extension agent said for us to try you." The gold-lettered sign on the door said Carter Biological Testing Services, but the reception room might have been a doctor's office, with its plastic tree and its old copies of *Field & Stream*.

"Yes, sir," said the blond in an eggshell drawl. She still looked bewildered by her visitors. "We do environmental testing of water sources. Y'all got a well that the water don't taste right?"

Taw set a paper bag on the counter in front of her, and removed from it a mason jar of murky water. "We need you to tell us what's in this."

She sighed. "Sir, we can do that for you, but we'll need more information first. Is this water sample from a well or one of the springs on your farm?"

Tavy's eyes narrowed. "Why do you need to know where it's from to tell us what's in it?"

The clerk sighed again, but it was from the enormity of her task, explaining all this technical complexity to two old men. She tried again. "See, there's a lot of things you can analyze for, and each chemical that you suspect requires a separate test. If you include pesticides, there are more than four hundred chemicals we could test for in a water sample, and each one of those tests costs somewhere between thirty and one hundred dollars. I don't think you want to spend half a million dollars finding out what's in your jar there, so I'm trying to help you narrow it down."

"Maybe she's already run a sample like this, Tavy," Taw suggested. "It would be cheaper to buy a copy of somebody else's test results."

Tavy shrugged. "Well, we ain't got half a million dollars, that's for dang sure. Okay, ma'am, this here jar is full of Little Dove River water. Now can you all offhand tell me what it's likely to contain, say, about fifty bucks' worth?"

She beamed at them, because they had now become somebody else's problem. "Let me call Mr. Carlsen, our lab manager. He might be able to help you. Wait right here."

When she had disappeared through the large metal door that led to the lab, Taw turned to Tavy and whistled softly. "Half a million dollars to run a water sample! No wonder these factories get away with murder. Nobody can afford the evidence!"

"The government can," grunted Tavy. A vague feeling of discomfort told him that his medication was beginning to wear off. He glanced at his watch, wondering how long he could afford to stay and talk.

Jerry Carlsen, a short young man with a crew cut and glasses, wore the chemist's badge of authority: a white lab coat. He introduced himself, insisted on shaking hands and repeating their names, and ushered them into a pine-paneled conference room adjoining the front office. Tavy brought along his mason jar of river water. He set it on the long conference table in front of him, and stared into it as he listened. *Put the pain in the water. Put the pain in the water.*

Carlsen intertwined his fingers, and settled back to listen. "I understand you gentlemen have a water sample from the Little Dove River that you want analyzed."

"Look," said Taw. "My friend here lives on the Little Dove River, and he's dying of cancer. We just want to know what's in that water."

"I see." He wondered what he ought to say to that. People were not Jerry Carlsen's strong suit. He was much more at home in his lab with clever, uncomplaining machines, where the intricacies of emotion and conversational subterfuge were not required. There was an honesty in science that was lacking in human contacts. Carlsen waited.

"We don't have a lot of money," Tavy explained. "And we're not a big company like most of your customers probably are. We're just regular folks with a problem. Somebody has poisoned our river."

Carlsen fidgeted in his chair. "I guess Doreen told you how expensive those tests are. High-priced equipment . . . specialized help . . . Water testing is more complicated than people realize. But I think I might be able to help you without violating any privileged information. You're not the first people to want an analysis of that river. One client made a deal with us: We gave him a fifty percent price break on the testing he wanted, and in return he authorized us to sell copies of the results to interested parties. Now those tests will not give you the identical readings you'd get from the sample in your jar here, because the river flow changes from day to day and the sampling site won't be the same, but the results of that test will give you a general idea of what chemicals are in the river."

"Fair enough," said Taw. "How much for a copy of their test?"

"A hundred dollars," Carlsen said. "But you'll be getting at least a thousand dollars' worth of water testing, and it will cover all the hazardous substances that you'd be concerned with."

"It's a deal on one condition," said Tavy. "When you give us the test results, you sit down with us and explain what all those figures mean."

"Sure, I can do that," said Carlsen. "If you'll write me a check, I'll go and get you a copy of the Little Dove analysis. Some coffee, too, if you'd like some."

"Depends," said Taw. "Where do you get your water?"

Ten minutes later, Carlsen was back with a manila folder balanced atop a stack of books. Behind him trailed Doreen carrying three white mugs on a plastic tray. With a nervous smile, she set them down on the conference table and hurried away to answer a ringing telephone.

"Okay," said Carlsen, settling down amid his fortress of books. "Here's your copy of the report. Now I'll show you what it means." He held up several gray-and-white paperbacks. "This set of books is the 1990 Code of Federal Regulations."

"Haven't you got an up-to-date one?"

"We're expecting the 1991 one any day now, but this thing is put out by the government, so it's not exactly efficient. You generally get an edition halfway through the next year. However, these regulations will not change. Okay, now, if you're interested in the Little Dove, what we need to check on is the Effluent Discharge into Surface Water for paper mills. That's your concern, isn't it? Titan Paper?"

Behind his coffee mug, Tavy nodded. "What's it say?"

"This thing is a bitch to use," grumbled Carlsen, flipping through pages. "There are so many volumes, and you have to keep switching from one to the other. Typical government document, written in lawyerspeak, of course. It lists the allowable limits for certain chemicals in parts per million. Then we should look up each chemical separately for further regulations. Basically, on this page there's a list of controlled chemicals for paper mills and what amounts they are permitted to discharge into surface water—that is, the river. I can photocopy this page for you, if you like."

"Thank you," said Tavy. "I'll add it to my collection."

"No problem," said Carlsen. "Now we want to look at the report results to see what chemicals we found in the river and in what amounts they appear. This sample was taken at the Tennessee line, so we assume that all this stuff we're finding came from North Carolina sources. Where did you get your water sample?"

"Under the railroad bridge in Wake County," said Tavy. "Near my house."

"You're farther away from the source, then, so the concentrations in your sample will be lower than the ones listed in this report. I guess that's some consolation."

"Not much," said Tavy.

Carlsen retreated to his texts. "Now, let's see what we've got here. Chlorine, sodium, potassium, iron—those aren't any big deal. In high concentrations they might affect the water's taste, but they aren't deadly. What you're going to be concerned with is mercury, dioxin, cadmium, and sulphur content."

Taw had put on his reading glasses, and was studying the report. "What's this BOD and COD?"

Carlsen smiled. "The letters are pronounced separately, Mr. McBryde. B-O-D: biological oxygen demand. C-O-D is chemical oxygen demand. These figures have to do with the ability of organisms to live in the water. The lower the number, the more oxygen the water can hold, which of course fish and plants need in order to survive."

"I don't know whether this is good or bad. Parts per million? Is this considered a low number?"

"No. It's pretty high. Bad news for the fish, I'm afraid." He smiled nervously. "Now, let's get to the chemicals. Mercury was formerly used in the manufacture of paper, but it isn't anymore. However, the mercury that was used was frequently dumped into the river during the manufacturing process. It's still there in the sediment, and it's still polluting the river. Mercury is pretty toxic. You know that phrase 'mad as a hatter'? Hatmakers used to use mercury in their craft, and exposure to it would eventually cause brain damage."

"Why don't they get the mercury out of the river, then?" asked Tavy.

"The companies claim that the cleanup would bankrupt them," said Carlsen in a carefully neutral voice. "They also deny that trace elements of mercury constitute a hazard."

"I'll bet they take care not to live downstream from the plant, though," said Tavy.

Taw consulted the report. "What about this line? Dioxin? I've heard of that before. Didn't they have some big evacuation because of that?"

Carlsen shrugged. "Dioxin. That's a touchy subject. It's a by-product of the bleaching process of papermaking. So is sulphur. Some tests have shown that dioxin is a very potent carcinogen, but more recent studies indicate that it is much less of a health hazard."

"What do you think, Mr. Carlsen?"

"Well, I tend to agree with the more recent studies. I

think it probably can cause cancer—hell, what doesn't?—but not in the minute concentrations they were claiming originally."

"But do you reckon the dioxin in the Little Dove River is a *minute concentration?*" said Tavy.

"According to EPA regulations, it's pretty high. So is the sulphur. The problem with sulphur is that it lowers the pH of the water, which decreases the ability of the water to hold oxygen."

"Kills the fish," said Taw.

"Pretty much."

Tavy scooted his chair close to Taw's and peered at the list of substances. "What about cadmium?"

"I'm not sure what its connection is with the paper company, but it is one of the more toxic heavy metals. In fact, its use has been severely restricted in Japan and Europe."

Tavy looked up from the report. "So, now we have a bunch of numbers here in parts per million. Can you tell us what it means healthwise?"

"That's this book," said Carlsen. "We call it Sax, for short, after one of the authors. It explains the health hazards involved with each chemical." He could have told them informally, but that wasn't his job. Better to keep it an impersonal transaction: Quote the book, and let them consider the implications of the printed facts. That way Carlsen would be left out of the human equation.

"Now we're getting somewhere!" said Tavy softly. "Go down the list, Mr. Carlsen. Tell us what the book says."

"Cadmium. There's a lot of technical stuff here. It's toxic. Definitely a carcinogen. Mercury. See page 746 . . . It causes liver damage. It's also a teratogen."

"What?" said Taw.

"Tumor causing," Tavy told him. "Now hush."

"According to this, it can cause reproductive effects as well," Carlsen continued. "You know, mutations."

"Birth defects," said Tavy. "And those misshapen fish in the Little Dove. What about dioxin?"

"Dioxin is a class of chemicals, not just one. There's more than seventy. The two most commonly found in paper mills are pentachlorophenol and trichlorophenol. They're high in your water sample, too, but it's hard to nail the company on that violation because the amount of the chemical allowed in waste water is determined by how much paper the company produces. The more paper they make, the more waste they're allowed. So if they exaggerate their production figures, the government can't touch them."

"Okay, what do those chemicals do to people?"

Carlsen shrugged. "The usual. They are carcinogens, teratogens, and mutagens."

Tavy leaned back in his chair and closed his eyes. "Cancer, tumors, and birth defects." He sighed. "Okay. We've got the bastards, right?"

"Got them?" said the lab manager.

"According to this water sample report of yours, Titan Paper is putting cancer-causing chemicals into the Little Dove River, exceeding the amount allowed by law. I want to know what we can do to them."

Jerry Carlsen hesitated for a moment, frowning more deeply than ever. Finally, he said, "Oh, hell! Look, that's a legal question, not a chemical one, so technically I don't have to give you an answer, and I'm certainly not an expert, but offhand I'd say . . . not much."

Tavy's weary expression did not change, but Taw reddened and burst out, "What do you mean, *not much*? They're guilty, aren't they?"

"It would be the job of the North Carolina EPA to crack down on the paper company. I doubt if there is anything in this report that they don't already know about."

"So why haven't they stopped it?"

"Truthfully?" said Carlsen, looking nervously at the

white face of Tavy Annis. "The paper company provides a lot of jobs to local residents, and it pays quite a bit of state and local taxes."

"It figures," said Taw, spitting out his contempt for all government with the words. "But they don't pay taxes in Tennessee, do they? Why doesn't our EPA nail them?"

"The pollution is not occurring in Tennessee. Bureaucratically speaking, it's none of our business."

Tavy sat up straight again, breathing anger. "None of our business? I got cancer. Can I sue the bastards?"

Carlsen picked up his cup of cold coffee, sipped it, and set it down again with a grimace. "Sir, anybody can sue anybody. But if you want my opinion, the paper company keeps squadrons of lawyers on retainer, and they will fight every motion, appeal every decision, and drag the case out for ten years easily. The legal fees would be staggering, and a decade from now, you wouldn't be much farther along than you are this minute."

"I haven't got that long," whispered Tavy. "I'm out of time, thanks to them."

Oakdale was a small village cemetery, with no iron gates to close against the darkness. Its frosted grass glistened at the flash of headlights from an approaching car. Beyond that circle of light, the old tombstones stretched away into the darkness, like a range of tiny mountains, dwarfed by the spreading oaks above them. Dry leaves skittered silently in the wind.

As he swung the car between the two stone pillars at the entrance, Mark Underhill switched off the headlights so that no one would see their shine from some distant hill and wonder why there were lights in the graveyard so close to midnight. In the dead of night, he thought, and the image made him smile. He drove around the paved entrance encircling the fountain, and steered the car up a dirt track that led to the newer graves. There was a grove of trees at a fork in the road. He would leave the car there. Beside him, Maggie shivered in the stillness, and tried to think about being somewhere else.

He stopped the car and turned to face her. "Are you ready?" No one was within half a mile of the car, but still he whispered. His breath hung in the air between them, as if his soul had leaked out of his body.

Maggie looked down at her hands. "I could wait here, Mark."

"No. We don't have much time. You have to help me dig."

He hauled himself out of the car, slamming the door behind him. The shovels and hand tools were in the trunk. Maggie huddled in the passenger seat until he tapped on her window with the handle of the shovel, and motioned for her to come out. She crept from the car, cinching her coat more tightly about her, and followed him down the hill toward the family graves. The wind whipped at her legs and made her face tingle with numbness.

Mark walked ahead, with both shovels slung over his shoulder and his overcoat pockets bulging with heavy hand tools. He was treading on the bronze markers in his path as if he were unaware of their significance. He was alone. Regally alone. Oblivious to the dead beneath his feet, or to the stumbling footfalls of his little sister, treading behind him.

Maggie Underhill was humming an old hymn, one that she used to sing in choir. "I am weak, but thou art strong; Jesus keep me from all wrong . . ." That song reminded her of Josh. He was always strong. When Daddy would yell at them or get out his belt, Maggie would always cry, and Mark would try to slip out of the room. Only Josh would stand his ground, waiting silently for the inevitable beating, not running and not crying. He would endure the beating

199

with a faraway look on his face, showing no emotion at all, which only made the major angrier. It was as if Josh went somewhere else when he was being hurt, so that the welts were inflicted on an empty body. Maggie could never manage his detachment. She would always end up screaming, even though she knew her father savored her pain. Sometimes Josh tried to protect her. Even if he wasn't the one in trouble, he'd stay and say the infraction was his fault, hoping to get Maggie a reprieve. Like as not, it would get him a harder beating, and Maggie would get one anyway. They had long since learned not to appeal to their mother when the major threatened them with punishment. She would shake her head and walk away. Sometimes she would even remind her husband of chores not done or infractions that occurred in his absence. Janet Underhill was no maternal refuge.

Paul Underhill had worn a wooden paddle as thin as a nail file disciplining his children. He made a ritual out of it. "Go and get Sergeant Rod," he would tell the offending child. He kept the homemade paddle on the fireplace mantel. Its handle was a foot long, and wrapped in black electrical tape to afford a better grip to the major when he hit his children with it. Its blade was painted red, but the paint had worn away over the years. It still hung in its accustomed place in the living room. Maggie wanted to throw it away, but she could not bring herself to touch it.

Maggie shivered in the darkness watching the shadowy form of her brother, trying to break frozen ground with his shovel. She wished Josh were here now. Then she would be all right. She didn't know whether Josh would go along with Mark or not—that was the trouble—but whatever he decided would be right, and then she'd know. She thought he might call her tonight before they left, but the telephone was silent. She began to hum louder, as if the sound could summon him here.

"Be quiet, Maggie!" Mark hissed at her in the darkness.

"Why?" she said in her normal tone of voice. "There's nobody here, and according to you, we're just reclaiming our property, aren't we?"

He shrugged. "I guess. It distracts me. I need to concentrate." He looked out at the white shapes of distant stones beyond the trees. "I have a flashlight in my jacket pocket, but I don't want to use it if we can help it."

Maggie shuddered as a gust of wind caught her. "It's too cold."

"You'll be warm enough when you start digging," Mark whispered. "I've loosened the dirt now. We have to hurry. At least we won't be visible from the road."

She knelt in the frosted grass and picked up the other shovel. She pushed its blade into the earth with her foot, but the ground was hard, yielding only a few clods of dirt to her digging. Mark was stronger. He had managed to carve out a small hole below the bronze marker, and he was busy enlarging it, piling the soil in a mound behind him.

They worked in silence, punctuated by the rhythmic chunk and scrabble of the shovels. Maggie tried to keep thinking about Josh—not his body, lying under another of the bronze markers, but of the voice that spoke to her still. She wondered where he was and wished she were there, too.

The thud of shovel point against a flat surface startled her out of her reverie. Mark jumped down into the hole, which was only knee-deep, and began to probe the soil with his gloved fingers.

"Get the light," said Mark.

So dark and so cold. Mark and his shovel made a dark shape in the shallow excavation. She could not see what lay at the bottom, but the hole seemed no more than three feet long. Then she remembered that the oak casket lid was cut in two sections, so that the mortuary could open only the top portion for viewing at the funeral. A half perfection couch, the funeral director called it. Mark would only need to uncover the upper half of the casket. The muscles of her face were taut with cold. Maggie picked up the flashlight, switched it on, and stretched it out to her brother.

"No. You hold it. At least until I need you to help me. Shine it down at my feet."

"The hole isn't deep," she said, staring into the small circle of light below her. "I thought they were put in deeper than that."

"Just as well," said Mark. "I still have more to dig, though. I wonder which side the catch is on."

Maggie stood with her back to the wind, teetering on the edge of the opening grave, as he opened a narrow trench along one side of the casket. The light wobbled in her hands as she looked out across the empty field and up at the stars above the shadows of mountains. The stars over Hamelin shone as clear as ice pellets. She had never seen so many. No haze of city lights diluted their brilliance.

Mark tossed the shovel up on the bank, and squatted on top of the casket, feeling along the newly excavated side for the brass latch. "Found it!"

One by one, Maggie began to count the stars.

Joe LeDonne had stayed an extra hour on patrol because it was Friday night, prime time for wrecks on back country roads. The Hamelin High basketball team had played an away game in Erwin, and LeDonne was afraid that hot-rodding teenagers would turn the two-lane blacktop into a drag strip on the way home. Tonight, though, they had been lucky: The switchback curves on the old Erwin road had claimed no young sacrifices, and now, after hours of cold riding past dark houses and frosted fields, LeDonne could call it quits.

He went back to the courthouse to pick up his old Volkswagen, and then headed for the one place in town that was open past midnight, the Mockingbird Inn. Most of the regulars would still be nursing beers, trying to drag out Friday night as long as it would go, but LeDonne took no interest in that. He wanted black coffee and a hamburger with tomato and mayonnaise before he went home to his own dark house. He'd see Martha on Saturday night, when Godwin pulled the night patrol.

As he walked into the noisy roadhouse, a sudden hush fell over a room filled with people who had been laughing and dancing a moment before. The sight of LeDonne's brown uniform had dampened spirits. He gave them a perfunctory nod to indicate that he wasn't there on business, and slid into an empty booth, feeling like the Angel of Death. From force of habit, though, he scanned the room. Some of the county hell-raisers were there, but they didn't look drunk enough to cause trouble. He saw mostly truckers on coffee break and Wake County's singles, shopping around between divorces. At the bar, though, sat Vernon Woolwine, dressed for an evening out in a black cape lined in red satin, worn over a threadbare dark suit. His black hair, slicked back across the crown of his head, gleamed like—and perhaps was—shoe polish. He was alone. LeDonne was thinking of going up and offering him a ride home when someone slid into the booth across from him, and said, "Long time no see."

It was Justin Warren, beer in hand, wearing a leather bomber jacket and a Stetson. None of his weekend warriors had accompanied him to the Mockingbird Inn. With an ironic grin, he lifted his mug in a toast to the scowling deputy.

"Long time no see," LeDonne agreed. "Lucky you. When I can get a warrant, I'll drop in on your little imitation boot camp."

Justin Warren shook his head. "I don't know why you want to take that attitude, Deputy. I'm a law-abiding citizen who pays property taxes."

"I don't think we need somebody importing trigger-happy toy soldiers into the county. Sooner or later, one of them will get shot, or you'll get careless with the drugs or the illegal weapons, and we'll be there waiting to shut you down." LeDonne looked around for the waitress. Where the hell was his coffee?

"Things must be pretty slow in Dogpatch if you have to worry so much about one law-abiding stranger. What do you do for fun? Round up stray dogs?" Warren laughed. "You poor guys can't even get a good murder case to chew on. The last one you had was the Underhill family, wasn't it? I read about them. And that crime solved itself before you got there."

LeDonne looked up quickly. "Maybe. Did you know the Underhills?"

"I knew the major. Met him in here about this time of night, once. He seemed all right. Too bad his kid went bezerk. I figured it for drugs."

LeDonne searched the man's face for a sign of strain. "Did you get along with Paul Underhill? Like him?"

"Didn't care one way or the other." Justin Warren smiled. "You really are afraid of me, aren't you?" he said. "You're hoping you can arrest me for something so that I won't haunt you anymore."

"Why should you haunt me?"

"Because you miss your old life. Your old buddies. Combat is a hard-on like nothing else. You still dream about it. You close your eyes and you're back in the jungle, and it's so real you can smell it. You're a cop because you're still chasing that rush. You want to come out to the camp in the night, and lose yourself in the woods with us. We can take you back to when you were alive, LeDonne. Join the hunt, why don't you? Where's the harm?"

Where was the harm? LeDonne was picturing himself in camos, crawling through the wet woods, reactivating senses he hadn't needed for twenty years: the smell of fear, the electric feel of someone hidden close by. Maybe he could go up one night and join in; it would be a good way to check the place out and see if they were up to anything. Make sure there were no drugs around. He could feel his muscles tighten at the thought of the hunt, and he almost smiled.

LeDonne's coffee arrived, but when he looked up to thank Crystal, he saw that she was not the one who brought it. Instead, LeDonne found himself staring into the solemn, pudgy face of a satanic Vernon Woolwine. In his present incarnation, Vernon had reddened his mouth to a gash, and ringed his mournful eyes with black eyeliner, in his best imitation of Bela Lugosi. The hillbilly vampire pointed to the coffee on the scarred pine table and ruffled his cloak with a flourish by way of greeting. "Going my way?"

"Just about," said the deputy, getting to his feet. He took a long swallow of coffee. "I reckon I can run you home, Vernon. I'm about through here." Suddenly, he wanted to go home. Not to his empty house. He wondered if Martha would still be awake.

In her iron bedstead with the hollow pipes at the head and foot of it, Nora Bonesteel was dreaming, her eyelids flickering in the darkness. Her hands were curled into fists as she struggled with the senses flooding her brain, but it was a blind dream. She saw nothing. She felt. The mattress beneath her turned hard as a board, and she could not turn over. The space seemed hardly larger than her own body.

She felt the itch of mold growing on her cheek and in the hollow of her throat, but she could not raise her hand to scratch away the patches of green. She knew, without seeing them, that the patches of mold were green. The color of wet and decay. The bed felt wet with a heavy cold fluid that was not water, but she could not sit up. When she tried to cry out for release, she found that her lips would not open. Copper threads tied her lips together, blocking her tongue. She could feel the wires attached to triangular points stuck into her inner lips, but there was no sensation of pain, only the bitter taste of copper against her shriveled tongue. Beyond that there was only immobility, and cold.

When she felt the cold blade of the hatchet cut through the skin of her neck, Nora Bonesteel sat bolt upright, tears streaming down her face, groping for the bedside lamp. She felt her face and her neck, and stretched her lips to reacquaint herself with the form of the sleeping woman that she was. She could see and move; the sensation of confinement faded as she returned to full wakefulness.

With shaking fingers she switched on every light in her house and then lit two candles on the parlor mantelpiece. She fiddled with the radio dial, usually set for classical music, until she found an all-night bluegrass station blasting out lively, familiar country songs, and there she sat till sunup in her blue Queen Anne chair, enveloped in noise and light to wall out the roaring darkness.

CHAPTER

12

The . . . house
Went up in a roar of flame,
As I danced in the yard with waving arms,
While he wept like a freezing steer.

—EDGAR LEE MASTERS,
Spoon River Anthology

They were on the sidewalk in Johnson City. Maggie Underhill kept trying to dodge the gusts of wind, pulling her short cloth coat tighter around her, but Mark seemed oblivious to the cold. He was wearing his blue blazer and a burgundy tie emblazoned with shields. He might have passed for a law student except that his hair was too long, and there was a glazed quality to his stare. He was clutching a white pillowcase wrapped around something angular. It jutted out through the folds of cloth, giving off fumes like rotten eggs mixed in kerosene. Mark didn't seem to notice the smell. He held the bundle to his chest as if it were a kitten.

"Let me do the talking," he murmured to his sister. "You just stand there and look sincere. Can you handle that?"

Maggie looked away. That's what Josh had been telling her, too. He had called that night when they got back from Oakdale, half-frozen and sick with the smell of formalin. After Mark parked the car under the oak tree, he had gone to the woodshed to hide the object of their quest. Maggie let herself in by the back door, and put the kettle on to make tea. She was warming her hands over the heat of the stove burner when the kitchen telephone rang. With a smile of relief, Maggie walked over and picked it up.

"It's going to be all right," she heard Josh say in his gentlest voice. "You just hold on, Maggie. I'm here. I'm with you."

"Did you see what we did?" Maggie asked. "Are you mad at us?"

She thought she heard him sigh, which struck her as odd, since ghosts didn't draw breath. "No, Maggie. I'm not mad at you. I'm just sorry it had to be this way. I want you to hold on, Maggie. Can you do that? Just keep on keeping on until spring, and then everything will be all right."

A new thought made her shudder. "Are you with Daddy, Josh? Is he mad at us?"

"He's not here. I have to go now. Just remember I care about you. And I'm with you. No matter how bad it gets."

"I couldn't run away. And I can't tell on Mark. We never told on each other. I wouldn't even get down the paddle for anyone else's whipping."

"I know, Maggie. Just hold on."

"Can I call you?"

"You don't have to."

After that she'd made herself some tea, and took a long, hot shower. When she came out, she heard Mark in the front room, pacing and talking loudly, as if he were arguing with someone, but she didn't go down to see. She was suddenly very sleepy.

That had been two weeks before. Now it was Valentine's Day. Maggie had passed the days watching television, a pastel blur of game shows, looking out the window, and waiting for Josh to call again, but he never did. She never went out into the woodshed to see by daylight their terrible acquisition. Nor did she speak of it to Mark. The days went by, and she thought perhaps he had forgotten about it, now that the urgency of retrieving it was past. At first she had been afraid that their vandalism would be discovered by a cemetery groundskeeper, but apparently his vigilance in winter was not great. They had reburied the coffin, and covered the earth with leaves. No one seemed to have noticed the disturbance. As each day passed, Maggie spent less time looking out the window at the gravel drive and the low-water bridge that led up to the highway. She stopped going cold at every loud noise. Gradually, television became more real to her than life, and she snuggled down in its bland warmth, safe again, as Josh had promised.

Mark let two weeks pass before he mentioned the money again. He came downstairs at eleven, hours earlier than his usual time of awakening, and announced that they were going to Johnson City after lunch. He was clean-shaven, and his hair was combed. Dress up, he'd told her. This was business. Without a word of protest, Maggie put on her navy blue wool and some makeup and followed her brother to the car without asking the purpose of the journey.

They drove the two-lane mountain road to Johnson City in silence. The pillowcase on the backseat reeked in the closed car until Maggie was ready to gag. She opened her window a crack, but the cold air was too bitter against her face. She hoped they'd be leaving the thing in Johnson City; she didn't want to know what it was. Mark pulled into a parking space on a quiet side street, and headed for a glass-fronted store, the pillowcase under his arm. Maggie fumbled in her purse for coins for the parking meter, but found that she hadn't any money. In the end, she trailed after her brother, wondering what "business" had brought them to town.

The sign on the window said Jewelry Store in flecked gold leaf. Maggie paused to look at a display of garnet rings—her birthstone—but Mark grabbed her elbow and ushered her into the store. "Good afternoon," he said to the shop's only inhabitant, an elderly man in a dark suit. Mark could sound quite affable when he cared to, which wasn't often. It was his public face, same as their father's.

"What can I do for you good people?" the old man asked. His soft Southern voice invited their confidence.

Maggie looked around her, at the silver tea sets, the trays

of diamond engagement rings, and the case filled with gold watches. She wished that they were shopping. She would have liked a birthstone ring or tiny gold earrings studded with garnets. But Mark seldom went into a store except to grocery shop when they ran low on powdered milk or bread, and on those trips he went alone. Dad had been like that, too, treating the house as if it were a fortress.

Mark had strolled up to the counter and placed his reeking pillowcase on the glass counter. The old man stepped back as the smell reached his nostrils. Mark smiled reassuringly. "We need some help," he said pleasantly. "There is a number carved in very tiny print, and we need someone with a strong magnifier to read it."

"What is it?" asked the old man, dabbing at his face with a linen handkerchief. Beads of sweat had appeared at his temples.

"It's a number carved on a tooth," said Mark. "Belonged to a spy. This is classified, you understand." He reached into the pillowcase and drew out the yellowed jawbone, now devoid of skin but still smelling of preservative. Maggie looked away.

"Where'd you get this?" asked the jeweler, making no move to take it from Mark's outstretched hand.

"Please. Read out the number for us. It's that tooth there." Mark pointed to a molar, shiny with a gold-tone filling.

The man looked at Mark, and started to say something, but thought better of it. With a shrug he took the jawbone, and carried it back into the office where he did jewelry repair.

Maggie touched Mark's elbow. "Suppose he reports this?"

Mark smiled. "He doesn't know who we are. Besides, it's our family fortune we're trying to recover. Surely people can understand that. If not, we can buy them off."

Maggie let her thoughts drift away from the conversation as she stared at the trays of rings in the glass-fronted counters. Perhaps Mark would let her buy one when he recovered the money from Switzerland. Mark was humming tunelessly. Every now and then he would lean forward to peer at the jeweler through the glass partition.

Several minutes later, the old man came out, holding the jawbone in his handkerchief, his arm outstretched to distance himself from the stench. "I don't understand," he said, blinking up at Mark. "I've examined every one of these teeth. There's no number on any of them."

"That's impossible," said Mark with a stubborn smile. "Did you use a strong magnifier when you looked at them?"

"I'm telling you: there's nothing there." The jeweler glanced at the telephone. "May I have your names, please?"

"No," said Mark. "We'll take our business elsewhere." He grasped Maggie by the elbow and hurried her out of the shop. When they reached the car, he sped away without even waiting to take the parking ticket off the windshield.

It was going to be a long winter. The solstice was six weeks past, but Laura Bruce still couldn't see any appreciable lengthening of the days. Cloudy days seemed dark even at noon. She looked out the kitchen window at the gathering twilight that blurred the shapes in the yard until they became gray shadows ebbing into the dark. Surely time was passing, she thought, touching her swollen belly.

She turned on the kitchen light to shut out the evening gloom. Time for a cup of tea, and perhaps a sandwich, not that she felt much like eating. She had been to the doctor in Johnson City again today. No change, he told her. He had measured for signs of dilation, listened for the heartbeat that wasn't there, and finally sent her away, counseling more patience. It wasn't time yet. He didn't look at her

much during the appointment. She had become an embar-
rassment to him: the specter of failure and death among the
happy mothers awaiting his care. He didn't ask how she
was feeling, and she volunteered no information. All that
mattered was *when*, and that he was unable to tell her. So
she drove home in the pale winter sunlight, and thought a
dozen times of aiming her car for the nearest tree. She
didn't, though. Despair was a sin. She'd read that somewhere.

Laura opened the refrigerator, and looked without favor
at its contents: plastic cartons of cottage cheese, a package
of hot dogs, and a bowl of homemade applesauce. She shut
the door. Just a cup of tea, then. She didn't feel like going
to the bother of cooking. After all, she wasn't eating for
two. And not getting any exercise, either, she thought, forcing her mind away from the pain of recollection. As soon
as some mild weather set in, she would go for walks, or
perhaps do a bit of gardening, setting out early annuals for
April color. Jane Arrowood could tell her what plants
would thrive in early March. She must remember to ask.

Meanwhile, there was television, and books from the limited supply of the Bookmobile. By default, because the library van contained little other than westerns and romances,
she had discovered C. S. Lewis's *A Grief Observed*. She
read it over and over, even renewing it, because she could
not bear to part with it. Reading Lewis was like talking to
someone who understood what she was feeling now. He
spoke of the *laziness* of grief. Yes, that was true. She felt
as if she had been moving in slow motion over the past few
weeks. The slightest task required great effort, and the many
small chores of living seemed altogether pointless. She fin-
gered a limp strand of hair that fell across her forehead;
she hadn't shampooed it for several nights, always telling
herself that another day's postponement would make no
difference.

She followed his chronicle of the stages of bereavement,

willing herself to move on to the next one, for she had to. Because no one could live where she was now, in such a spiritual twilight. So she reread Lewis, and took him at his word that there was an end to even the greatest pain. But it was hard to be brave in private.

She still hadn't told Will. But that didn't count as being brave. It was just a confrontation that she was avoiding. She wrote to him every other day, as something to do, and she missed him so much. If Will had been home, she would have confided in him, and let him comfort her. But trusting her sorrow to pieces of paper would mean reliving it, and putting aside her own sorrow for Will's sake. She wasn't ready to do that. Grief is a form of selfishness. Had Lewis said that, or did she work it out for herself? Laura had become quite adept at penning cheerful, newsy letters that betrayed nothing of her own despair. Will has enough to trouble him, she told herself. He needn't be burdened with this, too, when there's nothing to be done for it. She had managed to outlive the first shock of the tragedy, first as a sleepwalker, and then with mindless activity. *The bustle in the house the morning after death.* She had scoured the house, tidied the closets, and finally, in the momentum of housecleaning, she had set about turning the nursery back into a guest room, taking down the dinosaur curtains, and packing away the baby things. All reminders were gone now, save just the one that she saw each time she looked in the mirror.

The rumble of the kettle subsided, and a ribbon of steam sailed upward from the spout. Laura got a tea bag out of the canister, and put it into an earthenware mug. She glanced at the library book lying on the counter, and thought again about fixing a sandwich. She mustn't give in to the laziness of grief. Perhaps she ought to try to do some visiting.

She had avoided the Ladies' Circle, with their relentless chatter about pregnancy. And Nora Bonesteel. Laura had

215

not been back to the house on Ashe Mountain since she had learned of the baby's death. She had to work through her bitterness before she could face the old woman again. Did Nora Bonesteel know that the baby would die, and if so, why didn't she give Laura warning? Sometimes when Laura thought of Nora Bonesteel, she would become angry that this knowledge had been kept from her, and at other times, she would recall something else Nora had said. "I hardly ever get anything I'd set a store on knowing." So perhaps she hadn't known at all. And if she had received a premonition, what good would it have done to talk about it? It could only have given Laura added weeks of suffering. Laura had come to accept that, but the resentment lingered. She wouldn't go back to see Nora Bonesteel until she could work through her grief. And until she could deal with the well-meaning inanities of people who didn't understand about bereavement.

That thought brought an image of Mark and Maggie Underhill into her mind. When Laura had been called to comfort them on the night of the murders, she hadn't understood about grief, either. She hadn't known what to say to them, or how to act in the presence of their tragedy. She had felt embarrassed and tongue-tied in the face of so much loss. She had thought they might not want strangers around, but perhaps they needed people, whether they knew it or not. Will would have sensed that. He would have tried to befriend them. She hadn't done a good job of ministering to them, she thought, and personal sorrow was no excuse. Laura hadn't seen the Underhills since Christmas. She had not telephoned them or driven out to see how they were. Mark and Maggie had not tried to contact her, either. Grief is lazy; grief makes us shy. We want people around, she thought, but we don't want to make the effort to talk to them. I have been selfish, Laura told herself. I lost one person; they lost four. Now I can tell them that I truly do understand their loss. In a few days she would go and see about them. When she felt stronger. Perhaps she would take them the book.

The living room of Tammy Robsart's trailer was ten feet long, and was separated from the kitchen by a six-inch step and a wrought-iron rail flanking the kitchen table. The carpet was green and shabby, and the paneling was a bad imitation of pine, but she kept it clean and uncluttered. Better than most in the trailer park. In one corner of the room sat a straw clothes basket containing the toys of three-year-old Morgan. They had picked them up together before she sent him off to bed.

Now that it was dark and quiet, Tammy Robsart sat at the kitchen table, her hand cupped for warmth around a mug of coffee, watching its cloud of steam rise into the chill air of the trailer's living room. In the back bedroom, scarcely larger than the double bed itself, her Morgan was already asleep, tucked under a quilt and three blankets, fully clothed. It was too cold tonight for him to sleep in his own little room, so she had taken all the bedclothes in the house and piled them on the double bed. Snuggling close to Morgan under all those covers would give them both extra warmth.

The wind rattled the sides of the trailer, making it shudder on its underpinnings, and driving drafts of searing cold through every seam and crack in the metal casing. It couldn't be much colder outside, Tammy thought, sipping the coffee. Its warmth in her throat was momentary, but still comforting in the icy silence. She was wearing her bathrobe on top of her jeans and sweatshirt, and two pairs of Dale's socks under her bedroom slippers, but the cold encased her, reddening her cheeks and making her every move a conscious effort. Things would be better in the morning, she told herself. At daybreak she could call someone to check out the old wall furnace and see why it wasn't working. Surely they couldn't be out of oil already? She had just put in a hundred dollars' worth in January, and she couldn't afford another tankful. Maybe the church had some sort of emergency fund, though, for fuel oil. Or the county. She hated to think of taking charity, but she didn't see any way around it. Pride was one thing, but she couldn't let Morgan freeze just because there wasn't any money. Why did it have to be so cold tonight? And why didn't the furnace quit earlier, when she could have thought up someplace else to go for the night? The little kerosene space heater that she'd set in front of the door was giving off some heat, but not enough to heat a twelve-by-forty trailer in the dead of winter. It was better than nothing, though. She hoped the kerosene would last until morning.

Tammy's fingers itched for a cigarette, but there weren't any in the house. She'd given them up because they cost too much. She bought Morgan fresh orange juice instead. Dale still smoked, but in the Gulf they got cigarettes for free. Donated by the tobacco companies as a patriotic gesture. She tried not to begrudge him his warmth and his cigarettes; life couldn't be easy for him, either, and she couldn't blame him for not writing. At school, English had always been his worst subject, and he hated to put pen to paper, misspelling most of what he did write, and communicating next to nothing. But at least a letter would show that he still thought of them. Sometimes Tammy felt like one of those Middle Eastern hostages, all shut up in this jail of a trailer with no one but Morgan to talk to, and no money for anything except bills and groceries. When she was tired and sad, it was easy to believe that Dale didn't give a damn about them.

She was only twenty. She tried to imagine another forty years of such an existence, but her mind was too numb even for daydreams. She ought to go to bed and cuddle up with Morgan for warmth, but she wasn't sleepy yet, and to lie awake in the cold darkness would only make the day seem that much farther away. She might think too much about missing Dale and about how much Morgan had to do without, and then she would cry, which might wake him up and frighten him. Morgan hated to see her cry. He always thought it was his fault, or else he'd cry, too, thinking surely things are hopeless if Mommy is crying.

No point in wasting time staring up at the ceiling, Tammy thought. She could write to Dale, but she would find it hard to talk about anything other than the cold and the misery she felt, so perhaps she ought to wait and write him when she could be more cheerful. She supposed that she could try to study the GED textbook. She had been going to a night tutoring class at the county extension building a couple of times a week. The high school equivalency exam would be given again in March. If she could pass that, things might begin to get better. She flipped her fingers through the pages of essays and multiple-choice questions, wondering what she felt up to studying.

Reading comprehension, then. That was easy enough. Read a paragraph, and then answer a bunch of questions about what you had read. She found one talking about the solar system, and began to work her way through the maze of words, her lips moving soundlessly as she read. She was just puzzling over the first question, wondering what *heliocentric* meant, when the blaze of light made her look up, and suddenly the cold was a rope around her heart and ice in the pit of her stomach.

The kerosene heater was a black hulk encircled by flames. Sprigs of fire had climbed the curtains and slid up the simulated-wood wall beside the door, and now around it, blocking the exit. As dark smoke began to roll toward her, she felt the sting in her eyes, breaking the spell of shock.

Morgan. An instant later, Tammy Robsart was running down the hall toward the back bedroom, screaming out the name of her son.

She ran past the trailer's other outside door, in the hall across from the tiny bathroom. There was a bookcase in front of it now, holding all of Dale's record albums, and her own collection of old textbooks and tattered paperbacks. There was no time to worry about it now. On the wall above the double bed was a narrow window, farthest from the fire. She would try to get them out that way. At least they were still dressed.

"Morgan, honey! Wake up!" She shook him, and he tried to burrow deeper under the pile of blankets. "No, hon. We have to get out of here."

The smoke was coming down the hall now. She kicked the bedroom door shut, and crawled over her son to crank open the metal window. It didn't lift up the way windows in a house did. Trailer windows opened outward at a downward slant. There wasn't much room to fit a person through the opening, but Morgan was tiny. He would go first.

She shook him again. She could feel the heat from the front part of the trailer. "Morgan! Get up now."

He opened his eyes and looked at her. "What?" His voice was a tired wail.

"Listen to me," said Tammy, forcing herself to speak calmly, not to cry. "I'm going to put you out that window, okay? And I want you to run to Troy's house and beat on his door as hard as you can. Can you do that?" He was only three, but he was a smart little boy. He could memorize a commercial if he heard it twice. "I'm going to let you down out the window, and I want you to run away as fast as you can, Morgan."

He looked at her with big, sleep-smudged eyes. "Why?"

"Just do it. I'll come, too, but I don't want you to wait. You just run, okay?"

He nodded, no longer drowsy. The cold air from the open window made him shiver. "Run," he echoed.

"Run," said Tammy. "Fast as you can." She lifted him up to the window, and eased him through the slanted opening feetfirst, holding him first by the waist, then the shoulders, and finally lowering him by his wrists, so that his fall to the ground was only a few feet. "Run!" she screamed. She lay panting against the windowsill until she saw him get up, and stagger a bit away from the trailer. He looked back once, and called out something, but she screamed again, and he sprinted off toward the Etheridges' trailer, where his playmate Troy slept safely.

It had all taken less than two minutes, but to Tammy it seemed as if she had been living with the danger for hours, and she was weary of the terror. She pushed herself up, standing on the bed, and stuck her leg out the narrow opening. It wedged at the thigh. She pulled it out again, scarcely feeling the scrape of metal against her leg. She could hear the fire now, roaring now as it picked up speed from the fuel of pressed wood and pasteboard in its path. She tried to push herself out the window headfirst, but her breasts and shoulders held her fast. She could not afford to become stuck in the metal window frame, where she would burn like a pig on a spit. Not the window, then. How else to get out?

She eased open the bedroom door, hot to her touch. The back door, blocked by the bookcase, was only three feet away. The flames had not yet reached it. She had perhaps a minute to clear the exit and get out. She eased her way out of the bedroom, coughing as a wave of smoke reached her nostrils. She leaned into the bathroom, grabbed a wet washcloth, and pressed it against her face. Then she began

221

to push at the bookcase, but it would not slide away from the door. Empty it, then. She tore at the records first, pulling them to the floor, and kicking them out of her path. Another push. Still too heavy. The books, then.

She longed for the cold she had felt before. Now the heat was a palpable thing, a wave pulsing toward her, and the spreading flames sent sparks at her from the living-room ceiling. Tammy screamed at the flick of cinders, and flung the books on the floor. The fire had climbed the wall and set alight the ceiling.

She rocked the bookcase. It was light enough to move now. Sobbing with pain and terror, she shoved the empty shelving aside, and fumbled at the lock on the metal knob. It gave. She was free. She dared not turn around to see how close the flames had come. She was free now. One push would send her tumbling onto wet grass, and she would run and find Morgan and not look back. Suddenly, none of the possessions mattered.

She fell against the door, twisting the knob and sobbing with relief at her deliverance. It was like the final push when Morgan was born—one last great exertion at the end of rending pain, and then she would be free. The metal door swung outward. In an instant she felt the cold gust of night air, and she stretched her arms out toward the soothing chill. But as the cold wind reached her, it also reached the fire above her, suffusing it with oxygen. The flash of burgeoning flames engulfed the tiny corridor, and most of Tammy Robsart's body as she dived for the frosted grass.

She felt nothing in the first instant. It was only after she tumbled to the ground that she saw the flames and thought idly, as if everything were happening in slow motion, that the fires were still close, and she wondered if the grass were alight. Several more leisurely seconds seemed to pass before her eyes cleared, and she saw that it was her own bathrobe, her body that blazed in the cold darkness. She felt rather than heard herself scream, and then she began to roll and run away from the bonfire that had been her home. Had Morgan run far enough? She had to find him. Idly, she wondered when she would begin to hurt.

Spencer Arrowood was asleep when the call came. The night was cold, and he had burrowed down under his electric blanket, wishing that it wouldn't get light for two more days. He was that tired. He had spent a long day helping Joe LeDonne on a wild-goose chase. At the deputy's insistence, they had sent inquiries to the TBI, the FBI, and to the Nashville police department, checking for priors on Wake County's new citizen Justin Warren.

"You want to call Interpol, too, while we're at it?" asked Spencer, amused by LeDonne's intensity.

"I wouldn't mind," said LeDonne.

"It's not against the law to play soldier, Joe. Hell, it's not even against the law to screw a dog in Tennessee anymore." The repeal of the state's bestiality law was a running joke in Tennessee law enforcement.

The deputy shrugged. "Let's put in a request for Warren's service record while we're at it, okay?"

"It'll take a week or so, you know. We have to fax them on letterhead, and then wait until they feel like sending the information."

"Some things never change," said LeDonne.

After that, Spencer had night patrol around the county, checking out the Mockingbird for underage drinkers, and stopping a domestic war between a drunk and his enraged wife. By eleven o'clock, Spencer felt like he'd been dragged two miles down a gravel road. He was ready to go home and sleep for a week—or at least eight hours, which was equally rare. The call that pulled him out of bed at 1:00 A.M. was from Millie Fortnum of the Wake County Rescue

Squad. She called on his home number, meaning that it was urgent. Fire in the trailer park, she'd said. Meet you there.

He microwaved a plastic mug of coffee to wake him up as he drove. The trailer park: principal trouble spot of Wake County. That rural ghetto of aluminum racked up more than its share of domestic brawls, disorderly drunks, and petty thieves. He could put a name to almost every mobile home in the barren park. As he drove through the dark streets of Hamelin, Spencer idly wondered who tonight's victim was. Had Horton Wheeler got drunk again and fallen asleep with a lit cigarette in his mouth? Or did one of the old ladies overload the wiring in her tinderbox home?

He could see the red shine of a county fire engine as soon as he drove into the park. Near it, most of the population of the park was standing in a semicircle, staring at the smoldering remnants of somebody's home. His headlights illuminated old men in robes and striped pajama legs and a plump gaggle of women wearing bright head scarfs to cover nests of pink curlers. They opened a path for him, and he eased the cruiser through, and parked near the fire truck. The volunteers were still hosing down the fire, but not in an effort to salvage anything. There wasn't enough left of the mobile home to tell what it had been. Now the firemen's concern was to keep the wind from spreading the fire to the homes nearby.

In the glow of the embers Spencer could make out Faro Weaver, chief of the volunteer brigade. He looked around for the rescue-squad van, but it was gone. That was a good sign, he thought. If Millie Fortnum was in a hurry, somebody must have survived the fire.

"Whose home was this?" Spencer called out as he got out of his car.

There was a moment's hesitation, not because they didn't

know, but because this group of citizens did not consider
the law to be on their side most of the time. Not that they
had anything against Spencer Arrowood personally; it's just
that his badge usually spelled trouble for people in these
parts. Sheriff Department uniforms meant somebody getting hauled off to jail during a family argument or a too
loud, too drunk party. The sight of a man in that brown
uniform standing outside your house meant that the fi-
nance company had sent people to repossess your belongings and the man with the gun was there to see that they
got away with it. Whenever they showed up in your
neighborhood, it meant bad news, and tonight was no
different, except that the bad news had arrived first, in
the form of a fire.

Finally somebody called out, "Robsarts' place. He's overseas, though. It was just Tammy and her young'un."

Spencer nodded, trying to remember if he knew them. He
didn't think so—another good sign. They weren't troublemakers. "Did they make it out okay?"

A heavyset woman in jeans and a duffel coat stepped out
of the crowd. "The little boy did. He's asleep at my place
with my kid. Tammy got him out quick as she could. She
wasn't so lucky, though. Fire got her pretty bad."

Spencer thanked her. "Could you show me where you
live? I'll take the boy to the hospital if she asks to see him."

"Number twenty-seven. Double-wide, third on the right.
Name's Etheridge." The woman looked suddenly embarrassed and shuffled off in the direction she'd pointed.
"Reckon I'll head on back," she called out. People began
to follow her, drifting away from the fire, and murmuring
among themselves.

Spencer went over to talk to Faro Weaver. He had a
report to fill out, and a trip to the hospital ahead of him.
He knew it wasn't arson, though. The mood of the crowd
told him that. It was just the usual run of bad luck that

dogged the poor: Try to keep warm and your ramshackle house ignites around you. In neighborhoods like this it was too commonplace to be called a tragedy.

She could feel the heat from the examining-table light, and instinctively she tried to squirm away. "Stay still," said a man in green, shadowed by the brightness. "Can you hear me, ma'am? Are you in any pain?"

Tammy Robsart blinked up at him, trying to concentrate on his question. There was pain like a dull roar, but she couldn't figure out what exactly hurt. Something had been pressed across the lower part of her face. She took a gulp of pure oxygen, and nodded her head slightly, still trying to take in her surroundings. Beside the man in green, there was a bottle on a rack with a tube leading down toward her. She tried to sit up.

She felt gentle hands pushing her back down. She licked her cracked lips, and tried to speak. "The fire . . ." Her voice came out in a whisper. The interval between the opening of the door and the sirens—the ambulance was only a blur in her mind. Her throat felt like leather.

The man leaned closer now, and she could see that he was wearing a mask. Above it, white hair curled around his wrinkled forehead, and his blue eyes seemed as bright as the light.

"Can you say your name for me?"

"Tammy," she whispered. "Tammy . . . Robsart."

"That's fine. Mrs. Robsart, are you able to understand me? We need to talk."

Her lips moved again, soundlessly, but her eyes were open and clear. She was conscious enough to be frightened. The man looked away, heaved an audible sigh, and then leaned down again. His voice was gentler now. "You're in the hospital, Tammy. I'm Dr. O'Neill. I need to tell you about your condition."

Suddenly, she felt searing cold all the way to her bones, racking her body with a great shiver. She shut her eyes tight. "It's so cold."

"There's nothing to keep you warm. I'm sorry." He turned to a nurse. "Get me a blood sample and check for smoke inhalation. Try the right femoral artery."

"Morgan?" said Tammy, ignoring the roar from her body.

"That's her little boy," said a woman's voice from outside the light. "She's asking about him."

Dr. O'Neill nodded. "He's fine. You got him out the window, didn't you? Well, he did what you told him. Ran to the neighbors for help. They called the fire department and the rescue squad who brought you here. He's quite a little hero. And you were pretty brave, too." His eyes glistened in the bright light. "And you have to keep on being brave for a little bit while we talk about what you want to do."

Tammy Robsart tried to raise her head to survey her body, but straps held her to the examining table. Her lungs felt tight, and her throat was dry. The rest of her sensations seemed to come in red waves that subsided into haze. "Do I need an operation?" she said. Her words came out in a rasping whisper that she barely recognized as her voice.

"You're very badly burned, Tammy. We have a medical term called the Rule of Nines, to determine the extent of burn damage a patient has sustained, and I'm afraid you scored very high on it."

Tammy tried to smile. "First test I ever done good on."

"It's like golf, I'm afraid. A high score is not good. You have scorched lungs, and heat damage, as well as severe burns on your legs, back, and lower torso, and on one arm.

The flare-up must have hit just as you were jumping out of that trailer of yours, when the cold air got in."

"Yeah. It just whooshed, and it was like the fire stayed with me. I couldn't get away from it." She waited for him to go on, but he was silent. Finally, she asked it. "Am I hurt bad?"

"Yes. I'm afraid you are. I'm sorry. The extent of your burns exceeds the . . . the usual margin for survival."

"Dr. O'Neill!" It was the woman's voice, from outside the light. "You shouldn't—"

"Hartnell! Save it for church. We're fresh out of miracles. She's got a right to know."

"I feel okay," said Tammy. Dying ought to hurt a lot, and if you could stand the pain, and hold on through it, you didn't have to die. She was no stranger to pain. She was tough. Didn't she have Morgan by natural childbirth and not make a sound? She had chewed on ice during the contractions, and hung on to Dale's hand till it bruised.

"Lack of pain is not good, either, Tammy," Dr. O'Neill sounded far-off and weary. "It means the nerves have been destroyed, along with the rest of the tissue. The third-degree burns aren't hurting you, Tammy. It's the less serious ones that you're still able to feel. I'm sorry to have to tell you this, but I had to be honest with you, so that you could make a decision. Here are your options: We can spend the next eight hours trying all sorts of burn treatments, which will make you uncomfortable, and which will not help you, but we could try. . . . Of course, it would leave that husband of yours with a lot of debts. Or—" He swallowed hard. "We could put you in a private room, see that you don't feel too much pain, and let you spend that eight hours any way you choose. You can see your son, make provisions for him and for— Well, I guess the fire took care of most of your possessions. But you can have a telephone, and talk to whoever you want. Someone will stay with you in case

228

you need anything, but no one will disturb you. You can spend the next hours any way you wish."

"And then what?" whispered Tammy. The cold was spiraling around her bones like a piece of silver wire.

"It's just about certain that either way . . . in about eight hours, you will drift off to sleep, and you won't wake up."

"Dr. O'Neill!" It was the woman's voice again, harsher this time. "You can't expect a patient to make a decision like that. Shouldn't we airlift her to the burn center in Knoxville? They've made great progress lately in burn cases, and—"

He shook his head. "I called Knoxville. The air-rescue chopper can't come. One was put in the shop for routine maintenance, and the other one got engine trouble and had to be grounded for repairs. Without them, we couldn't get her to the burn center in time. We're two hours from Knoxville by road, and we couldn't do much for her in transit. We could only give her a lot of pain and waste her remaining time in a useless ambulance run." He turned his back to her, and his voice was low. "Besides, what kind of life would it be? Her hands and feet are almost gone. And she's a Robsart. They don't have the money for the upkeep of a hopeless invalid. I'm not going to sentence that little girl to living hell. I say let her go."

"You can't tell her there's no hope, Dr. O'Neill! Even if it's true. We have to make every effort—"

"We have. Short of the Knoxville burn center, we've done it, and it won't save her. She needs to know that."

"I'm twenty," she said. "I'm real strong."

"I know." He leaned close to her, and his voice was gentle. "I wish that would help, but your body can only do so much."

"I'm gonna die?"

"Yes. You need to tell us how you want to spend the time you have left."

"I want to see my boy. And the county sheriff. Spencer Arrowood. Will he come?"

"I'll call him myself," O'Neill promised. "Anybody else? Do you have family?"

"Just Dale. My husband. He's in the Gulf. Can we call over there and try to find him?"

"Yes. Give us his unit, and we'll put somebody to work on it while we're getting you settled in your room."

"Wait!" Tammy Robsart tried to reach for his hand. "Gotta ask you. Do I look horrible?"

O'Neill hesitated. "Your hair was burned some, but your face is all right, minus eyebrows and eyelashes. Is that what you were concerned about?"

She blinked up at him, crying but tearless. "My little boy. I didn't want Morgan to remember me looking like a monster. I'm ready now. It won't hurt, will it?"

"Not as bad as it once would have. We've put a catheter in at the base of your spine, so that we can control the amount of painkiller you need. There's another needle in you replacing your fluids, or trying to. If it gets too bad, and you want to go to sleep, you just tell Hartnell here, and she'll see to it."

"I want to see my son first. Just give me that much time. I can hold on until then."

CHAPTER

13

... you must wear your rue with a difference.

—Hamlet

Spencer Arrowood stood in the hallway of the hospital, wondering whether it was the disinfectant smell, the shade of green on the walls, or the nature of his business that made him feel like puking. A stubble of blond beard on his chin indicated the haste with which he'd been summoned. He had forgotten his badge. He had outlasted his fatigue, though. A cup of black coffee, provided by a passing nurse, had jolted him into full alert. He'd be up for the rest of the night, no matter what, but he wished he could be someplace other than here. Naomi Judd had worked as a nurse for years before she got her break in country music. He wondered how she had stood it. How did any of them?

He looked down at the wooden waiting bench where a small form in tiny jeans and a blue sweater was curled up, butt in the air, eyes closed. Spencer took off his sheepskin jacket, and spread it over the sleeping boy, Morgan Robsart, until only the blond curls were visible.

Dr. Peter O'Neill emerged from intensive care, looking as if he'd been up for days. His white coat was rumpled, and the lines on his face were etched deeper than before. County Hospital was understaffed, of course. He worked many more hours than other physicians his age, but somebody had to tend to these people. He didn't see anybody else volunteering. The region had a lot of poor people without medical insurance; not exactly an inducement to young physicians, who preferred both the glamour and the income of big-city jobs. Not to mention the state-of-the-art equipment. It was tough to lose a patient that somebody else could have saved. O'Neill had that feeling on a regular basis. Like tonight.

He thrust his hands into his pocket and surveyed the two visitors with weary concern. "Is that the boy?" he said, nodding toward the sleeping toddler on the bench. "Maybe I ought to take a look at him."

"Morgan Robsart," said the sheriff. "I picked him up at the trailer park. He's fine, though. Mrs. Etheridge looked him over and said there's not even a red spot. The mother must have got him out of there first thing, before she worried about herself. How is she?"

Peter O'Neill sat down on the other end of the bench, pushing gently at the child's legs to give himself room. "She's not going to make it. We're doing everything we can, mind you. Replacing fluids, counteracting the pain—except that she wants to be awake to see her son, so we can't give her as much morphine as I'd be otherwise inclined to. She's a fighter, though."

"Will that help?"

"No. She's burned over eighty percent of her body. There's not enough of her left to put up a fight. Even if we could have gotten her to a burn center, they'd have lost her. She'll last a few hours, though. The Red Cross is trying to locate her husband. She's been asking for her son." O'Neill's thoughts seemed to wander as he looked down at the child, all but hidden under the sheriff's coat. "Does he know what's happening?"

Spencer looked away. "He's only three. I thought she might want to tell him in her own way."

"Well, you'd better wake him up, Sheriff. I don't know how long she can keep going on reduced morphine. I'll get a gown for you. Should mask you, too, but what the hell does it matter?"

Spencer put his coat back on, and lifted the sleeping child. "Morgan," he murmured. "Wake up, son. I know it's late, but you have to wake up now. It's real important."

The little face burrowed into his shoulder, and blond curls brushed his chin. Morgan Robsart smelled of cocoa and peppermint, traces of an earlier consolation that he was not aware of needing. Over the child's head, he asked the doctor, "Before he wakes up any more, how bad does she look? Is he going to be able to take this?"

"All you will see is her face,' said O'Neill. "I'll come in with you. Don't let the boy out of your grasp. He can't hug her or anything. The burned areas of her torso are beginning to harden now into eschar, and—"

"Okay. Let's go." Spencer repressed a shudder of revulsion. Burning had to be the worst way to go. The only thing he prayed for concerning death was that he not die by fire. He shook the child gently. "Morgan, we're going to see your mama now." He wondered what you could say to a dying woman. Naomi Judd would know.

Tammy Robsart was sitting propped up in bed, an oxygen mask pressed against her face. Her skin looked sunburned, and the top of her head was swathed in bandages, but she was still recognizable: He realized that she had been the woman he'd spoken to at the Christmas train. How old was she? Twenty-one? He hugged the boy tighter, remembering his intention of buying the child a toy at Kmart. He hadn't gotten around to it. He would, though, tomorrow.

When she saw him at the foot of the bed, holding Morgan, the green gown surrounding both of them, she sighed and closed her eyes for a moment. Dr. O'Neill pulled a chair up close to her and asked how she felt. "Take this mask off," she said in a voice just above a whisper.

Her eyes were different now. Not just the lashless intensity of her stare but the expression in them as well. The
woman at the railroad tracks had been shy, a little wary of
authority figures, and finding it hard to cope with all the
demands on a grown-up with a child. This solemn woman
who stared right into his eyes had no more time for the
niceties of age or social position. She was dead; she out-
ranked them all.

"I'd better talk to you first, Sheriff," she said
quietly. "Don't break in on me, though. I'm running out
of time."

He nodded, cowed somehow by her calmness. There was
no emotion in her voice. She had time only for facts now.

"All right. I got no family except Dale, and he's— Well,
he's overseas now, and even if he wasn't, he wouldn't be
much good. Not for Morgan. He didn't want a child like I
did." She looked up at her son, and her face crumpled. "I
can't hold him, can I? No. Okay. Sheriff, my boy is beautiful, and he's as smart as they come. I want him kept safe.
Better than safe."

Spencer started to speak, about social services and distant
relatives, but a stern look from her silenced him.

"I don't want him living in any trailer from now on.
And I don't want him to ever be cold or have to eat
brown sugar on bread for breakfast 'cause that's all there
is. I want you to give him to somebody smart that can
help him do good in school and will send him to college.
And buy him toys." Her voice softened. "He just loves
them Ninja Turtles."

Spencer shifted the child to his other arm. Morgan was
groggily awake now, looking at his mother, but afraid of
the strangers, the unfamiliar surroundings. Tammy Robsart
glanced at her child, but her gaze was fixed on Spencer
Arrowood, willing him to carry out her wishes.

"Well," he hesitated. "You know, your husband is the child's legal guardian, and—"

"You tell Dale what I said. You tell him!" She looked at the telephone on the nightstand. "If they can find him, I'll tell him myself. I want Morgan to be all right. He's losing me. He ought to get something. All the family pictures got burned up, I reckon. Can you get him one of me? High school yearbook—two years back. . . ."

"You might pull through—" Spencer began.

"No." She took another breath of oxygen. Dr. O'Neill leaned over and adjusted the catheter. The look he gave the sheriff said, *Don't waste her time.*

Spencer brought the child closer to the bed, and knelt down so that Tammy could be close to her son. He was wide awake now, but frightened by the adults' solemn faces. When he was close enough to Tammy to whisper, he said, "I had cocoa."

"That's good, son." She almost smiled. "I have to talk to you now about something big. Okay?"

Morgan nodded, but his eyes kept straying to the strange objects around the room.

"I have to go away soon," said Tammy.

"In a spaceship?"

"No, hon. Like the angels in your Christmas book."

"Can I go, too?" He held his arms up like the angels with the wings of eagles hovering over the valley.

"You have to stay here. But I want you to remember me, and to remember that I love you. I don't want to leave you, Morgan, but I have to."

"Uh-huh." He was fascinated by the tubes and bottles, barely listening to her.

"The sheriff will be your friend, and I'll be watching you from—from heaven, I guess."

"Okay." He tried to reach for the oxygen mask, but Spencer leaned away so that it eluded his grasp.

"Can I have your best kiss?" Tammy Robsart whispered.

"Yep." He dangled beside her in the sheriff's arms, and kissed his mother's cheek. "Can I eat now?"

"Yes. You go eat. Anything you want. . . ." Tammy's voice trailed away. "Good-bye, Morgan."

Dr. O'Neill motioned for them to leave the room. "I increased the morphine," he murmured. "She's suffered enough."

On the bedside table the telephone rang.

Spencer carried Morgan out into the hall, and down to the nurses' station. "Can you get this young man some ice cream?" he asked one who didn't seem to be working. "I have some calls to make."

A pretty dark-haired nurse smiled and held out her arms. She looked a little like Naomi. "Why, sure. Come with me, big fella. The cafeteria has three different flavors. Would you like that?"

Spencer smiled and waved until they disappeared around the corner of the hallway. Then he went into a stall in the men's room and cried.

Morgan Robsart was not yet back from his expedition to the hospital cafeteria. It was a slow night at County, evidently. Spencer Arrowood sat at the desk in Peter O'Neill's office, staring thoughtfully at the black telephone. Who do you call in the middle of the night in such an emergency? He had thought of taking the boy home with him, but in the life of a county sheriff, nothing is certain, least of all off-duty time. At any hour he might be summoned to a crime scene (probably wouldn't, but the possibility was always there), and he knew that he could neither take the child along nor leave him unattended. Besides, Morgan might be frightened, and Spencer was mortally afraid of his own inexperience with children. What could he say or do to comfort this motherless child who liked Ninja Turtles and Ghostbusters. *Who you gonna call?*

It was past midnight. Someone in the trailer park? *"I don't want him living in any trailer from now on,"* Tammy Robsart had said. He saw her dead eyes looking at him, willing him the care of her son, and he knew that he would have to do better than that. Cradling the receiver between his ear and shoulder, Spencer punched in his mother's number, and listened to the succession of unanswered rings. Where the hell was she? What was today, anyhow? Then he vaguely remembered something about a trip to Asheville with a couple of her bridge-playing friends. She had told him about the trip—a road-company theatre production or an antique exposition, something like that; Spencer had barely heard her, absorbed as he was in the current of his own life.

He put down the receiver, double-checked a number, and tried again. After three rings, he heard Martha's sleepy voice mumble hello.

"It's me," he said. "I'm at the hospital."

"Oh, God," said Martha, jolting to wakefulness. "What is it? You're not hurt, are you?"

"No. There was a fire at the trailer park, and I'm here with a little boy who lost his mother tonight. I need somebody to stay with him. I know there has to be a magistrate's hearing to decide what to do about him, but we've got forty-eight hours to attend to that. Meanwhile, he needs a friend."

Silence. Then he heard Martha sigh. "Oh, Spencer. Don't pick on me. I don't know a thing about kids, and I've got enough on my hands as it is. Joe's here. He's—he's had one of his nightmares."

"Well, I hate to ask you in the middle of the night, but . . ." Spencer waited, hoping that Martha would relent to break the silence, but nearly a full minute passed without

239

a word between them. Finally, he said, "I'm sorry. I'll keep trying." He hung up before Martha could make any well-meaning suggestions. He drew the line at calling strangers in the middle of the night. He sat for a moment listening to the dial tone, and then dialed a new number.

After two rings she picked it up, a little breathless. "Yes? Will, is that you?" She didn't sound like someone just awakened.

"This is Spencer Arrowood," he said. "It seems like I'm always calling you in the dead of night to ask a favor."

Laura Bruce sighed. "I can't go out to a crime scene to-night, Sheriff," she said. Her voice shook a little, with what emotion he could not tell.

"No, that's not it. I have a little boy here that needs a place to go. He's three years old." He explained about the mobile-home fire, and about Tammy Robsart's instructions for the care of her son. Laura Bruce listened without com-ment. "I tried a couple of other people first," he said. "I'd take him myself, but I wouldn't know what to do with the little feller, and besides, I'll be on duty tomorrow. It's just until there's a formal hearing." He let the silence stretch out again.

Finally she said, "Do you know where I live?"

"Yes. Can I bring him over now?"

"All right. I'll make up the bed in the spare room." She paused for a moment. "I'm glad you called me. It will be nice to have company."

"I'll be there in twenty minutes."

"Wait! Does he have any clothes? No, of course he doesn't. Never mind, Sheriff. I can see to that tomorrow. He can sleep in one of Will's old T-shirts tonight."

Spencer thanked her and set the receiver back in its cra-dle. Tomorrow he would have to see the magistrate about a hearing for the orphaned boy. He would also make time to go by Kmart and pick up some clothes for Morgan, who had just lost everything in the world. He hoped the store was well stocked with Ninja Turtles and Ghostbusters.

When she hung up the phone, Laura Bruce closed her eyes and tried to think of a prayer. Was this divine compensation, she wondered, or God's idea of a joke? Lose a child, gain a child. She had not yet finished her mourning and here was Spencer Arrowood trying to yank her back into the world. She looked down at the curve of her belly, hard and still beneath the velvet robe "Why couldn't I have *my* child?" she asked of no one in particular. She had told no one of the loss of her baby. When someone called to say they hadn't seen her about, she said that she was feeling under the weather. What she felt was that she was only part alive. She hugged her grief to herself, unwilling to share it with these mountain strangers, or even with Will, who had his eternal summer and his glorious little war. But they couldn't leave her in peace, even in her sorrow. Spencer Arrowood had found another orphan to foist on her, and she must be strong in deference to the needs of others. When was it her turn to be comforted? Why didn't God find somebody else to do His errands?

Stifling a yawn, she stood up and ambled toward the hall closet. She must make up the bed in the guest room before the little visitor arrived. Then she would make cocoa. She deferred her own grieving for later.

CHAPTER

14

From too much love of living,
    From hope and fear set free,
We thank with brief thanksgiving
    Whatever gods may be
That no life lives forever;
That dead men rise up never;
That even the weariest river
    Winds somewhere safe to sea.

                    —SWINBURNE,
        "The Garden of Proserpine,"

Tavy Annis sat at his dining-room table, sifting through a stack of white envelopes. "I reckon that about does it," he told Taw, tossing him the most recent addition to the pile. "North Carolina Environmental Protection Agency. I sent them the Little Dove analysis we bought from Carter Biological, and they thanked me for my concern, and said that the matter had been taken under advisement."

"Well, they may do something about it eventually."

"Not within my lifetime," said Tavy.

Taw McBryde looked away, pretending to study the deer in the painting above the stone fireplace. Not in Tavy's lifetime. How long was that? Two weeks? A month? Lately he had seemed to fade like a parchment drawing, until the only thing alive about him was the anger that still smoldered in his eyes. He wouldn't speak about the pain, but the lines at the corners of his mouth deepened, and he was given to long silences that seemed to indicate an inner struggle between himself and the thing inside him, but Taw knew better than to tell him to give up the struggle. Tavy was not ready to let go yet, with nothing accomplished. But now it was hopeless. He had hung all his hopes on the EPA, and they had shunted him off with a form letter. His body was running out of time; even rage could not fuel it indefinitely. In spite of everything, he was weakening. The EPA would have to go into that factory with axes this afternoon to accomplish anything within Tavy's lifetime.

"What now?" asked Taw. "That's about everybody, isn't it? You've tried them all. What else can you do?"

"I'm not quitting. I never was one to do that. Do you remember the time that Doyle Weaver broke my Barlow knife on purpose, and I swore to get even with him?"

"I didn't know you ever did," said Taw.

"It took a while. We were growed up by then, and you were long gone, but I got him. We were fishing from the railroad trestle over the Little Dove, and I noticed the spinning reel was loose on his new fishing rod. Didn't say a word. A couple of casts later, he throws that rod over his shoulder and swings it out over the river, and splat! Off goes the reel into the river, and he's so off balance with the shock of it, that he goes and drops the rod in after it." The memory made him smile. "We never did find it. Course I didn't look too awful hard, myself."

"Well," said Taw. "I guess you can figure that sooner or later, somebody will give that paper company its comeuppance. I reckon I could—"

"That's not good enough. Now I've tried every way that's peaceable and reasonable to get some justice in this. I even wrote them to personally plead with them to clean up their mess—wrote to Roger W. Sheridan, the president of the company. Not a word. Not even a form letter. And now I'm done with being reasonable. I'm out of time."

Taw rubbed his glasses against his sweater and put them back on. "All right," he said. "I'm with you. What are we going to do?"

Tavy Annis tottered to his feet. "There's a gun in the top drawer of that sideboard. You can put that in your coat, while I get us a couple of decent-looking neckties out of my chifforobe. And you can drive that new car of yours. We're going to North Carolina."

"Of all the damned days for Spencer to be off!" said Joe LeDonne, helping himself to a peppermint from the jar on Martha's desk.

"What brought that on? The phone call?" said Martha. She switched off the electric typewriter, and leaned back in her chair. "Whatever it was, I'm sure you can handle it by yourself. Don't begrudge Spencer his concert. He can use a break from this place."

LeDonne perched on the edge of her desk, rubbing his chin with a thoughtful frown. "Yeah, but this is weird. You know I hate weird stuff."

"What was it?" Martha smiled indulgently. "The weekend warriors out there on the mountain?"

"No. That call was from a police officer from Johnson City. He's checking on a complaint from a jeweler in town. According to him, two young adults entered a jewelry store with a human jawbone and asked the store owner to read a serial number on a tooth filling."

Martha's eyes widened. "People were toting around a human jawbone in Johnson City? That's about the last thing I'd expect. It sounds like Satanists, doesn't it?"

"I guess," said LeDonne.

"There aren't any Satanists around here, though, are there?"

"Not that I know of. Johnson City hadn't heard of any, either. But they got interested enough to look into it. Then, a couple of days later, somebody there in Records noticed that a parking ticket had been issued to a car registered to the Underhills of Wake County. Thanks to those murders last fall, the Wake County Underhills are notorious all over east Tennessee. They got to talking about it around the station, and this officer who called me—J. D. Lane—thought there might be a link between the couple with the jawbone and the Underhills. Just a hunch, but he asked me to check it out."

Martha's look of skepticism turned to a thoughtful frown. "Young adults? What sex?"

"Male and female. Dark-haired Caucasians."

"The two surviving family members were a teenaged boy and girl."

"Yeah. Lane knew that. He'd looked up the case in the *Press-Chronicle*. That's why he called us. He could have come over and checked it out himself, but as a courtesy, he notified us instead. I told him I'd check on it."

Martha was unable to contain her laughter. "As a courtesy? Did you believe that?"

"Hell no," Le Donne growled. "I know why he called me. He thinks this case is going to be a can of worms, and he doesn't want to get near it. So he's trying to dump it in my lap."

"And you'd like to dump it in Spencer's lap, wouldn't you?"

"Yeah, but I won't." LeDonne straightened his tie. "I'm going out to the cemetery and take a look at the Underhill graves. I hope to hell I don't find anything."

"Call me on the radio," said Martha.

He zipped up his sheepskin jacket and ambled toward the door. "You bet."

A four-lane interstate, less than twenty years old, meandered through the wide valley into North Carolina with all the effortlessness of a flatland road, with mountains on the horizon only for scenery. It came out just below Asheville and would take them across the state line in an hour or so, but they were in no rush, and the old, familiar two-lane road over the mountains was their road; the new featureless swath through the valley belonged to another generation; people who were in a hurry, mostly to get somewhere else.

Taw pulled out of Tavy's gravel driveway and turned the car away from town, trying not to think what the trip might do to his Mercury's suspension system. The view, though, would be almost worth it. The old-timers still called the one-lane blacktop the Drovers Road, a fading memory of its original purpose when it was only a trail cut along the ridges. When Appalachia was the West, there had been great herds of cattle and even buffalo ranging in these mountains, fattening on the maist of the chestnut trees. Great cattle drives had followed mountain trails from Greeneville, Tennessee, to Greenville, South Carolina—more cattle than ever went up the Chisholm Trail in the farther West of the late nineteenth century. Now the road was an indifferent blacktop, meandering along the ridge of the Smokies, and crossing the state lines without benefit of a welcome sign.

The Drovers Road began as a green tunnel, shrouded by oaks from the forests on either side. If you were good at noticing things off to the side, you might see deer skittering through the trees close to the road, spooked by the engine noise. After a few miles of gradual incline, the road leveled off on the top of a long, high ridge, where overgrown fields and crumbling barns testified to the ruined farmsteads that had once crowned the heights. The meadows were empty now, but beyond them, in the distance, lay miles of golden valley, flanked by an endless roll of mountains, green with pines, hazing to blue on the horizon. It was the top of the world; and they were alone in it.

"I had a mind to live up here once upon a time," said Taw, slowing the car to a crawl as he looked out across the mountains. "When I was stuck up in De-troit, I used to see this view in every country song. When anybody said *home*, I pictured this."

"Why didn't you move up here, then?" asked Tavy. "I reckon somebody would have sold you a couple of acres."

"I'm too old for it now. The heights is for young people. Looking out across that empty space there to those far-off mountains is like looking into the future, and I don't want to see that far anymore. It scares me a little. I think about getting snowed in come winter, and the winds that would whip across that valley and rattle the house like a Dixie cup. I think about getting sick up here alone with no one to look in on me. And having to drive ten miles for a loaf of bread. I'm too old for it."

Tavy snorted. "Young people can't live up here, either, Taw. Too far to commute to their jobs. No school bus to take the kids to school. No phone lines." He nodded toward the brown ruin of a saltbox house. "I guess nobody can live up here but ghosts. Maybe I'll take up residence here."

Taw reddened and set his jaw. "Don't talk like that!"

"Like what? About dying? It's not exactly a surprise ending, is it? It's not like I'd live forever if I didn't have cancer. I am looking at the future out there, like you said, and that's what I see."

"I know. I just don't like to hear you talk about it. It sounds like you're giving in."

"Nobody solicited my opinion," said Tavy. "But I don't reckon I mind all that much. I'm a little tired of the world these days, with its silly music and its all-fired self-important technology. It's not worth all the pain I'm having to see another few months of it, I can tell you that. I think I'd rather see what comes next."

Taw almost said, What if nothing does? but he caught himself in time. It was not a subject to speculate on with the dying.

After five or six glorious miles of sprawling vistas like the view from heaven, the road began to twist downward again, between banks of pine trees, and they were enclosed again in forest, heading for the valley they had just seen spread out before them. It would take another six miles of switchbacks to reach it, though.

"Reckon we're in North Carolina yet?" asked Tavy.

"Near about," said Taw. "After that, it will be another twenty miles or so before we run into the four-lane that'll take us to Titan."

Tavy settled back in the passenger seat and closed his eyes. "Give me a shake when we get there."

In later spring even the valley would have been beautiful, with a sweep of green meadows curling around the rocky river, and cows lazing under white-blossomed apple trees, but in the last weeks of winter the fields were yellow with dead grass or brown with mud, and the black trees were bare. A crossroads hamlet huddled around a post office the size of a toolshed, as bleak as the end of the world. Taw flipped on the radio; the sightseeing was over.

Oakdale Cemetery was already tinged with green. Gold-tinted leaves sprouted at the tips of oak and maple branches scattered throughout the well-kept lawns, and green shoots of grass laced the brown stubble around the grave markers. Joe LeDonne tried not to think about why. He parked the patrol car on the circle near the new part of the cemetery, and threaded his way among the plots, reading the lettering on the bronze markers.

He avoided cemeteries when he could. Too many of his friends had ended up there well before their time, and he wondered sometimes if it was a form of arrogance to stroll among the dead, pretending that you would last forever. There was enough danger in his line of work without taunting fate. LeDonne believed in fate. In a twelve-month tour of duty in Vietnam, he had seen smarter men, braver men, and better men than himself go to their deaths, for no reason that he could discern, while he had been spared. He had learned not to question death's choices, but its presence made him uneasy. Sometimes he thought he might be an oversight and that if he got in death's way, it would notice him, and come back to tidy up the loose end.

He didn't pretend that this was just a scenic park, either. He had learned to respect death. But he wanted to get out of there before it noticed him. And before any of his old buddies dropped by for a visit. The way they did in his nightmares. Lanier or Mullins or Edmiston would appear, sometimes back in the jungle, sometimes in his house in Hamelin. Sometimes the spectral visitor would be his regular old self, smiling and cracking jokes like nothing happened, and sometimes, Mullins wouldn't have a face, or Lanier would be gone from the waist down, and the sound of the Bouncing Betty would still be echoing around them. Then LeDonne would have to fight his way back from the place of dreams, and abandon his friends to the darkness. Again. Then Martha would brew him coffee, and hold him, telling him again and again that it was over, and he would nod and pretend to be convinced. Yeah, he thought, it's over, but it has a half-life of twenty years and counting.

In Southeast Asia people believed that ghosts were spirits of the dead who had died too suddenly to make the transition from one plane to the next. Those who died violently were the ones who walked. If that were true, the Underhills probably weren't resting in peace, either, he thought. But at least they didn't have to cry out for justice. Their murderer had sentenced himself and followed them into the next world. He hoped he would find an undisturbed grave.

Underhill. One double marker bearing the names of Paul and Janet, and on either side of them two smaller plaques for Joshua and Simon. Four identical dates of death. No flowers, not even plastic ones, adorned these graves, and unswept leaves had drifted into the plot, making the site look long abandoned. How long had it been? Six months?

LeDonne knelt on the marker, and began to brush the leaves away from Josh Underhill's grave. As he did, a sharp March wind swirled a new assortment of leaves in the wake of the old ones. He pushed those aside, and examined the earth beneath. It was tightly packed. No sign of disturbance. He turned to the parents' grave, and began clearing the leaves away, using his fingers like a rake. The leaves were cold and wet, and stuck to his hand like dead skin. He shook them away, and ran his fingertips through the dirt. There was no grass beneath this leaf pile, and the soil crumbled at his touch. He brushed more leaves from the plot, and saw that clumps of clay were still heaped near the slope of the hill. This was not last year's gravedigging, done by the cemetery workmen. The soil was newly disturbed, and hastily replaced.

LeDonne stood up, and brushed bits of red clay from his trousers. There was no need to go further just yet. He had probable cause now, enough to start asking questions. But not of the Underhills, not yet. He would have to do much more investigating before he was ready to confront them. This crime, this sign of mental disturbance, changed everything. Now the open-and-shut homicide case of last October was beginning to look much more complex.

Back in the car he radioed Martha that he had completed the 10-96. He asked her to phone the district attorney to say that he'd be stopping by in twenty minutes. Martha wanted more information, but he signed off, and drove out of the cemetery, feeling like a trespasser.

After forty-five minutes of driving through the river valley, Taw McBryde's Oldsmobile passed through a row of well-

kept white houses in a larger village. He slowed down, looking for signs. At a gas station and post office crossroads, a
shield-shaped blue sign directed him to the interstate. After
that, the scenery swept past in a featureless blur, punctuated
by green road signs announcing the distance to the next
three towns. Town number two was Titan Rock, home of
a large and prosperous paper company. Taw speeded up to
sixty-five, and even then the trucks whizzed past him.

It was after four when he took the exit ramp for Titan
Rock, leaving the monotony of the interstate to the long-
haulers and the commuters. In an hour it would be dark.
He looked out over the dingy factory town, with its garish
strip of fast-food joints and glass and neon filling stations.
Everything in Titan Rock was either old and dirty or plastic,
and towering over the crumbling town was the factory, a
brown fortress straddling the riverbank. One mushroom
smokestack was emblazoned with Titan Paper, as if there
could be any doubt about it. Taw aimed the car for the
smokestack, and followed the narrow streets to his destination. With one hand, he shook Tavy's shoulder. "We're
there, old buddy."

Tavy was awake in seconds, alert. "Good," he said, peering up at the smokestack in front of them. "Let's go over
it again."

Philip Withrow had been elected district attorney because
there had been Withrows in Wake County since before the
Civil War, because he was young and energetic enough to
campaign for the post, and mostly because Wake County's
other lawyers already had good practices and couldn't be
bothered with the job. It wasn't as if the position would
lead anywhere, except maybe to a job as a state senator a
dozen years down the line. Meanwhile, it was a dreary term

prosecuting drunk drivers, two-bit thieves, and assault cases. Like the sheriff, he tended to see the same people over and over, and he had come to the conclusion that crime ran in some families the way lawyering ran in his.

He still looked like a kid, despite his premature balding and his charcoal wool suit with the yellow spotted tie. There was a looseness about his clothes that made people think of a kid playing dress-up. He had been reading the Sharper Image catalog, trying to decide which electronic gadget he was going to give himself for Father's Day, when LeDonne showed up. He slid the magazine in his drawer, and leaned back in his red swivel chair, trying to look authoritative and calm. He didn't feel calm around LeDonne, though. He always suspected that there was a sneer lurking behind the deputy's impassive face.

"Hello, LeDonne!" he said in politician friendly. "How's business?"

"Steady," said LeDonne. "But not what you'd call pre-dictable." The deputy ignored the leather captain's chair beside Withrow's desk, and stood at parade rest, as remote from the attorney as he was from the people he arrested. "I need some advice about a point of law."

"That's what I'm here for," said Withrow happily. He had a wall filled with law books to get him out of this one. "What's your question?"

"It's two questions, really. The first one is, is grave rob-bing a misdemeanor or a felony?"

Whatever Philip Withrow expected, it was not this. His mouth opened and closed without uttering a sound, and for a second he stared at the deputy, waiting for the punch line. LeDonne was silent. "You're serious about this?" Withrow said at last. "*Grave* robbing? Oh, you mean Indian bones from an archaeological site? I think we can—"

"No, sir." LeDonne's expression did not change. "I mean

robbing a grave in Oakdale Cemetery. I have reason to believe that one has been disturbed, and that bones were removed from the site."

"I think— Well, I'd have to look it up, but I think it's a
misdemeanor. Teenage boys, you mean? It's like vandalism,
isn't it?"

LeDonne shrugged. "That brings me to the second question. I have reason to believe that the graves were opened
by the deceased's next of kin. Now, does that mean that
the bones are the property of the heirs, and is it in fact not
vandalism or theft at all in that case?"

Withrow leaned his head back and exhaled a long, loud
breath. "Okay. Tell me who we're talking about and what
has happened." When LeDonne finished explaining in his
precise, emotionless way, the district attorney sighed again.
"I could look it up if you're dying to know, LeDonne. But
all you really need to know is this: There's no way we're
prosecuting on this one. Make it go away, you hear? Get
them counseling. Get them to commit themselves. Whatever.
I don't want to be the first east Tennessee D.A. to make
the supermarket tabloids. Just make this one go away."

It was after four-thirty in the gathering twilight when the
two old men stepped into the reception area of the Titan
Paper Company. They were nicely dressed, with dark ties
and suit jackets, and they were smiling pleasantly at Sarah
Watkins, the receptionist, weary with the boredom of her
undemanding job. She wanted nothing more than to beat
the traffic out of the plant's parking lot, and get to Food
Lion before nightfall. Visitors, at least, would take her mind
off the second hand of the clock. She summoned up a smile.
"Can I help you all?"

"I was hoping we might catch Roger," said Taw McBryde,
returning the smile. "Mr. Sheridan, that is. I've got an old

friend here who'd like to see him. We're just back from the doctor's in Charlotte." He nodded toward Tavy, inviting the receptionist to understand the finality of this visit. "We can't make the stockholders' meeting, but since we were passing through, we thought we'd drop in and say hello. Now don't tell me the old rascal is busy." He twinkled at her, sharing the joke on self-important old Roger.

The receptionist looked doubtful for a moment, and her gaze wandered to Tavy, looking gaunt behind a bony smile, and clutching a paper bag to his chest. "Brought him a little something from home," he said hoarsely. "You don't reckon he's too busy for that, do you?"

Sarah Watkins grinned. "Well, he's by himself, anyhow, and his phone light's not on. Shall I announce you, or do you want to surprise him?"

By now Taw had spotted the hallway that she had glanced toward. There was no one else in the reception room. No guards anywhere. Not much crime in Titan Rock, he reckoned. "We'll sneak on back and surprise him," he whispered. "We can't stay too long, anyhow."

They hurried off down the corridor before she could think better of the unannounced visit. The walls were lined with pictures of old men in suits—the board of directors, maybe, or past presidents of the company. They look about the same age as Tavy and me, thought Taw McBryde. Maybe that's why the receptionist let us through. To a gal her age, all old men must look alike. He kept hustling down the hall as fast as he could without looking suspicious. If he stopped to think, he might realize the folly of their intentions. There was no use asking Tavy to reconsider, though. Planning this day had kept him alive for weeks now, while his skin faded to transparency with illness, letting the rage shine through him like an aura. They were in it now. As they reached the door bearing Roger W. Sheridan's brass nameplate, Taw slid the pistol out of the pocket of his jacket.

The siege was accomplished in less than a minute. One moment Roger Sheridan was standing at his door, trying to figure out who his visitors were, and the next instant he had a gun in his ribs, as he spoke into the intercom telling Sarah that he wasn't to be disturbed.

"Who are you?" he asked, staring up at his captors. He was a short, stocky man in his early fifties, red-faced, with eyes like huckleberries. Droplets of sweat trickled down his shiny forehead, and his expression was a study in outrage mingled with terror. Taw didn't think Roger Sheridan was a good bet to make sixty-five, a fact that cheered him. His contempt for the pompous little man made it easier to hold the gun steadily and convincingly against his temple.

"Who are we?" Tavy repeated. "We live downstream from your paper company, that's who." He looked around at Sheridan's showplace office. A well-carved Thomasville desk and bookcases gleamed with furniture polish, and the red-and-gold fabric of the tapestry sofa matched the drapery material covering a Palladian window. Sheridan was sitting at his desk now, while Taw stood beside him, holding the gun. Tavy sank down in the visitors' chair, holding the paper bag between his knees, breathing a little heavily from the exertion and excitement.

Sheridan was still trying to make sense of the intruders. "What do you want? Is this a robbery? Did you used to work here?"

"No," said Tavy. "It's not a robbery. We don't want your money. And I wouldn't work here for any salary, including yours. I wouldn't want this place on my conscience. We came to talk to you about your plant's water pollution, Mr. Sheridan."

The company president blinked. "You're environmentalists?"

"Not really," said Tavy. "Didn't used to be, anyhow. I'm just a man dying of cancer, and I wanted to tell you a few things about your paper mill." He reached into his jacket pocket and pulled out the Carter Biological water analysis. "Did you know that you are releasing into the Little Dove River mercury, dioxin, sulphur, and cadmium? Did you know that you are exceeding federal EPA levels for each of them? Did you know that three of those substances are cancer causing?"

Sheridan shrugged. "That is not my area of expertise. I have engineers who take care of that sort of thing. And lawyers."

"But they report to you. You have to sign the papers for the EPA reports. You have to know what you're putting into that water."

Sheridan turned to stare up at Taw, impassive behind the gun. He seemed to be trying to decide which of his captors to reason with. The dying man had nothing to lose; maybe this one. . . . "It's a very complex business," he said, trying to sound friendly. "Lots of confusing government regulations; highly technical information from many departments. I'd be happy to get someone to talk to you about this. They'd know more than I." He ventured a smile. "Look, fellas, I have grandchildren. I don't want to mess up the world any more than you do."

Taw did not respond to his smile. The gun did not waver.

"We don't need information," said Tavy in a harsher tone than before. "We came to tell you that the stuff you put in the river causes cancer. What are you going to do about it?"

Sheridan's smile was as oily as a politician's. "Our studies do not confirm that allegation," he said smoothly. "Of course, we are concerned about the environment just like everyone else, and my engineers have assured me that the emission levels of this plant are perfectly safe and legal. Now, I understand how you might feel, having cancer and looking for someone to blame. Do you smoke, by the way?"

"No," said Tavy. "I used to fish, though. So you're telling us that the Little Dove is not a health hazard?"

"That's right," said Sheridan. He started to stand up, but Taw pressed the muzzle of the gun against his temple, and he slid back into the leather chair, glistening with sweat. "The river is perfectly safe," he finished weakly.

"Well, for your sake that's mighty good news," said Tavy Annis with a bitter smile. "Mighty good news." He set the paper bag down on Roger Sheridan's shiny mahogany desk, and took out a mason jar filled with murky brown liquid, the color of tobacco spit.

Titan Paper's CEO stared up at his interrogator, nervously licking his lips. "What's that?"

"Why, Mr. Sheridan, that's a jar of harmless Little Dove River water," said Tavy. "Now, drink it."

Sheridan's mouth dropped open, but no words came out. Finally, he said, "You're joking!"

Taw touched the muzzle of the gun to the captive's sweaty temple. "You heard him," he said. "Pick up the jar and drink, or we'll blow your goddamn head off."

Tavy picked up the jar, sloshing the liquid a little, as if it were a snifter of brandy, and held it out to the gasping man. "Go on, now. Drink it all. Chugalug."

Roger Sheridan summoned up a trace of his old authority. "You can't do this to me!" he spluttered. "I'll have you arrested for this!"

"Really?" Tavy grinned, motioning for him to drink.

Sheridan brought the jar to his lips, inhaled, and jerked his head away as the reek of dead water slammed into his nostrils. "I'll get you for assault!" he whispered. "I'll have you charged with attempted murder."

Tavy Annis nodded pleasantly. "Please do, Mr. Sheridan," he said gently. "Please take us to court, and say that making you drink a quart of Little Dove water is attempted murder. I want that statement to be a matter of public record."

Taw had to prod Sheridan in the temples once again, and finally cock the gun, before he would drink the water, but when Taw began to count slowly, a weeping Sheridan thrust the jar against his mouth, and began to gulp down the foul liquid, coughing and crying as he drank. "Please! Please!" he sobbed between swallows. Mucus ran from his nose, mixing with the water and his sweat, but his captors remained impassive, and would not look away. At last he managed to drain the jar, his body heaving from the ordeal. His blue suit glistened with sweat and foul water. Sheridan slumped in his chair, hand over his mouth, taking deep, sobbing breaths. "I'm going to throw up!" he wailed.

"That might be the best thing," Tavy told him. "In the long run. You can keep the jar as a reminder, Mr. Sheridan. You're forcing people to drink that water every single day. Think about it." He stood up and walked away, motioning for Taw to follow him. As they opened the door, they heard the sobbing turn to retching, but they did not look back.

Morgan Robsart was sitting on the braided rug in Laura Bruce's living room, watching the Ninja Turtles take on the bad guys in a sewer battle. He seemed oblivious to the conversation of the two women seated on the sofa behind him. The light from the color television bathed his upturned face in an aura of light. Laura Bruce looked at the sturdy little form and longed to hold him.

Barbara Givens, in a coat and skirt of patchwork suede, was writing on a notepad balanced on her plump knees. Beside her, on the end table, a cup of tea sent wisps of steam into the air. "It's not all that hard," she was saying.

"I've raised enough young'uns to know. He's three years old, isn't he?"

"Yes," said Laura. "But I was an only child. I don't know much about little boys."

"Three years old," Barbara said again. "He's potty trained. He talks good. There's not a whole lot to raising boys, you know. Keep 'em fed, and keep 'em from breaking their necks. That's about it. You'll do fine."

"I hope so," said Laura. "I want him to be safe and happy."

"He's a sweet little boy. I don't reckon you'll have any trouble, but if you do, give a holler. And if you ever need a sitter, my oldest girl would be glad to come over."

Laura smiled. "Maybe when I have a doctor's appointment. Other than that, I wouldn't think of leaving him. It's wonderful to have him here."

"How long do you have him for?"

"I don't know." Laura tapped Morgan on the shoulder and handed him another cookie. When she turned back to Barbara, she spoke softly so that he would not overhear. "I went to a hearing before the magistrate, and I told him I'd be willing to keep Morgan for as long as anyone wanted me to. His only relative is his father, who is overseas. They called him, and he seemed relieved that someone wanted Morgan. So maybe when Will gets back, we can see about making it permanent. He's a special little boy."

"Well," said Barbara. "He's been through a lot. How's he taking it?"

Laura shrugged. "It's hard to tell. He wet the bed the first couple of nights, which was understandable. He had nightmares, too. And of course his misses his mother. But he's very sweet, and he's smart as a whip. He loves to be read to."

"I've got some old children's books up in the attic," said Barbara. "I'll hunt them out for you. They'll come in handy for the next one as well."

Laura turned to look at Morgan, still absorbed in his cartoon. Suddenly, he turned and grinned at her, and she smiled back. "There's something I ought to tell you, Barbara, about the next one," Laura said quietly.

Late that night, Tavy Annis was sprawled in his morris chair, grayer than mole fur. His breathing was heavy, but he wouldn't let himself be put to bed. He huddled under a tartan blanket, exhausted from the day's events. "Reckon that's about it," he said to Taw McBryde, who was stoking the fire, and pretending not to notice his friend's discomfort.

"It sure felt good to watch that fellow drink his own muck," said Taw. "Wish they'd come take us to court about it. I'd love to say in open court why we did it."

Tavy smiled a little. He had given himself a morphine injection on the ride back to Hamelin, but it had worn off now. He was trying to fight the pain so that he could stay awake a little longer and savor the triumph. "I wish I could be there to see it, Taw."

"I wish so, too." said Taw. There was no point in arguing anymore about death. You could see it now in Tavy's face. Hear it every time he drew breath. It wouldn't be much longer now, which was just as well.

Tavy drew the old blanket closer about him. "You know we didn't really solve nothing today. What we did won't even make that Sheridan bastard sick. You've got to drink it regular to get what I've got. And the plant won't do a multimillion-dollar cleanup just because somebody attacked their office boy."

"No. But at least we did something. We tried every other way we knew and got nowhere. At least we made him listen to us."

Tavy nodded. "Yeah. They may have got me, but at least I got in one good punch."

"You think Sheridan will report it?"

"Maybe not. He's not hurt, and he won't want the publicity, especially with a dying man ready to accuse them of murder. I wish I could have stopped them, though."

Taw stood up and set the poker back in its brass rack. The fire was blazing merrily now, but Tavy still shivered. "I've got time. I haven't finished with Titan Paper yet," Taw said.

Tavy sighed. "Hope you bought yourself a water filter."

"We need to warn people about the river. We need to make the goddamn bureaucrats care. Can you take being bothered, or do you want things peaceful from here on out?" he asked.

"Hell," said Tavy. "Might as well postpone peace and quiet while I can. Gonna have a lot of it directly. What did you have in mind?"

Taw McBryde grinned at his lifelong friend, and walked to the telephone. "Why, I thought we might turn ourselves in."

Spencer Arrowood sat in a metal folding chair on the floor of the civic center—section F, row 24—with a Judds Farewell Concert program, photo, and a cassette tape resting in his lap. Beneath his feet a soft protective surface covered the wooden floor of a basketball court, and high wooden bleachers lined the walls, but tonight the steel-raftered coliseum was neither a sports arena nor a convention site. For one night only it had become a secular cathedral. The massive slabs of sound equipment and lighting systems flanking the stage heralded the coming event, as did the hucksters selling T-shirts and albums in stalls near the back of the room. Spencer looked down at his newly purchased eight-by-ten photo of Naomi and Wynonna Judd in fringe and turquoise, posing in a Southwestern landscape of red sandstone cliffs. Their costumes suggested the Navajo style of dress, which struck him as odd, since the Judds were descended from an east Kentucky family that went back well over a century in the Southern mountains. He wondered why the city people who decided such things thought that the Arizona desert was exotic but that Appalachia—despite its ghosts and gold mines, Cherokees and Civil War legends, cougars and Child ballads, moonshine and white water—was not.

It was ten minutes until showtime, and still people were filing in. There was hardly an empty seat anywhere. Spencer glanced about him, a little embarrassed to be here at all, and hoping he wouldn't be seen by anyone from Hamelin and hailed as a country-music groupie. He looked at the assortment of faces in the rows near his seat, wondering if he had anything in common with any of them. Aside from this one mutual obsession. They weren't the concert crowd he'd expected. There was a smattering of teenagers, but there were just as many people over sixty. Most of the audience seemed to range in age from twenty-five to fifty: heavy-set women with frizzy hair, urban cowboys in Harley-Davidson T-shirts, dowdy suburbanites wearing polyester finery and brass chain necklaces from Leggett's, and a smattering of wheat-germ folks with tanned, preppy faces and jogging suits. Spencer wondered if he was overdressed for the occasion. He was wearing his tweed jacket and the navy fisherman's sweater that his mother had given him for Christmas. The Judds would be decked out in sequins, but it wasn't as if they could see into the audience. Everyone else looked like they had just come from Kmart. He wondered if he still looked like a cop out of uniform. He still thought like one. He studied the faces, looking for images from mug-shot books, signs of drug taking, or the hostile leer of a mean drunk. He wasn't even in Wake County. Strictly speaking, trouble here would be none of his business, but still he looked. He hoped there wouldn't be any trouble, though. She deserved better than that.

A local disc jockey, pressed into service as master of ceremonies, climbed up on the stage, clutching the microphone as if he were tempted to burst into song himself. The thunderous applause was not for him. It was all anticipation for the Judds, the main attraction. But there was more between the crowd and their idols than the disc jockey in the velvet tux. To justify the eighteen-dollar ticket price to an audience for whom that was half a day's pay, another act was booked into the concert for padding, and they must be endured before the magic could begin.

Spencer sighed, and put his program away as the houselights dimmed. He'd already read it through twice, but he'd rather go through it again than have to wait in darkness with nothing to keep him occupied except the warm-up group.

The cowboy band that opened the show received a flurry of polite applause. Spencer forgot their name as soon as he heard it. He listened impatiently to the blare of noise from their guitars, and wished that the promoters had used the time to show a Judds video, or slides of their career. He didn't want to be distracted from the object of tonight's concert. He felt the impatience all around him as well.

He sat in the blaring darkness trying not to think about death. The tensions of the past few weeks wouldn't go away; it was one of the hazards of his job. He was supposed to be off-duty, relaxing at a concert, and yet he felt that he was attending a memorial service. This was the Judds' farewell tour, because Naomi Judd had been stricken with an incurable disease, and now a host of her loyal followers had crowded into the coliseum to say good-bye. It was a funeral with T-shirt sales. He felt like a fool for being there, and even more because he minded so much that Naomi Judd was dying.

Spencer felt a twinge of guilt. Had he minded this much about Tammy Robsart? He had felt genuine regret at her terrible death, and for Morgan Robsart's loss, but the sorrow had not lingered. He'd even caught himself thinking that the boy might be better off with a middle-class guardian; that maybe it was his only chance to escape the cycle of crime and poverty that sucked every generation of Robsarts down to the bottom of society. He remembered seeing Tammy and her son on the hillside in December, waiting for the Santa Claus train. There had been such a light of pride in the young mother's eyes when she looked at the little blond boy. She never had a chance at a better life. She had died because she was too poor to get by without a space heater, and because her ramshackle trailer was a death trap. And now she wouldn't even know how her beloved son's life turned out. Surely hers was the greater loss.

At least Diana Ellen Judd Strickland had taken a wonderful ride on the cosmic carousel, before she lost her balance. In a career spanning eight years, she and her daughter had won the Country Music Association Vocal Duo of the Year Award six times, and just about every other honor in the business as well. Four Grammys, a slew of awards from *Billboard* and *Cashbox*, and tributes from half a dozen other arbiters of musical achievement. They had made it.

It was an Appalachian fairy tale. At twenty, Diana Judd must have seemed as doomed as Tammy Robsart. She was already pregnant when she married at seventeen. At twenty-five she was divorced, and raising two kids on too little money. But she managed to beat the odds. First nursing school back in Morrill, Kentucky, then a nursing career, and finally a kitchen-table demo tape of her singing with her teenage daughter, in the tight mountain harmony like spun gold. At the hospital Nurse Judd badgered a patient's father into taking the demo tape to RCA, and from that

came an audition. A series of small, random moves suddenly
made everything fall into place, transforming pretty nurse
Diana into the Queen of Everything: Naomi Judd. She could
have reigned for decades on her voice and her style, but she
developed an illness, and that was the end of it. The glory
hadn't lasted long enough, but at least she had been given
it. If she died young, she would become the female Elvis, a
bluegrass Madonna canonized by the love of her fans, because they had to keep believing that dreams came true for
people who lived in trailers.

The roar from the crowd shook the rafters. Spencer stood
up with the rest of them, and applauded as the two auburn-
haired women walked to center stage and greeted the cheering darkness. Naomi Judd was as beautiful as ever in her
gold lamé costume with a full skirt that made him think
of square dancing. Wynonna, her rawboned daughter, was
dressed in black, and carrying her guitar, but Spencer barely
spared her a glance. This was Naomi's night. He watched
the way she slinked across stage, like a cat dancing among
the footlights. When Wynonna sang lead, Naomi would
stand like a candle in her pink spotlight, with such serenity
that you never realized that she must be counting measures,
and thinking of the notes she would sing. She glowed. She
laughed. She teased the stagehands. He had never seen anyone look so radiant, so far from death's door. He tried to
remember every detail of the performance, to save the joy
of it for later, when—wherever Diana was—Naomi would
be gone.

Toward the end of the performance "Mama Judd"
thanked the crowd for their support and their prayers. She
talked about faith and beating the odds against chronic ac-
tive hepatitis. Then Wynonna chorded a note, and they
began to sing a slow, sad song. It was several moments
before Spencer glanced away from the stage, his attention
caught by the flicker of lights in the darkened hall. People in

the bleachers were standing up, holding lit matches, candles, cigarette lighters. Their tiny flames flickered in the darkness, illuminating tears on the solemn faces: burning prayers or just an eternal flame to say good-bye?

Spencer fumbled for his cigarette lighter, the one he used to light emergency flares at wrecks. He held the sputtering flame aloft, feeling not at all foolish in this steel-raftered cathedral with concrete floors and bleachers. He felt his eyes sting, and a tightness gather in his throat, but the sadness was gone. He was paying tribute to a legend. If God granted miracles by majority vote, Naomi Judd would live another hundred years.

On Ashe Mountain the wind shook the tree branches, and the windows rattled. Nora Bonesteel's white house seemed to huddle on the mountaintop facing the dark shape of the Hangman, invisible on this cloudy night. The dry grass of winter rustled in the meadow as if unseen feet were trampling in the darkness, but in the surrounding forest all was still. No deer moved in the thickets, and no rabbits scurried beneath the trees to become owl's prey. The only life on the mountaintop centered around the flicker of orange light reflected in one window of the little house.

Nora Bonesteel's face shone in the firelight. She had moved her chair close to the hearth, both for warmth and for illumination to work by. In her lap lay a quilt of velvet and satin, catching the light in patches of emerald and crimson. Her fingers worked silently amid the moving shadows, unraveling a seam of black thread with the point of a needle. She could not sleep. Each time she closed her eyes a swirl of faces and voices would close in on her, driving her back to full consciousness. She felt cold from the inside out.

Finally, she got out of bed, built up the fire with applewood and hickory, and took out her basket of needlework.

After a few minutes of embroidery on a tea towel, she realized what she wanted to work on: the graveyard quilt that
she'd made last fall when the hovering feeling had come
over her and wouldn't go away. She took the quilt out of
the cedar blanket chest in the hall and looked at it in the
firelight.

The blue satin mountains shone against the white muslin,
and the embroidered cemetery was flawlessly stitched together with tapestry thread in rich jewel colors. She had
finished the quilt last autumn. The edging was done, the
detail of the scene was picked out in tiny, even stitches, and
the design was balanced, needing no further elaboration.

Why, then, did she feel compelled to work on this finished
piece? She ran her fingers along the velvet border, searching
for imperfections. When her rough forefinger touched satin,
she stopped. Two satin rectangles remained on the black
border of the graveyard quilt. Four others were sewn firmly
into place beneath white embroidered headstones in the
center.

With a sigh, Nora picked up an unthreaded needle and
began to pick away the loosely stitched thread from one of
the remaining coffins on the hem. The quilt was not yet
finished.

CHAPTER

15

I have a rendezvous with Death
On some scarred slope of battered hill,
When Spring comes round again this year
And the first meadow flowers appear.

—ALAN SEEGER,
"I Have a Rendezvous with Death"

The rains began in March, always a wet month in the Southern mountains. Sometimes it was snow—once, when Spencer was in grade school, it had snowed every Monday in March without melting in between, giving the children the best sledding of their lives and keeping them schoolbound till mid-June, making up snow days. Lately, though, the winters had been milder, and the rains brought out the daffodils and the redbud before winter was over. There had been one good snow last week, and it was still sitting on the ground waiting for a thaw when the rains began. "Bad combination," the old-timers said. "Better set up the flood watches tonight. Them creeks is gonna go."

Spencer stood at his office window watching the leaden sheets of rain pelt the street. The rain made shining puddles in the asphalt, and swirled along the curbing like tiny mountain streams. It had been raining for three days now, and the pall of slate skies and pervading damp penetrated even the fluorescent brightness of the sheriff's office, creating a chill that belied the thermostat. Spring seemed a thousand years away.

Joe LeDonne strolled in, flipping through the mail, and glanced out at the curtain of rain. "Is that supposed to be a costume or not?" He pointed to Vernon Woolwine, who was hurrying toward the café for his morning doughnut.

He was slouched low against the onslaught of rain, hands thrust deep in his pockets. He was wearing a yellow plastic raincoat and matching rubber boots.

"Could be Paddington Bear," called Martha, who had been observing Vernon from her own window.

"Or Spencer Tracy in *Captains Courageous,*" Spencer suggested.

LeDonne turned away. "Maybe he just doesn't want to get wet."

Spencer reached for the pile of letters. "Anything interesting?"

"Letter from the army," said LeDonne, trying to sound disinterested. "Probably a response to my inquiry about Justin Warren. About damn time."

"Well, unless he's wanted for mass murder, you'd better be prepared to put his case on the back burner for a while," said the sheriff. "We may be on flood duty before long. How are you doing on the Underhill investigation?"

"I talked to my psychologist in Knoxville. He says they may be suffering from a form of delayed shock, a reaction to the murders. Definitely they need counseling. He thinks we may be able to persuade them to get help by offering not to prosecute them for grave robbing if they seek treatment for mental disturbance. Not that we're going to prosecute, anyway, if it's just grave tampering, because Withrow doesn't want the word to get out that we have ghouls in Wake County."

"You haven't spoken with the Underhills yet, have you?"

"No. I wanted to take my time with this one. Check out the laws. Get the cemetery to exhume the body. Talk to the shrink. Talk to the jeweler in Johnson City and get him to identify their photos. All that is done now. I'm just trying to figure out what it means."

Spencer nodded. "Just how crazy are they? Were they the ones who killed the family?"

"That's what I've been trying to decide. And I just don't know yet. Remember that dead rabbit at the scene that we couldn't make sense of? That could be another indication of Satanist behavior. Animal sacrifice."

"Did you talk to their teachers?"

"Yeah. They weren't much help. Nobody noticed any signs of cult behavior in either of them."

"Being a teenager *is* cult behavior," said Martha. "The girl was a churchgoer, though. Remember, Joe? She sang at the Christmas service."

"I wouldn't expect it to be her, anyway," said Spencer.

LeDonne said, "I guess I'll take a ride out there if this rain ever lets up. Figured you might need me around, though, while the weather is this bad. If the temperature drops five degrees, we're going to have more wrecks than John ever saw."

Spencer smiled at this use of a mountain expression. His mother sometimes used that phrase, too, but as far as he could tell, no one who said it remembered who "John" was.

"We may have more trouble than wrecks," said Martha from the doorway. "If this rain doesn't let up, every creek in this county will leap the banks. We'd better start calling around for boats."

Spencer took his khaki raincoat from the oak coat stand by the door. "I think it's time we started riding the roads," he said. "We may have to block off some sections where bridges are submerged. Martha, start phoning people with boats, and rounding them up for emergency duty. We'll radio in to tell you the trouble spots, and you mark them on the county map there."

"The Underhills' house is pretty close to the Little Dove. It's not much of a problem normally, but with all this rain, it might be," said LeDonne. "Maybe I ought to get them out of there."

"Not yet," said Spencer. "Let's wait and see how bad things are first."

The hospital room seemed to be composed of shades of gray. Even the window, with its view of distant hills, offered only pewter-colored variations: a sheet of rain and a clabbered sky. Taw McBryde was tired of the bleakness, not so much for his own sake, but for Tavy. His last glimpse of earth should be a better sight than this one. He wished his friend could hold on until spring, when the world would be green and gold and warm, but perhaps such a glorious place would be harder to leave behind than this one.

Tavy seemed to have left the world already, though, the way he lay there, parchment-faced, staring at nothing. For days now he had been letting go, an inch at a time, and now he was nearly ready to fall back and let his life slip away. He seldom spoke. Maybe he didn't even care if there was anyone in the room with him or not, but still Taw felt that he could not leave. He wouldn't have it on his conscience that he had left his best friend to die alone. So he sat in the plastic chair next to the bed, sleeping in catnaps, and waiting to see if Tavy needed anything, or had any final message to impart before he moved on.

Taw had hoped that the crusade against the paper company would fuel Tavy's resistance and make him want to live, but the hopelessness of a decade of litigation had not proved inspiring. Fighting a major corporation took more strength than most people had, and the victories were few. Tavy no longer seemed to care. When Taw tried to start up a conversation on the subject, his friend would answer in monosyllables, without even bothering to turn his head.

Taw looked up at the blank television screen, wishing

that something besides soap operas came on in the daytime. He had tried everything he knew to amuse Tavy, even a round of five-card stud, but nothing could penetrate the cotton wool between Tavy Annis and the world.

The tap at the door came as a welcome relief. He went to let in the visitor, expecting someone from the church with another potted plant, but he found that it was their lawyer, Dallas Stuart, who had stopped by to pay his last respects. Stuart was a few years older than they were, but they remembered him from the old days. Nobody had reckoned him exactly brilliant, but he was decent, and he worked hard. Taw hadn't considered hiring anybody else when he thought they might need a lawyer. He stood there now in his hat and a dripping black raincoat, looking like a man who has made a left turn into a funeral procession and can't think how to get out. He opened his umbrella and set it under the sink to dry out and then approached the sickbed with a look of solemn apprehension.

"How is he?" murmured Stuart, glancing toward the still form on the bed.

"He can still talk," said Taw. "He's just dozing right now. I'll wake him up."

Before Stuart could protest, Taw walked to his friend's bedside, and gently shook him awake. "Mr. Stuart's here," he said softly. "He's probably going to tell us there's a posse surrounding the hospital right now."

A smile flickered on Tavy Annis's transparent face. "Never take me alive," he rasped.

"So what's the good word, Counselor?" asked Taw. The bravado was for Tavy's sake. "Do we old desperadoes have to flee to Bolivia, or what?"

Dallas Stuart ran his fingers around the brim of his felt hat, looking nervously from one man to the other. He sat down in the straight-backed chair beside the nightstand and thought for a moment about what he ought to say. "Boys,

I'm just a simple country lawyer," he said at last. "I'm not any Ralph Nader or a muckraker like that fellow on *60 Minutes*, so I might not be the best person in the world to advise you in this matter. But you know I care about you and about the rest of the people here in the valley, so I'm doing what I can." He shook his head. "I have to tell you, though, y'all are the first clients I've ever had that flat-out *tried* to get arrested."

Taw laughed and slapped his knee. "How are we doing so far?"

"I don't know what to tell you boys," said Dallas Stuart. Men of his generation called their peers boys at any age shy of a century. "You can't force a man to press charges, and I hate to tell you this, but Roger Sheridan of Titan Paper Company claims he never heard of you two. Swears it never happened. I believe your side of the story, because I don't think you could make up anything that outlandish, but I can't get anybody to arrest you without a complaint, and there's not going to be one from Titan."

"What do they think we are—cranks?" Taw's voice was too loud for the little white room.

"No," said Tavy in a whisper like dry grass. "Martyrs. And they're afraid."

"We need to get arrested, Mr. Stuart," said Taw.

"I don't think you can count on it, boys. The paper company doesn't want the publicity."

"Then we'll think of something else," said Taw.

Dallas Stuart nodded toward the eggshell man swallowed in the bedsheets. "I don't think he can fight anymore," he whispered.

"No," said Taw. "But I can."

Maggie Underhill pressed her nose to the front window, and stared out at the sheet of water stretching from the edge of the far woods to the house itself. There should have been a field, a county road, and a concrete low-water bridge between the Underhills' home and the stand of pines on an upland slope, but those landmarks had vanished beneath the tide of coffee-colored river water spilling over its banks, swollen with runoff from the mountain streams. The river had jumped its banks a day ago, and the bridge was swallowed by the deluge sometime during the night. Now the torrent was swirling around the porch railings, and Maggie could see objects floating past: logs, porch chairs, wooden crates, and tires. Once she saw the side of a white metal object sailing through the original channel; a refrigerator, perhaps, or an old washing machine. Was it a junked appliance, or had someone's house washed away?

Maggie wasn't afraid. She couldn't imagine a house being swept away by something so harmless as the Little Dove. She could remember seeing the cows wading in the river in the dryest days of summer, when it was hardly more than ankle-deep and so studded with rocks that you could walk from one side to the other without getting your feet wet.

The brown tide that surged past her now looked nothing like last summer's sluggish stream. But there was a silky look to it; smooth, as if you could snuggle down in it and go to sleep. She wondered if she and Mark ought to do anything about the flood. Call someone? But the phone didn't seem to work anymore. The only one who ever called was Josh, and when Maggie tried to dial a number, the phone was silent in her ear, so she had given up trying. She wished Josh would call her now, and tell her what to do about the water. There wasn't any point in discussing anything with Mark. He stayed shut up in his room now, playing music so loud that she could feel the vibrations in her chest. He no longer talked to her about the money, or his plans to find the number of the bank account. Now he stalked past her in the hall as if she were a stranger, muttering to himself. She wondered when he ate and slept, and if he ever bathed. If she told him about the torrent of water lapping against the house, would he listen?

Maggie felt a rush of cold at her feet, and for an instant she thought that cold fingers had reached for her ankle, but when she looked down, she saw that rivulets of water were sliding across the wooden floor. Water seeped in under the front door, and up through cracks between the pine boards, making the floor shine like a mirror. She ran for the stairs, calling out for Joshua.

Shiloh Church sat on high ground, just at the crest of a rolling hill, so expertly graded by nature or the road builders that the incline was hardly noticeable. Now, though, nature had made its lofty aspect apparent: The church and its parking lot sat ringed by oaks and yellow fields, an island in a muddy sea that stretched across the valley from ridge to ridge.

Half a dozen muddy cars were in the parking lot; mostly four-wheel drives. But nearest the door sat Laura Bruce's little white Chevrolet. She had arrived at nine that morning, with Morgan Robsart, sporting a blue-and-yellow rubber raincoat and new boots, in tow. He was in the Sunday school room with two little girls and his entire arsenal of toy weapons, while Laura and a handful of volunteers readied the church to become an emergency shelter.

"Of course, it may come to nothing," Jane Arrowood had told Laura that morning when she phoned. "But my son Spencer said he'd be patrolling the roads today, looking for flooded sections and washed-out bridges. Usually at times like this we get the church set up to take flood victims, and to dispense coffee and hot meals to the rescue workers. I can stay as long as I'm needed. If you don't feel up to it, I'm sure we can find enough Circle members to handle it."

"Of course I'll come," said Laura. "I'll bring all our extra food and blankets and meet you there in half an hour."

"Are you sure you're all right?" Jane asked. "It could be a very long day, and if heavy flooding comes, we may not be able to get you home tonight."

"Never mind," said Laura. "I'm tired of looking at these same walls, anyhow."

Fortunately, there were no bridges to cross between her little house on the ridge and Shiloh Church, but still Laura drove slowly, watching for the shine of water on the pavement ahead, and marveling at the strangeness of the familiar road. Fields and fences had vanished beneath a brown coverlet, making it difficult at times for her to tell where she was. Once, she saw white chickens perched in tree branches at the side of the road: someone in the lowlands had turned his livestock loose to fend for themselves until the waters subsided.

Beside her in his child seat, Morgan Robsart gazed solemnly at the clacking wiper blades diverting the rain into streams at either side of the windshield. "It sure is raining hard," he remarked at one point.

"Sure is," said Laura. "But we'll be all right."

"I know," said Morgan. "If it keeps raining like this, there can't be any fires."

Jane Arrowood was already at the church when Laura arrived. By the time they had got the coffee going in the church's forty-cup percolator, Barbara Givens came in, followed by her sister-in-law. Marynell Weaver, the scoutmaster's wife, arrived at ten, with her four-wheel drive loaded down with sleeping bags and the troop's supply of camping food. Two more owners of four-wheel drives arrived during the course of the morning, bringing preschoolers who were sent off to the Sunday school room to play with Morgan.

"How bad is it likely to be?" asked Laura. She smeared

another slice of bread with peanut butter. The metal tray in front of her was piled high with newly made sandwiches.

"It was worse in the old days," said Jane Arrowood. "The TVA put dams on the wildest rivers. Now it's just the Little Dove, which usually doesn't amount to much, and the little creeks that overflow when it rains too hard and too fast. Everyone should be all right if they don't try to drive across submerged bridges. We almost always lose somebody whose car gets swept away in the current. I don't know why people never learn."

Laura thought it over. "There's an unreal quality about it," she said. "People cross a bridge every single day, and then one day the sleepy little creek drowns the bridge. But tomorrow it will be safe again—a two-second drive to get to the other side. What can happen in two seconds?"

"A lot," said Jane. "Other than that, people ought to be all right. Some of the houses on the floodplain will have underwater living rooms, but most of those folks are used to it by now, and they'll have enough sense to get out. I'm expecting the Arnetts to walk in any minute now, bringing the baby, the cat, and the color television. They're used to it."

"Why don't they leave?"

"It's their land. Besides, they know the signs. Lowlanders can smell a flood long before the rest of us know it's coming. If you live next to a creek, you get to know it."

Laura set down the knife. Her eyes were wide. "Suppose you lived by the creek but you *didn't* know the signs?"

"Then somebody would have to come and get you," said Jane, opening another loaf of bread. "That's why the volunteers are out rounding up boats."

"But suppose they don't reach the house in time?"

Jane Arrowood shook her head. "They do the best they can. That's all any of us can do."

Laura was already untying the apron from around her

waist. "I have to go," she said. "When you were talking about people who live in floodplains, I suddenly thought of the Underhills' house. It's not more than a hundred feet from the riverbed. And they wouldn't know to get out."

"We'll tell the first group of rescue volunteers we see," said Jane. "Or I can call Martha at the sheriff's department and have her radio a message to Spencer. Don't you try to go—in your condition."

"I'm the guardian of Mark and Maggie Underhill," said Laura. "They're my responsibility. Besides, it would take too long to wait for the volunteers to show up, or to call the sheriff. Who knows what part of the county he's in? And he may have enough to handle right now. If I go now, before it gets any worse, I can have them here in half an hour. You'll watch Morgan for me, won't you?"

Jane Arrowood sighed in exasperation. "I hope the Lord thinks a lot of you," she said. "At least take one of the four-wheels instead of that dinky little thing you drive!"

Spencer Arrowood felt the chill all the way to his bones. He had spent a long morning navigating rain-slicked roads, trying to gauge the severity of the rising water. In Hamelin the problems were confined to flooded basements and low spots in a couple of residential streets that had turned into ponds. He'd closed the flooded section of those streets with wooden barricades, and then radioed Martha to make sure that the school board had decided to release the county's students early that day. The rain showed no sign of letting up, and he didn't want those school buses waiting another hour to depart. The streets of Hamelin were no problem, but the county roads, some of them gravel surfaced, could be treacherous.

Spencer's inspection of the main county roads and bridges had been punctuated by calls from Martha, with reports of

stalled-out cars, and one fender bender. By the time he finished rescuing the stranded motorists, he was soaking wet,
and starving, but he still had miles of territory to cover, so
he stopped at a country store for a candy bar, and checked
in with Martha to let her know where he was.

"I think we'd better get the boats out," he told her. "People in the low parts of the valley are going to be treading
water soon, if they aren't already."

"I'm way ahead of you," said Martha. "I asked the radio
station to air a request for volunteers. Le Donne and Millie
Fortnum are meeting with them at the rescue-squad building. We've got an emergency shelter being set up at the high
school gym, and your mother called to say that Shiloh
Church is accepting refugees out in Dark Hollow. Anything
else?"

"That's fine, Martha," said Spencer, taken aback by his
dispatcher's efficiency. "You've done a good job." Martha
seemed to be gaining in confidence lately, and she was
showing initiative and ability beyond what anyone expected
in a dispatcher. He wondered if she had been reading self-
help books, or if proximity to LeDonne was giving her
strength. Whatever it was, he was pleased.

"I'm heading out to Dark Hollow now," he told her.
"Maybe I'll stop in and say hello to my mother. See if they
need anything out there."

"Ten-four, Sheriff," said Martha cheerfully. "Get a sandwich while you're there."

If it had been any other errand—a drive to work or a run
for groceries—Laura Bruce would have turned back before she had gone a mile. Even in Barbara Givens's four-
wheel, she felt frightened. The wind blew ripples of water
across the road, forcing her to drive at twenty miles per
hour even on the straightaways. She tried not to look at

the shining fields and woods, inundated by floodwaters that crept higher and closer to the road with each passing minute.

She put her hand to her abdomen, where the dead child lay. She would not have risked this journey if there had been another life at stake besides her own, but then she would have had to endure the guilt of not going. The odd thing was that she was glad to be out here, despite the danger, the cold, and her own diminished physical strength. She had a mission. She was needed. She had always resented the male characterization of war: that man the warrior would go off to perilous shores and have adventures, while the Penelopes of the world waited at home, safely tending the garden, mending clothes, and putting their lives on hold until the heroes returned. Yet there was Will in a tent somewhere in the Gulf, watching television, playing cards, and trying to drum up a little business for God, while all the adventure lay back home. She could have— *should have*—waited for the county rescue squad to evacuate the Underhills, but she had been seized with the idea that God meant her to go. It was just like Him to let the trained professional in His service sit around, and then draft some complete amateur to do the job. She smiled into the soggy gloom, and thought of the consoling letter she would write her husband: *They also serve who only stand and wait.*

By the time she crept around the bend to the Underhills' road, Laura had convinced herself that she was a warrior of the Lord, equal to just about anything except parting the waters. The sight that lay before her dimmed that belief to a flicker. Fifty feet in front of the car, where the road sloped down off the hill and into the bottomland where the Underhills' house stood, there was a swift brown river gliding along where there should have been a road, a bridge, and a yard. Logs, crates, an old car flowed past her, pulled by the current of the swollen river. Two hundred yards away the white farmhouse stood like an island in the newly spawned river, dividing the current with its bulk. The waves were as high as the porch, but the water on the other side of the house seemed shallower, perhaps because it was farther from the riverbed. Beyond the house the land rose upward into a hill that was still well above the flood line. Laura could see a dirt track used by hunters snaking its way up the side of the hill, but there was no way to get to it through the torrent of rushing water in the once placid river.

"Maybe they've had enough sense to get out," she said aloud. "They could go out the back door of the house, and go up the ridge to safety."

She blew the horn, four long blasts, to alert anyone who was in the house that help had arrived—or tried to. An upstairs curtain moved, and she saw a face—she wasn't sure whose. They were still there.

Laura thought for a moment about the roads and ridges of the county back country. What was on the other side of that range of hills? She closed her mind, picturing the roads and the connections between clusters of houses. That must be 283 on the other side, she thought. There's a general store and half a dozen houses somewhere along that stretch of road. How do I get there?

Mentally, she retraced her steps. *Go back up the hill and continue on the main road until you get to the 283 turnoff.* The bridge there was a high metal span with overhead supports. It would still be well above the crest of the flood, and just past that bridge, the road began to climb onto a plateau between the mountains. They would be far removed from the dangers of the current.

Carefully, she began to back the car up the road. She didn't want to risk turning around on the narrow one-lane road surrounded by the relentless brown tide. Then she would cross the high bridge to 283 and walk over the ridge to the Underhills' back door. God always had to do everything the hard way.

Joe LeDonne was warm and dry in the rescue-squad building, clipboard in hand, and surrounded by a score of people in rain gear, all talking at once. He would rather be anywhere else. Not that he liked water. When he was a kid in Gallipolis, Ohio, LeDonne had heard the old-timers talk about the floods that used to sweep through the town before they built the flood walls. He had learned early on that water couldn't be trusted. In LeDonne's world, not much could.

Most people never seemed to learn to distrust water, though. A little way south of his hometown, there was the Tug River, on the Kentucky–West Virginia border: it would flood every year, driving the same families from the same little bottomland houses. They'd shovel the mud out and move back, and every third year or so, the house would wash away altogether, and they'd build again in the same damned spot. He never could figure out why people were such damned fools as to live in a floodplain, and worse— fool enough to go back again and again.

It wasn't just the folly of it all that annoyed him, though. He had been jumpy and irritable for days. This endless spring rain, and the flooding it caused, took him back to Southeast Asia, where it seemed to rain perpetually. He hated the sound of the rain and the feel of wet socks against his skin. He wanted very much to get out of this building, and start heading up a rescue operation. His dislike of water was nothing compared to his hatred of being bullied by his past.

"Excuse me, Deputy. I heard on the radio that you could use some volunteers."

LeDonne looked up from his clipboard and found himself face-to-face with Justin Warren, the weekend warrior. He was wearing an olive-drab raincoat and combat boots. Behind him stood half a dozen of his "recruits," also decked out in foul-weather gear.

"Stallings here has a boat," Warren said.

LeDonne's eyes narrowed. "*You* want to join the rescue operation?"

"Sure. It's good experience. Command situation, dealing with danger. Needs discipline and good reflexes. Besides, we're in good shape, and we know the terrain. Tell us what you need done."

Millie Fortnum appeared at LeDonne's elbow. "More volunteers? Good! Come with me."

"Put these guys with my outfit," LeDonne told her. "We'll take a couple of the boats and do evacuations." He turned to Justin Warren. "I thought you might need some supervision. And I believe I outrank you, Warren." He said it slowly and then waited, as if he could say more but wasn't going to.

Justin Warren nodded. "I expect you do."

The records check on Warren had come through clean. He had no criminal record or history of bad credit. He had no military record, either. None. LeDonne had been planning a ride out to Justin Warren's camp to share this news with the sunshine soldiers, but this wasn't the time to go into it. At least this new willingness to help was a healthier pastime than Warren usually practiced. LeDonne wanted to see how he behaved in a real emergency.

"Come on," said LeDonne. "Let's see what they want us to do." A group of volunteers was climbing into the back of a covered pickup truck, ready to be driven out for flood duty. LeDonne saw Vernon Woolwine, still dressed like Paddington Bear, hoisting his bulk over the tailgate, yellow boots waving in the air. For the first time all day, the deputy smiled.

Maggie Underhill turned away from the window in the up-stairs hall. She had heard the car horn and looked out, but she could not tell who was there. They couldn't get across, though. The brackish river had come back from the dead. She looked out at the swirling currents eddying among the oak trees in what had been the front yard. It reminded her of something. What was it?

"Who was that?" Mark Underhill stood in the doorway of his room, unshaven and disheveled. "What did they want?"

Maggie twisted a strand of her dark hair. "It was a car, up on the road. I expect they wanted us to come out on account of the water."

He didn't seem to hear her. "Government agents," he said, nodding to himself. "They know that I have the num-ber of the secret bank account. They've come after it."

"They can't reach us," said Maggie. "The bridge is under water."

"I'm going to get the tooth," said Mark. "They might try to sneak into the shed when it gets dark."

Maggie looked out at the wooden toolshed in the side yard under an oak. Water was swirling around it, but it seemed solid enough. "I'll go with you," she called out. He was already clumping down the stairs. She heard the splash as he reached the ground floor. The water was now an ankle-deep stream, the color of coffee with milk. Maggie went down the stairs, still trying to talk to Mark, but he wasn't listening.

The water lapped at the baseboards of the downstairs rooms, and eddied around the chairs. Tin cans, cups, and other bits of flotsam drifted along in the current. Maggie waded into the swirling brown water, holding the skirt of her velvet robe above her knees as she went. Mark splashed over to the front door and pulled it open, ignoring the crest of water that surged inward. He swayed a little, and nearly fell as he lurched onto the front porch. Maggie called after him, but the door slammed behind him, leaving her alone.

Suddenly, the phone began to ring.

With a last look at the door, Maggie made her way through the icy water to the kitchen, and picked up the receiver. She hoped Josh couldn't see the crusted food on the table, and the empty cans lying about on the coun-tertops. Mark never threw anything away, and lately she hadn't seemed to care. It seemed easier to stop eating.

"Hello, Maggie." His voice was as calm and comforting as ever.

"Hello, Josh. I'm sorry about the mess. I'll clean it up later. Listen, I have to go and help Mark. He's outside, and—"

"No, Maggie. Don't go out there."

"But he just went to the shed, and there's water all over the yard, and—"

"Mark isn't your problem, Maggie. Let's worry about you. If you do as I say, everything will be all right. I'm here. I'll take care of you. I always took care of you."

Maggie pulled a kitchen chair close to the phone, and stood on it. Her feet were freezing. She wanted to ask more about Mark, but she could tell from Josh's tone of voice that he didn't want to talk about it. Just like he never wanted to talk about Mom. "What should I do, Josh?"

"Stay here and talk to me, Maggie. Just keep standing on the chair. The rain can't last forever. Why don't you sing something? A hymn would be nice."

It took Laura Bruce forty-five minutes to reach the other side of the ridge. As she had predicted, there was little evidence of flooding in the higher valley. The ditches beside the road were overflowing, but except for a few sloping patches, the road was clear. When she reached the tiny grocery store in Boone's Run, she stopped, and ran in to ask for directions.

The old man behind the counter looked pleased to see a customer, but when he noticed that she was pregnant, he said, "You oughtn't to be out in weather like this."

Laura nodded. "I'll be in quick as I can. I just need to know where to turn to find the hunters' road that comes out at the Underhills' farm."

The storekeeper shook his head. "Never heard tell of that place," he said.

"Well, do you have a county map?"

He shook his head. "Never needed one. Lived here all my life."

Laura turned to leave when another thought occurred to her. "Wait," she said. "You probably know that farm by its old name. What was it? I know I've heard people say it a dozen times. The Tylers? Tillers?"

"Tilden?" said the old man. "You mean the Tilden place over the ridge in Dark Hollow? Well, there's an old dirt logging road that goes over the mountain, but you don't want to take that in this weather. It's awful steep, and there could be mud slides."

"I'll be careful," Laura promised. "But there are children in that farmhouse, and that's the fastest way to get them out." Seeing the doubt on his face, she added, "My husband is with me. We'll be fine."

"That's all right, then," he said happily. "I reckon a man can handle it. It's down the road about three-quarters of a mile, just past the red barn on the left."

Laura Bruce thanked him and hurried away before he could follow her to the door and see that she was alone.

Three minutes later, she spotted the barn, surrounded by

a dejected group of muddy Herefords standing knee-deep in mud. She turned off at the gravel road that twisted through fields and up the wooded mountainside in a series of twists and turns. She would drive as far as she could, as long as there was no danger of getting stuck or sliding off the mountain. She hoped she wouldn't have far to walk. She wasn't sure how long a wooden house could hold against the current, and if the water behind the house was more than knee-deep, she wouldn't be able to get to them at all.

When Spencer Arrowood arrived at Shiloh Church, he was dripping with mud and shivering. The church kitchen and meeting room were filling up with bedraggled people, wrapped in blankets or winter coats. Some of them were drinking coffee or eating a bowl of Barbara Givens's home-made vegetable soup.

Jane Arrowood saw him in the doorway, and the corners of her mouth twitched, but she managed not to laugh. Instead, she picked up a plastic tablecloth and hurried over to him. "I can't have you messing up a good blanket, Spencer." She held it out to him at arm's length. "Go and wash up while I fix you a sandwich. Then you can tell me what happened to you."

"Nothing to tell," said Spencer, shrugging out of his raincoat. He draped it on the back of a chair. "Some fool woman got her car stuck, that's all. I had to put my shoulder to the bumper to get her out." He went over to the sink and washed the mud off his hands and face. "Can you spare a bowl of that soup?"

"That's what it's here for," said Jane. She handed him a bowl and a teaspoon. "How are things out there?"

"We haven't lost any lives yet. Not that I know of. But the rescue squad has started getting people out of some of the houses along the creeks." He sat down on one of the benches, and began to eat the soup. "You've got a good crowd here."

"Yes. They'll have some shoveling out to do tomorrow or the next day, but at least they're safe and warm for now. Barbara has half a dozen little ones in the Sunday school room. She's telling them jack tales. Morgan Robsart is there, Spencer."

The sheriff's spoon paused in midair. "What's he doing here? The pastor's house is on high ground. Oh, of course. Mrs. Bruce is here helping out. Where is she?"

"I was hoping you'd seen her. She went to get the Underhill children."

"How long ago?"

"An hour, I think. Things have been so hectic here."

Spencer stood up. "I'll radio in, and see if the rescue squad knows anything about them. If nobody's gone out there, I'll go after her. What did you let her go for?"

Jane Arrowood sighed. "I hoped she'd have the sense to go for help if the way was blocked."

"Maybe she has," said Spencer. "I'll call and see."

The four-wheel drive made it up the hill to the crest of the mountain, and down the other side to within sight of the Underhill farm. Laura parked in a wide clearing on one of the cuts in the mountain. The ground there was too rocky to get stuck in, and she would be able to turn the vehicle around when it was time to leave. She got out of the car, and began to walk slowly down the mountain. She had the waddling gait of late pregnancy, and she had to work at keeping her balance on the slippery slope. *"I'm in no shape for heroics,"* she said aloud. *"You should have thought of that, Lord."* The cold rain trickled down her neck, and droplets clung to her eyelashes.

The slope of the hill ended about thirty feet from the

back porch of the house. Laura could see that the water covered the backyard, but she wasn't able to tell the depth of it. She was near enough to call out to Mark and Maggie, though. She hoped that they could get across. She cupped her hands around her mouth, and called out Maggie's name. Her voice echoed above the rush of the water. Laura waited. The house looked like a derelict in the bleakness. Its paint was peeling, and there were rust spots on the roof, but it looked sturdy enough to stand against the tide. It would be cold and dark, though. No place for anyone to stay. She called out again. "Maggie! It's Laura Bruce! I've come to get you."

A minute passed. Perhaps two. Then the back door opened a little way, and finally Maggie Underhill stepped out, looking as gaunt as an old woman. She wore a rumpled black velvet robe, and her dark hair lay in tangles about her face. This is my fault, thought Laura. But there's no time to worry about it now. I mustn't frighten her.

Aloud she said, "Hello, Maggie! It's time to leave now. Can you tell how deep the water is between us?"

"I can't leave!" Maggie called out. "Josh is with me."

"Mark, you mean," said Laura, edging a few feet farther down the slope.

"No. Mark went out to the shed, and he hasn't come back." Maggie pointed to the side yard.

Laura looked in the direction she pointed. There was an old tree towering about the water, but no outbuilding. Churning water surged along where the shed had been. Laura closed her eyes for a moment. She mustn't think about that. She must get Maggie out.

"Please come over here, Maggie," she said, straining to keep her voice loud but calm. "We need to go to the church."

"I have to stay with Josh. He takes care of me."

"No, Maggie! He killed everyone else! He's not taking care of you. You have to come with me."

Maggie smiled. "You don't understand," she said. "He did it for us."

Spencer Arrowood knew better than to try to reach the Underhills by the low-water bridge in front of the farm. That would have been submerged hours ago. But he had to drive down there, anyway, just in case Laura Bruce had managed to get stuck or go off the road trying to reach the house. He radioed Martha to let her know where he was, but he didn't ask for backup; everyone else was busy enough with their own rescue operations.

He turned his windshield wipers to a slower speed. Was it his imagination, or was the rain slacking off? If the downpour would just stop, the floodwaters would recede in a matter of hours. If it didn't, they might have to call in National Guard troops to help with the crisis.

He reached the turnoff to the Underhill farm, and started slowly down the incline, searching the brown water for signs of a submerged vehicle. He saw no sign of Laura Bruce in the current or on the road ahead. Perhaps she had gone to phone for help. But he had to see about the Underhills. That meant taking the steel span farther downstream, and crossing the ridge from the other side. He picked up the radio transmitter to tell Martha that he'd be another hour at least.

Laura Bruce didn't know how long she could stand on the muddy hillside in the cold rain arguing with a mad girl, but she couldn't think of any alternative. She could not abandon Maggie Underhill. She wiped the rain out of her face with her forearm, and tried to think of something else to say. Maggie was standing on the covered porch stoop, insisting that Josh would take care of her. She was too far away to be reasoned with. They could only shout across thirty feet of floodwaters. If only she could get Maggie to wade over to her. *But*, thought Laura, *who in their right mind would wade out into a flooded, polluted river?*

The idea occurred to her then. It was worth a try, anyhow. After that, the only thing left would be for Laura to try to go across herself, or to turn back and waste an hour or more in summoning help. Laura called out, "Do you still remember your lines from the play? Can you say them now?"

Maggie Underhill looked puzzled. "Which lines?" She had not expected the conversation to veer in this direction.

Laura tried to remember the crucial part. "The lines that begin with 'There's rosemary, that's for remembrance . . .' "

Maggie Underhill nodded. " 'And there is pansies, that's for thoughts . . .' "

"Good. But can you act it out?"

She watched as Maggie parodied the giving of the flowers to various members of the court. The words of the speech were indistinct in the sound of the waters, but she could hear the change in cadence when Maggie began to sing. "Hey nonny, nonny," the song she sang as she went to her death.

"And then what did she do, Maggie?"

Maggie was already moving forward, though. Down the steps of the porch, and into the water, strewing imaginary flowers as she went. There was a serene smile on her face. It would probably be easier at this point to be the mad Ophelia than to be Maggie Underhill. The losses were fewer and less intense. *I'll have to go in and get her, though,* Laura thought. *Ophelia doesn't come out.*

She could see that the water was only knee-high on

Maggie, and that this far uphill from the swollen river, there was no current, just spillover from the channel. No heavy objects carried along by the flood. All the debris was borne by the current farther down the slope, at the front of the house. Laura held out her hands as she stepped off the bank and inched forward into the chocolate water. Maggie Underhill looked up at her and then beyond her to a spot on the hillside. She stopped strewing imaginary flowers into the tide.

"Josh!" she said, pointing to the muddy slope. "He's up on the hill."

Laura turned around. She saw the red four-wheel drive parked in the clearing, muddy to its chassis. She saw bare, wet trees lining the road and clumps of brown grass sticking to the red clay in the hillside. There was no one there. The hillside was as lifeless as the river itself.

It didn't matter, though. Maggie Underhill was walking toward her now, oblivious to the water surging around her. She moved steadily forward, smiling happily. Laura stood still and waited for her to come.

Maggie would have walked past her in her eagerness to reach her vision, but as she drew near, Laura took hold of her, and hugged her. "It's going to be all right now, Maggie," she said. "You're safe."

Maggie Underhill nodded absently. "Josh always sees to it that I'm safe."

Laura held on to Maggie, and they waded out of the flooded yard and began to climb the rain-slick slope. Once Laura fell, but Maggie helped her up. "I didn't really think I was Ophelia," she said. "I used to wish I could think so, though. But way back in my head, I'd know different."

"Good," said Laura. She felt an ache in her abdomen, and she took a gulp of air to counteract the feeling of being pulled inward. Then it was gone. She hadn't done so much, after all. Just a long walk in the rain, and a few minutes in dirty water. Maggie would probably have been all right, anyway, if she had stayed upstairs. But it was over now, and she'd done it. Maybe it hadn't amounted to much, but it was about all she could manage, considering.

"Mark is dead, I think," said Maggie calmly. She balanced herself on a rock, and held out her hand to Laura Bruce, helping her up. "He went out the front door, where it's deep. I almost went with him, but Josh wouldn't let me."

They had reached the car by then. Maggie slid in to the passenger seat, and leaned back, wiping the rain from her cheeks. Laura slumped behind the steering wheel, trying to catch her breath before she had to battle the mountain road. "Why do you think Josh is helping you?" she said between gasps. His name called to her mind the sight of bloodstains on the white walls, and gray matter splattered across the living-room floor. Surely he was a monster, and not a savior. "Didn't he kill your family?"

"Yes," said Maggie. "But he had to. Mark and I understood that. It was the rabbit, really, that made him decide that it had to end. The dead rabbit." Her eyes were glazed, and she looked off into the distance as though she were watching the events take place on a movie screen. "Dad had always beaten us. I never had any short-sleeved outfits, because Mother was always afraid that the bruises might show. But Josh got it worse than the rest of us. He was the oldest, and Dad thought he was a wimp. He wasn't, though. Sometimes he'd take the blame for things that the rest of us did just so Dad wouldn't hurt us."

"Why didn't you tell someone, Maggie?"

"I did once. A teacher. She asked my dad about it, and he took his belt to my back until I bled. After that, I never told."

"What about your mother? Didn't she try to protect you?"

Maggie shook her head. "No. She'd even tell on us sometimes so that he'd have an excuse to hit us. I think she was
afraid he'd get mad at her if he wasn't mad at us. I have
scars on my back. . . . I used to wear a T-shirt, even when
I went swimming, to cover the scars."

"Why would your brother get so upset about your father
killing a rabbit, though?"

Maggie sobbed. "No. Dad didn't kill the rabbit. Simon
did!"

"Simon?" The littlest Underhill. A little blond boy of
seven or eight. Laura remembered his face from the family
photograph in the den. He looked restless in the picture,
and his mother had her hand on his shoulder, trying to hold
him still.

"That evening, when we were at play practice, Josh went
out to the shed and found Simon torturing the rabbit. Then
he knew that it had to stop. Simon was going to be just
like Daddy. First animals, and then people. If something
wasn't done, it was just going to go on and on. So while
Mark and I were gone, Josh took Daddy's gun and shot
Daddy and Mother because they hurt us so much and because they had turned Simon into one of them."

"How do you know this, Maggie?" The pain sounded
again in Laura's body, but she wouldn't listen. "Was there
a note?"

"Josh told us," said Maggie softly. "He was still alive
when we came home. He was waiting for us."

Laura shivered. She reached out to touch Maggie's arm,
but the girl seemed unaffected by the memory. "Did he try
to hurt you or Mark?"

"Of course not!" She was scornful. Such a foolish question. "He protected us. Always. He waited for us so that
he could explain why he had to do it. To make sure we
understood. He told us about finding Simon and the rabbit,
and he said he loved us, and that we would be safe now

that Dad was gone. And then he went upstairs and shot himself."

"You let him?"

Maggie nodded. "He wanted to. I wanted to think up a lie about burglars, but Josh said that the police would know better, and then the secret would get out. Before he went upstairs, he made us promise not to tell what happened. He told us to call the sheriff, and to say that everyone was dead when we got home."

"But why? Why would he want people to think he was a crazed killer?"

Maggie Underhill said, "I don't know, but I think he felt sorry for Daddy."

Laura put her hand on Maggie's arm, and they sat in silence for a good while, until Spencer Arrowood tapped on the window of the car, and asked if they were all right.

Laura Bruce looked up at him with a pain-dimmed smile and said, "You'd better get us both to a hospital."

CHAPTER

16

Now the green blade riseth from the buried grain,
Wheat that in dark earth many days has lain;
Love lives again, that with the dead has been:
Love is come again like wheat that springeth green.

—JOHN MACLEOD CAMPBELL CRUM,
"Easter"

On Ashe Mountain the sun was warm, and all the world looked green. It was one of those early April days that might as well be June, filled with birdsong and the scent of flowers carried on the wind. The sky was a brilliant blue, and the trees were in full leaf.

Nora Bonesteel had taken her needlework and her rocking chair outside, so that she could have good light to sew by and the beauty of the day for company. Across the sprawling green valley, the rock called Hangman shone in the glare of the sun.

She heard the car when it was still out of sight below the crest of the hill, but she didn't get up. At Nora's age it was best to let things come to you. She did another twenty stitches of her needlework while she waited for company. No need to scurry about. The cookies were baked, and the lemonade sat in the good glass pitcher in the refrigerator. Only when she heard the footsteps on her concrete sidewalk, and the sound of their voices, did Nora get up and wave a welcome to Laura Bruce and the little blond boy at her side.

"Hello!" said Laura, giving the old woman a hug. "Now that winter is over, I thought I'd come to see you." She was slender again, in jeans and an East Tennessee State T-shirt. Will Bruce's alma mater. Her hair glinted gold in the sun, and she was smiling.

"You're looking good," said Nora Bonesteel. "Are you feeling all right?"

"Yes," said Laura. "I guess you heard about the flood. Bet it didn't do any harm up here, though."

"No," said Nora. "I reckon I'm safe from floods till the Lord revokes the rainbow. I used to think I was safe from everything up here, being so far removed from civilization, but the world has a way of getting smaller. New York reached out with the chestnut blight and got me, and now the river comes into the valley, bringing the taint with it."

Laura sat down in the grass beside the rocking chair, and looked out across the blue hills. "I lost the baby. I guess you know that. And it may be because of that poisoned river."

"There's nowhere safe in the world," said Nora. "But we're safer than most."

"I know. I've accepted it. For a while I was angry, because you didn't tell me, but then I thought, What good would it have done?"

Nora Bonesteel said, "Knowing is one thing. Changing is another."

"I know. And I couldn't blame you for keeping it from me. I kept it from Will. After it was over, I called him. He took it really well. He thinks he'll be coming home soon."

Morgan Robsart was standing patiently beside Nora's chair, looking politely bored. His blond hair was neatly combed to make him presentable for company, and he was wearing a red knitted sweater with a circle of green designs around the collar. It fit him perfectly.

Nora turned to the child. "Look here, boy," she said. "On my front porch I've got a basket of dried apples that I've been saving all winter. If you'll go get you one of them, there's a mighty hungry whistle-pig in the field out back who'll eat it right out of your hand."

"She woke up!" said Laura.

"Yes. Persey's back. It's spring. And look yonder." She pointed to a tree near the front porch. It was hardly bigger than a fishing pole, but it had sprouted leaves on tiny branches at the top. "The chestnut made it through the winter."

"Can I go get that apple?" asked Morgan. "Where's that whistle-pig?"

"Out back, near the pond. Her name is Persey. Short for— Well, never you mind."

Laura Bruce waved him away. "Just be careful of that groundhog. Make sure she gets apple and not fingers!" She watched him as he ambled off. "He's so wonderful," she said. "Will says we can start the formal adoption procedure when he gets back. That is, if Morgan's real father is willing." She paused for a moment, waiting for Nora Bonesteel's reply.

"It's likely," the old woman said at last. "So you've got your hands full these days?"

"Oh, Morgan is no trouble, but I've been to the hospital in Knoxville twice to see Maggie Underhill. She's going to be all right. She's in therapy now, and they think she'll be able to go off to school next year. I've also been getting more involved in community matters."

"Ladies' Circle?" asked Nora with a trace of a smile.

Laura made a face. "Not a chance. I tried. Honest I did, but that just isn't me. But this evening there's a meeting of the Little Dove Action Committee down at the church, and I'm going to that. Taw McBryde is getting up petitions to take to our senator in Washington." Laura looked away. "I've been working on a letter to send with the petition, telling the senator that I think the river might have been responsible for my stillborn child."

"Bring me up a petition, and I'll sign it," said Nora.

Laura looked at the piece of cloth in the old woman's lap. It was a pillowcase, carefully embroidered with vine leaves and red flowers. She wondered if Nora Bonesteel was making wedding presents, and, if so, did the recipients know yet that they were getting married? She didn't ask, though. She leaned back, enjoying the feeling of warm sunshine and the silence of the mountaintop.

Nora Bonesteel stood up. "Would you excuse me just a minute?" she said. She walked down the hill a little ways, toward the clump of apple trees just past the vegetable garden. Over near the pond, she could see Morgan Robsart sitting in the green grass with a lapful of apples, the groundhog at his side. Persey was up on her hind legs, holding a shriveled apple between her paws.

Nora turned back to the grove of trees, and took hold of an apple branch. Tavy Annis was standing amid the new leaves, looking back at her with a pleasant expression, as if he'd dropped by to pay her a call. He was wearing his red flannel jacket, gray work pants, and a baseball cap with fishing flies stuck in the bill.

"Guess you'll be going up on the ridge now," said Nora, looking out across the waves of mountains rippling on toward the horizon, blue and purple and gray. "You go ahead on. Things are being taken care of here. Godspeed."

She turned away and went slowly back up the hill to sit in the sun.

ABOUT THE AUTHOR

SHARYN MCCRUMB is rapidly becoming one of the most acclaimed of American women mystery writers whose work transcends genre. She won the coveted Edgar in 1988 for *Bimbos of the Death Sun,* and her nationally lauded novel, *If Ever I Return, Pretty Peggy-O,* was named a New York *Times* Notable Book for 1990. It also won the Macavity Award and was a finalist for the Anthony and the Nero. McCrumb's most recent novel is *Missing Susan.* She lives with her family in Virginia.